THE FIRE MAIDENS

The Secret Sirens Series
Book Three

D. R. Bailey

THE FIRE
MAIDENS

Published by Sapere Books.

24 Trafalgar Road, Ilkley, LS29 8HH

saperebooks.com

ISBN:

I would like to dedicate this book to my niece, Maria. A drama teacher, bringing passion, professionalism and dedication to her work, Maria has also been the director on many youth theatre productions where I was the producer. She has been an inspiration to many students under her aegis.

CHAPTER ONE

The English Channel, Autumn 1943

I stared at my navigator, Assistant Section Officer Maria Preston, as the ink-black waves of the Channel lapped against the side of the life raft. Behind us, the hulk of our ditched Mosquito was slowly sinking beneath the surface of the water.

"Well, Anna," said Maria prosaically, "you know what Laurel and Hardy would say."

"What would they say?"

"Here's another fine mess we've gotten ourselves into."

She laughed and so did I. Laurel and Hardy films were often shown on film nights back at Hawberry Hall where our squadron, the Sirens, was stationed. Although the three-storey manor house seemed a long way off right now, her humour served to lighten the mood. There was, however, nothing for it.

"I suppose we'd best try paddling back to Blighty," I said.

"I suppose we had."

Maria retrieved a pocket compass from her flying suit and we began to paddle in the direction she indicated, with no idea how far we were from the English coast. We worked at a steady pace, one on each side of the raft to keep it straight. We did so in silence, as it was quite hard work, and my thoughts turned to how we had arrived at our current predicament.

The pre-mission briefing had been straightforward. Wing Commander James Donnington, the CO of the Sirens, had taken his usual place on the raised podium at the front of the briefing room, alongside the two spies from MI6 who had helped to form the Sirens, and who we called the Marx Brothers. They bore the nicknames Harpo and Chico, which had apparently been given to them by someone from another squadron. With them was Wing Officer Gloria Shepherd, James's second-in-command, and Flight Lieutenant Henry Peterson, our lead instructor.

"The Sirens have been requested to provide a diversionary raid to keep the Germans guessing while our Lancasters bomb their target in Rouen," said James.

This revelation was met with an attentive silence.

"Naturally, your target will also be in Rouen," said Henry.

We were no strangers to Rouen, having hit the port not long ago in an effort to decimate the Kriegsmarine headquarters and, with it, the German Naval High Command. Unfortunately, we had lost two planes on that mission.

There was a photograph on the wall of the intended target, an airfield on the outskirts of the city. It was the type of bombing run we'd carried out many times before.

"You'll be going out as a full squadron of twelve, led by Flight Officer Anna Nightingale," Henry continued, glancing in my direction. "A bit of an overkill, but we want you to make a big noise and take attention off the real target. The Lancasters will be following in close behind you."

What the Lancasters' target was, we weren't told, but that was typical of wartime secrecy.

We took off in the dead of night and flew fast and low to the target. At the appointed hour we hit it full force: a single bombing pass over the airfield.

"Vipers, attack formation," I said as we barrelled over the countryside on our approach. Vipers was our mission codename.

The Mosquitos fanned out in a line. I eased off the safety on the guns. Then I opened the bomb bay doors. I felt the familiar adrenaline surge as we approached the target.

"In two," said Maria as the buildings and grounded planes loomed ever closer. "In one…"

Without warning, all hell suddenly broke loose. Searchlights came on, ack-ack and machine guns firing.

"Incoming!" It was Viper Four, my sister, Section Officer Jennifer Nightingale, who was piloting one of the other Mosquitos.

"Vipers, stay on target," I said over the radio. Fire or no fire, we had mission orders, and I had been entrusted with fulfilling them.

The incoming flak was heavy and since we could not avoid it, we just had to hope we weren't hit.

"Now," said Maria as we passed directly over the target zone.

"Bombs away," I said, releasing our deadly payload.

Twelve Mosquitos let loose their ordnance on timed fuses. In seconds the place would be an inferno.

"Full throttle, Vipers. Let's get the hell out of here," I said, accelerating away.

"Bearing zero four six," added Maria, the squadron's lead navigator.

As I wheeled around along with the rest of the flight, there was a tremendous bang and the aircraft rocked. I struggled to bring us back to level flight.

"What on earth was that?" I asked Maria.

"We've been hit," she informed me. "The starboard engine…"

I looked around. "Christ!" I exclaimed as I saw the engine on fire. I automatically reached for the control and killed the engine. The propellor continued to turn uselessly without power, but at least the fire would go out.

"That's torn it," said Maria.

She wasn't wrong. We'd be much slower on one engine. Then she delivered more bad news.

"Looks like a chunk has been taken out of the wing too."

"Damn!" I said, thinking fast. There was nothing for it.

"Viper Four," I said to Jennifer. "Take over the flight and get them home."

"What?" said Jennifer.

"You heard me, Viper Four. That's an order. We'll catch you up."

Standing orders were to leave badly damaged planes behind. Jennifer wouldn't like it, but orders were orders, and there were eleven planes to get back safely. "Roger, Viper Leader. You'd better damn well make it home," she said. There was a slight catch in her voice.

"Off you go, and don't spare the horses," I replied. "Keep the kettle hot for us."

"Vipers, on me," said Jennifer to the rest of the flight. "Let's go."

In a very short space of time, the rest of the squadron had vanished into the gloom, leaving Maria and I alone with a damaged aircraft in enemy territory.

"Are we going to make it?" Maria asked me.

I glanced at her briefly and read the concern on her face. "We're not going down in France if I can help it," I said with what I hoped was a reassuring smile. "Just keep us on course."

"You're the boss."

I knew she had faith in me. The question was, did I have faith in myself? Fortunately, the Mosquito was quite a resilient aircraft, even when badly damaged.

I dropped the Mosquito as low as I could to avoid being detected by enemy radar. As we flew, the familiar hazard-spotting routine kicked in as the terrain flashed by. Maria called out the hazards as we came up to them.

"Lines," she said, as some telegraph poles came into view.

"Seen them," I replied as we passed over them.

"House."

"Got it."

It was a good discipline and kept us focused as we made our way back towards the Channel.

"Don't look now," said Maria suddenly, "but I think we may have company."

I glanced off to the right and sure enough, the running lights of two or three aircraft could be seen above us. If they had their navigation lights on, then it was certain they were Jerries. We always had ours off over enemy territory.

"That's all we need," I said with a sigh.

We would become sitting ducks if they spotted us. We couldn't outrun them or even try to outmanoeuvre them, considering we were now underpowered.

There was a good chance they might not spot us. The Mosquito was well camouflaged paint-wise and it was a dark night. As long as there wasn't too much flare from our remaining engine, we'd be almost invisible. I decided to ease back the throttle a little.

"Is that a good idea?" asked Maria, noting what I was doing.

"It's the only one I've got," I said. "We're done for if they see us."

Agonising moments crawled by as the enemy planes passed overhead. At any moment I expected them to turn and attack. Fortune, however, was smiling on us and it was with some relief that we watched the lights disappear into the distance.

"And here's the coast," said Maria with a grin.

"Thank goodness for that," I replied.

We were halfway across the Channel, skimming the waves, when Maria said, "I do believe we're going to make it."

The port engine immediately cut out and she gasped.

"Oops," she said. "Me and my big mouth."

"I'm going to have to ditch," I told her. "As soon as we're down safely, we need to get the hatch open and deploy the raft."

"Yes, Boss," said Maria, rummaging in front of her for the life raft.

Since we were already flying at low altitude, ditching proved to be fairly straightforward. The Mosquito, being made of wood, floated easily and we had time to pop open the escape hatch. Fortunately, it was a warm autumn night and the Channel was calm.

Before we left the cockpit, I made one last radio transmission to Control.

"Control, this is Viper Leader. We've ditched in the Channel, approximate position…"

Maria gave them the coordinates, then we climbed out and slid onto the wing. We inflated the life raft and eased ourselves into it. Thus began our somewhat perilous journey home.

After a while — paddling on a dark night and with no land in sight — fatigue began to take its toll on both of us.

"Shall I sing?" said Maria suddenly. "To keep our spirits up?"

"All right," I readily agreed. Maria had a great voice.

She started up a rendition of 'We'll Meet Again' by Vera Lynn. After two verses, she stopped.

"I can't do any more, Boss, sorry," she said. "Plus, I'm kind of hungry."

"What have we got?" I asked.

Maria rummaged in her flying suit and pulled out the emergency pack we had been issued with. The pack contained Horlicks Tablets, chewing gum, Halazone tablets to disinfect drinking water, Benzedrine tablets to improve alertness, V matches, a canvas bag, and a small compass. This was in addition to the field compass that Maria always carried with her.

"No food?" I asked.

"No food," she replied.

I knew why we had no rations. It was the same reason we all carried cyanide pills and grenades. If we were shot down and unable to return, then the grenades were to be used to destroy the aircraft and prevent it from falling into enemy hands. The cyanide pills were for us. However, sitting in the life raft, I felt the lack of food to be something of an oversight, and determined to take up with James, *if* we ever made it home.

"Oh well," I said, trying to ignore the gnawing feeling in my stomach.

"Fear not, Boss," said Maria. "Because I have this."

With a flourish, rather like a conjurer, she produced a bar of chocolate from another pocket. I stared at it with relish.

"Oh, my goodness," I said. "Where on earth did you get that?"

"It's for emergencies, and this is probably an emergency," she said with a hollow laugh.

"I could kiss you!" I replied.

"Save it for James," came the sly retort.

James and I had been conducting a clandestine relationship for some time. Maria knew all about it. I wondered how many others at Hawberry might know. I pushed it out of my mind. James would be worried when the rest of the Sirens arrived back without us, but it wasn't the time to think about that.

"We'll have to ration it," Maria was saying. "Perhaps one square each an hour or so? When this is gone, I haven't anything else."

I nodded, eager to taste the sweetness and assuage my hunger just a little. I had not had the foresight to bring anything myself. I would not make that mistake again.

Maria broke off two squares and handed one to me. I took it from her gratefully and popped it in my mouth.

"Oh, my giddy aunt," said Maria as she replaced the chocolate in her pocket and buttoned it up. "I never tasted anything so good."

We started to laugh, easing the tension of our predicament. When the chocolate had gone, we both had a small drink of water from our canteen. At least we wouldn't die of thirst. Maria looked at her watch.

"What are we going to do, Boss? We can't both paddle all night."

I thought for a moment. "Perhaps we can take turns. One of us can sleep, the other paddle, then swap, how's that?"

"Good plan," said Maria. "I'll take first shift and after an hour, I'll wake you. Perhaps we can even have another square of chocolate."

"All right," I agreed. I was tired and even though I felt I should take the lead, I knew Maria would argue the toss. So, I huddled down in the life raft and closed my eyes.

It didn't seem that long before Maria woke me.

"Time to paddle, Boss," she said softly.

I sat up and stared at her for a moment. It was still dark. I had been in a dreamless sleep and forgotten where I was.

"We're still in the Channel," she said, seeing my disorientation.

"Yes…"

Maria retrieved the bar of chocolate from her pocket and we went through the same routine: a square each followed by a drink of water. Maria was about to hunker down when she hissed a warning.

"What's that?" she whispered.

"What?"

She pointed. "Over there."

I turned to see a black hulk silently cutting through the water. The shape was unmistakable. It was a U-boat.

"Get down," I said.

The two of us lay as flat as we could in the raft, not daring to breathe. We listened to the thrum of the engines, which got louder and louder.

"What do we do if they see us?" whispered Maria.

"Play dead," I replied, "and hope they go away."

My hand slid into hers and she squeezed it tight. The noise of the engines stopped. Then there was a shout, raised voices speaking in German.

A spotlight came on briefly and flashed over us. We held our breath. I wondered if our time was up. Would we be captured, imprisoned … executed? I remembered the cyanide capsule we all carried in our pockets.

There was a hurried conversation going on over in the U-boat. I had no idea how far away the German submarine actually was. After a few more anxious moments, we heard what sounded like orders being given, and the engines resumed. The U-boat, thankfully, didn't come any closer.

Nevertheless, we lay there listening as the sound of the engines grew fainter. Finally, I plucked up the courage to peek over the side of the life raft. The U-boat was nowhere to be seen — it had disappeared into the black night.

"It's all right," I whispered to Maria. "I think they've gone."

"Thank heavens for that," said Maria. "I really thought we'd had it."

"Let's hope there are no more," I replied.

The U-boats were known for hunting in packs. They wouldn't usually risk surfacing in the English Channel during the daytime, but at night it was another story. We waited a little longer in case there was another one, but after a while, there was nothing for it but to carry on.

"It's my turn to paddle," I said to Maria. "Get some sleep. If I see another Jerry, I'll wake you."

Maria nodded and lay down. I picked up the paddle, checked the compass, and started off once more.

CHAPTER TWO

Paddling by the light of the moon was a rather eerie experience. I was surprised not to have seen any ships, other than the German submarine. I had no idea where we were anymore, so I just kept heading north and hoped for the best. Jennifer had ditched in the Channel not long ago, but she'd put her Mosquito down reasonably close to shore.

We were nowhere near it.

I wondered if the current would take us off course. Fortunately, there wasn't any kind of a swell. I prayed that would continue. Contending with large waves in our little raft would be a perilous adventure.

After an hour, I woke Maria and we swapped places. The cold grey light of dawn was on the horizon when I once more took over the paddle from Maria. Shortly afterwards my eyelids began to feel heavy. Fatigue and lack of food were taking their toll.

I jerked myself awake several times, and then I lost the battle with sleep. Suddenly I was in an endless dream of U-boats and planes and then James was there, his hand on my arm. He kept saying my name: "Anna, Anna, Anna…"

I became aware of being shaken awake. I opened my eyes. Maria was looking at me, concerned.

"Anna," she said. "Are you all right?"

"Yes… Damn it, I'm sorry, I must have dozed off," I said, blinking in the bright light of day.

The sun was up and glistening on the water, which was starting to get a little choppy.

"Where's your paddle?"

Startled, I looked around, then shot her a guilty look.

"It must have slipped from my hands as I slept," I said. Now we had only the one paddle.

"No matter," Maria said with a smile.

"I'm a poor example of a leader," I said, contrite.

Maria wasn't having any self-castigation. "No, you're not, and what's done is done. The question is … where on earth are we?"

We must have drifted with the current. We could be anywhere, which was a sobering thought. There was no land to be seen, and we had no way of discovering our position.

"I have no idea."

Just then I heard the distinct thrum of several aeroplane engines in unison. I was pretty sure I knew that sound.

"Are those what I think they are?" said Maria, who had heard it too.

"I think so."

I shaded my eyes and peered into the distance. Closing fast with our position were six Mosquitos flying low over the water.

In moments the planes swooped over us and banked around for another pass. The leading plane dipped its wings.

"It's the Sirens!" I shouted joyfully. "The Sirens!"

"We're here," said Maria, frantically waving her arms. "We're over here!"

The planes circled us one more time, dipped their wings again and then flew away, leaving us alone.

"Do you think that was Jennifer in the lead?" I asked Maria. I could tell it was a radar plane because of the shape of the nose of the Mosquito. It was blank and rounded off without the usual gunports. Jennifer piloted one of two of our radar planes.

"I'm sure of it," she replied. "Which means we're going to be rescued very soon."

The pilots would have radioed our position to Control. Now it would be the task of a nearby ship to head for our position and pick us up. I had no idea when that would be.

Maria reached into her pocket and pulled out the bar of chocolate.

"Breakfast?" she asked, holding out a piece to me.

It was the last two pieces. I took one square gratefully and savoured it, hoping that we'd soon have something more substantial.

The time seemed to pass interminably after that. The wind started to get up and the little raft rose and fell on the rising swell.

"I hope someone comes soon," said Maria.

"They'll come," I told her, with more confidence than I felt. "I know it."

The sound of a ship's horn pierced the air. In the distance, we could see a British Navy destroyer and some other ships.

I pulled out the Very Pistol containing a distress flare. I held it up and fired it into the air. There was an answering sound from the leading ship and then they turned towards us.

"We're saved!" said Maria.

"In the nick of time," I said, relief washing over me.

Not long afterwards, Maria and I found ourselves aboard the Navy destroyer which had found us. We had been given some overalls to wear and were seated in the Officers' Mess in the company of a Navy lieutenant, whose name was Christian Jones. He was interested to know why two WAAFs were adrift in the English Channel, but waited politely while we polished off a double ration each of eggs and bacon along with a mug of hot tea.

He wore a faintly amused expression at our predicament. Fortunately, the fact we'd not had to explain ourselves right away gave us time to think.

Having assuaged my hunger, I pushed the plate to one side and sipped my tea. Maria was still eating.

"So," said Jones at length, "do tell how you came to ditch a plane in the Channel."

"Well," I began, "we were supposed to deliver the Mosquito to a base on the coast and we went a little awry."

I didn't officially have to address him as 'sir' since we were of equivalent rank.

"But you were flying at night, as I understand it? Isn't that a tad unusual?" he continued.

"Yes, but it was an urgent delivery," I said smoothly, "and apparently, they couldn't wait. So we volunteered to do it."

Maria, who had now finished her breakfast, added, "Night navigation is difficult."

"You're the navigator, I take it?" Jones said.

"Yes, sir."

To my annoyance, he persisted in questioning us further.

"Even so, why did you have to ditch? You're lucky you didn't end up in France with those navigation skills of yours."

I felt Maria bristle beside me and hurried to intervene.

"There was an engine malfunction," I told him. "It caught fire. We had no choice."

"Were they also female mechanics, fitting out the engines?" he asked.

I caught the drift of his question. "Some of them, yes," I said truthfully and without rancour. "But some are also males…"

He didn't hold a high opinion of women doing skilled work, and it seemed he set no great store by women in uniform, but since we were in his domain, we had to let it pass.

"Oh well, no matter," he continued, dismissing the subject. "We'll get you safely back to Blighty. That's what's important."

"Thank you, we appreciate it," I told him, forcing a smile.

"You're welcome." He frowned momentarily, as if recalling something. "Funnily enough, we picked up another flyer some time ago. Spitfire man, ditched up in the North Sea. Lucky that we found him. Mackennelly his name was, from a squadron called the Mavericks. Odd name for a squadron … thought so at the time."

"So you make a habit of picking up downed pilots?" I quipped.

Jones laughed. "Well, not precisely. Anyway, what unit did you say you were from?"

I exchanged a glance with Maria. We couldn't exactly make it up.

"We're from the Sirens," I said.

"The Sirens? I can't say I've heard of them."

"We're just a small unit, transporting planes and training pilots," I said, dissembling as much as possible.

"Yes, I see. Well, anyway, we've got you a cabin where you can rest up. Your clothes are being valeted and should be with you shortly. I'm sure that our skipper, Commander Marley, will be delighted to have your company for lunch. It might be a while before we make port."

"Where exactly were we when you found us?" I asked him as we stood up.

"We picked you up just south of Falmouth," he said. "Any longer and you would have been heading out into the Atlantic."

"Goodness!" I exclaimed. "That's a long way from where we ditched."

"The tidal streams can be a little wicked," he said. "Easy to drift a lot further than you think."

"We were lucky then," I said.

"You certainly were."

We were conducted to a well-appointed cabin with two bunks and a bathroom. Maria and I were both tired and elected to lie down for a while.

"I'll give him navigation skills," grumbled Maria once we were alone.

"Leave it," I said. "You'll just have to wear it."

Having a combat role in the war meant that I and the rest of the Sirens risked our lives every day, even if no one knew it. It was just a fact of life for us as a top-secret squadron. I closed my eyes and let sleep claim me. It wasn't long, however, before we were woken by one of the ratings. He handed us our clean and dry flying suits, which we gratefully donned.

"I've been asked to escort you to luncheon, ma'am," he said when we emerged from the cabin.

"To meet Commander Marley?" I enquired.

"Not exactly, ma'am, no," he replied.

"Oh, then who…?"

"You'll see," he said enigmatically.

We walked along several corridors, eliciting curious glances from the ship's personnel. Then we climbed up some stairways and onto the deck. We passed through a door, then along another corridor. Finally, the sailor held a door open for us and ushered us into a large cabin.

A thickset man in uniform was standing with his back to us, looking out of a window. Smoke danced in the sunlight coming through the window, and I smelt the distinct odour of a cigar.

"You're from the Sirens, I understand," said the man.

The drawl was unmistakable — it was Prime Minister Winston Churchill. He turned to face us and smiled. Maria and I both snapped to attention and saluted.

"Never mind all that," he said, waving his cigar around with an air of affability. "Let me shake you ladies by the hand."

He walked over and extended his hand to each of us in turn.

"It's an honour to meet you, sir," I began.

"Oh flummery," said Churchill. "There's no need to stand on ceremony. Come and sit down."

The cabin was rather spacious and there was a table laid with a white cloth, silver cutlery and white china. He indicated that we should be seated at the table and so we complied.

"Now then," he continued, "who do I have the honour of addressing?"

"I'm Flight Officer Anna Nightingale, Flight Leader of the Sirens," I said.

"And I'm Assistant Section Officer Maria Preston, lead navigator for the Sirens," said Maria.

"Welsh, eh?" rumbled Churchill, picking up on Maria's accent. He paused for a moment to puff on his cigar and then continued. "Luncheon will be served shortly, but in the meantime, tell me about the Sirens."

"You know about us, of course, sir?" I asked in surprise.

"Yes, yes, but I want to hear it from you, on the front lines, so to speak."

Maria and I spent an animated half an hour talking about the Sirens and the missions we had undertaken, while Churchill listened quietly. He poured himself a shot of whisky from a glass decanter on the table. We declined the offer of one ourselves.

The conversation was interrupted by the arrival of lunch, served by one of the stewards. It consisted of roast beef with all the trimmings. We tucked in with relish.

We resumed our tale and Churchill asked us pertinent questions now and then. A dessert of apple pie and custard was served along with tea.

"That's excellent information," said Churchill when we'd told him everything.

"Thank you, sir."

He poured himself yet another good measure of whisky and sat back in his chair. "You know, I haven't been a great proponent of women in the forces," he said. "Certainly not initially, but the exigencies of war and all that." He took a long puff on his cigar. "I wasn't entirely convinced about your unit either, if you want the truth. However, your accomplishments have certainly shown me otherwise. Now, I'm even more determined that your unit will keep flying."

"Thank you," I said again. "We're glad to be of service."

"Indeed, it shall be the best kept secret of the war," he said with a smile. "Never fear."

Lunch being concluded, we were escorted back to our cabin after saying farewell to Churchill.

"Well I never," said Maria as we sat together on our bunks.

"I wasn't expecting that," I said, laughing.

"I don't suppose we'll ever see him again," said Maria with a sigh.

However, in that assumption, she was proven wrong. After we made port, Churchill insisted on personally escorting us back to Hawberry Hall, along with his entourage, announcing that he wanted to see the place for himself.

We arrived at Hawberry in Churchill's Humber Pullman. He had insisted we travelled with him and kept us entertained with stories of his exploits all the way there. Due to the top-secret nature of the Sirens, only Churchill, his private secretary, and Air Chief Marshal Charles Portal — who was Chief of Air Staff — accompanied us into the Hall. The rest of his entourage was despatched to find a local hostelry while Churchill conducted his visit, so that the inner workings of the Sirens was kept to a select few.

Sergeant Martha Pryde at the front desk snapped to attention and tried her best to maintain her composure on seeing the Prime Minister enter the atrium at the entrance to the Hall. She was on the phone to James at once while Churchill remarked on the fine architecture of the building.

James arrived with Flight Sergeant Judy Royston, his adjutant.

"Sir, this is a surprise," he said to Churchill, saluting him and Portal.

"A good one, I trust?" rumbled Churchill.

"Yes, sir, indeed."

"Excellent, well, a couple of your team dropped in and I felt it incumbent upon me to pick them up and return them whence they came." Churchill took a puff on his cigar. "Perhaps you'd give me the grand tour, if you would?"

"Yes, sir, we'd be delighted. Perhaps a little fortification in my office first, while we get organised?" suggested James. "I have a tolerable whisky, if you're partial?"

"Now you're talking," said Churchill. "Lead on, Macduff."

"FO Nightingale and ASO Preston, good to see you back safe and sound," said James, flicking a glance in our direction.

"Thank you, sir," I replied with a smile.

His eyes held mine a moment longer, promising a better reunion later on.

As James led Churchill away, I turned to go up to my room when Jennifer barrelled into me, enveloping me in a big hug.

"Thank goodness you're safe," she said. "I was so worried about you."

She was immediately joined by my familiar motley crew, ASO Shelly Cartwright, SO Patricia Batley, SO Susan Bell, ASO Pamela Hartley, SO Sandra Brown, ASO Lucy Morgan, and ASO Connie Broadbent. They all started asking questions nineteen to the dozen.

"One at a time," I laughed. "Let's go to my room and we'll tell you everything."

A little while later there was a knock on the door. It was Judy.

"Anna, Maria — the Wing Commander requests your presence for lunch with the PM."

"Now, that's not something you hear every day," said Connie with a grin.

She and Jennifer were sitting by the window as usual, sharing a cigarette. They sat close to one another, and there were affectionate touches between them. I didn't give it a second thought anymore.

Maria and I accompanied Judy to what had at one time been Hawberry's original dining room. It was a large room lined with wainscoting, pictures on the wall and a marble fireplace. A large table which ran almost the full length of the room was covered with a white tablecloth and set with several places. James, the Marx Brothers, Churchill and his entourage were seated around it. Various dishes of vegetables were being passed around.

"Ah," said Churchill. "The gallant duo. Have a seat."

Cooked ham was served along with the vegetables. It was obvious that the kitchen had worked overtime to provide the meal at such short notice. There was red wine, but I declined it, and Maria did the same.

Churchill talked in complimentary terms about the facilities. It was clear he'd been on a guided tour of the base. He seemed to be a man for details.

"Air Commodore Laxington came for an inspection not long ago," said James during the conversation.

"Did he, by Jove?" said Churchill. "And what, pray, did he have to say?"

James hesitated and I stepped into the breach.

"He said what a good job we're all doing, sir. Then he told us that he had great admiration for the brave women in the Sirens putting their lives on the line in the course of their duty to King and Country."

James shot me a grateful smile. The real story of Laxington's visit could never be told.

On hearing this, Churchill almost choked on his wine. "He said *that*?" he spluttered.

"Yes, sir."

Churchill glanced at Air Chief Marshal Portal. Then he roared with laughter. I took it that Laxington's reputation had reached the PM's ears after all, though protocol would prevent him from saying more. After Churchill had recovered somewhat, he said, "You must have mightily impressed him."

"I think we did," I replied.

"Wonders will never cease," muttered the PM.

The conversation moved on to other things, and then Churchill said he'd like to say a few words to the Sirens before leaving.

Shortly afterwards we assembled in the briefing room with James, Gloria and Henry on the podium along with the Marx Brothers. I had noticed that at lunch the Marx Brothers had seemed rather pally with the PM. I had no doubt there were wheels within wheels where these two were concerned.

"I've gathered you all here," James began, "because, as you no doubt already know by now, we have had an unexpected but very welcome guest. He's asked to have a word and so without further ado, I'd like to introduce our Prime Minister, Winston Churchill."

We all burst into spontaneous applause as Churchill and Air Chief Marshal Portal took to the podium. Churchill was smoking a cigar. He paused for a moment, surveying us all. Everyone fell silent as we waited for him to speak.

"You know," he said, "I wasn't really planning to come here today, but it so happened that I picked up a couple of your aircrew in my ship. Which was, as it turns out, most fortuitous indeed."

He took a puff on his cigar and then blew the smoke out.

"Fortuitous because it has given me the opportunity to see this unit, the Sirens, first-hand. I must tell you what a damn fine unit it is."

He paused again, looking around. His ability to command the room kept his audience listening with rapt attention.

"I must admit that I was not entirely convinced about bringing women into the forces, let alone putting them in combat. However, war is a great leveller and in war one must think on one's feet. One must revise one's opinions and beliefs, and understand that a time of crisis requires new thinking and sometimes *different* thinking."

He stabbed his cigar in our direction to make his point.

"That is why I authorised this unit, against, I may say, some considerable opposition. However, opposition be damned. You have proven yourselves as worthy as any other serviceman in the RAF in the line of duty and in the line of fire. You have done a great service to King and Country."

I glanced at Maria. She was smiling.

"Rest assured that nobody shall interfere with the operation of this unit for the duration of the war, however long it may be. You have my personal guarantee of that. You also have my admiration and respect for what you have done and for what you will do. I thank you, and your country thanks you too."

He finished his speech with a flourish and smile.

"Three cheers for Mr Churchill!" shouted Shelly, suddenly getting to her feet. "Hip hip hooray!"

Churchill continued to smile benignly as the cheers echoed around the room. Shortly afterwards he took his leave, and with the excitement over, things returned to normal.

Later that night I snuck up to James's room and slipped quietly inside. I couldn't resist the chance to be with him. The desire was mutual. Besides which, we'd not long ago declared our love for each other.

He was sitting in an easy chair and immediately stood up to embrace me. I was reminded how handsome I found him with his black hair, moustache and brown eyes. We were soon lost in a kiss.

"Did you miss me?" I whispered when our lips parted.

"Like the devil," he replied.

"Well, now you can show me how much…"

CHAPTER THREE

I stole back to my own bed in the early hours of the morning. Only a select few knew about my relationship with James, and I aimed to keep it that way, at least for now. Neither of us had agreed on how we might take our relationship forward. James had mentioned the idea of marriage, but I was still unsure about it.

I climbed into bed and snuggled up to Jennifer. She stirred and opened her eyes.

"I was worried sick about you, when you went missing," she murmured. "I made James let me take the squadron out at first light to look for you."

"I'm very glad you did, or we might have been lost forever," I told her, only half-joking.

"No, you can't do that," she said, hugging me tight. "You can't ever do that."

I held her in my arms and wished I could reassure her in the way I would like to. I knew it was impossible. With war came loss. As I drifted off to sleep, I wondered what the future would bring for us.

Breakfast the next morning was the usual boisterous affair. Shelly and Maria were bickering. Connie and Jennifer shared a cigarette.

"Chocolate? Was that all you had to eat?" Shelly was saying.

"What did you expect me to take, a three-course meal?" Maria shot back.

"I would have taken a tin of something…"

"And opened it with what?"

I half-listened to their squabble as I tucked into eggs, toast and baked beans. Those long hours in the raft, when all of this was almost snatched away, made me suddenly appreciate the camaraderie more than ever.

"We're happy you're back, Boss," said Shelly, breaking off from her banter with Maria. "Jennifer was far too bossy."

"I was not," said Jennifer with a laugh.

"Power went to her head," said Patricia, joining in with the joke.

I was about to intervene on Jennifer's behalf when Judy appeared at my elbow.

"Wing Commander wants to see you, ma'am," she said.

"All right, thanks, Judy," I replied, ignoring the others, who were smirking.

I pushed away my empty plate and followed Judy up to James's office.

"He's not alone," Judy confided before opening the door to let me in. She knew about our relationship and was wholeheartedly supportive. I gave her a brief nod and walked in.

James, Gloria, Henry and the Marx Brothers were seated at the meeting table.

"Anna," said James with a smile. "Glad you could join us. Have a seat."

I saluted out of protocol and went to sit down. I wondered what was in the offing.

"Don't look so worried," said Harpo, taking a drag on his cigarette. The two spies smoked like chimneys. Perhaps it was the stressful nature of their job.

"I'm not worried, precisely," I said with a smile. "Just curious as to what's afoot."

"Well, wonder no longer," said Chico. "We're here to discuss a mission with you before breaking it to the squadron."

"All right." I regarded him with interest.

"It goes without saying that what we are about to tell you is top secret," said Harpo rather unnecessarily, since everything we did in the Sirens was secret, but I inclined my head in acknowledgement just the same.

"Ever heard of the Mimoyecques Fortress?" asked Chico.

I hadn't, of course, and said so.

"Not many will have," said Harpo. "As it's a top secret German military complex."

So saying, he leaned back in his chair and resumed smoking. Being used to their slightly exasperating ways, I waited patiently for them to continue.

"This fortress is being constructed as we speak," said Chico. "We happen to have obtained some plans and intelligence as to what its intended use is."

Harpo took up the refrain. "The fortress consists of a network of underground tunnels in a limestone hill which can potentially house up to twenty-five extremely high-calibre cannons, all aimed at London. These cannons have the capacity to fire at a rate of up to ten rounds per minute. You don't need to be a mathematician to work out that this would result in six hundred rounds per hour hitting the capital — a massive and devastating bombardment on par with the Blitz, or worse. Unlike the Blitz, we wouldn't be able to stop it."

"Good grief," I said, staring at him in shock.

"Naturally," said Chico, "we must prevent this fortress from being completed at all costs."

"So, you want us to bomb it?" I asked.

"Yes," said Chico.

"And no," said Harpo.

They laid out some photographs on the table, which showed cutaway plans of the fortress. There were deep shafts cut into the side of a hill. These angled shafts would take the extremely long cannon barrels, and the cannons would be fired from deep underground. In fact, the entire fortress was subterranean in nature and thus an extremely difficult target.

"As you can see, it's almost impregnable from the air," said Chico.

"Then how do we destroy it?" I asked him, nonplussed.

"You've heard, no doubt, of the Dambusters raid?" asked Chico.

"Yes, of course," I replied.

Everyone in the country had heard about the audacious Lancaster bomber raid on the dams in the Ruhr valley, carried out only a few months previously.

"The famous bouncing bomb," said Harpo with a grin, tapping the ash from his cigarette into an ashtray.

The bombs had been designed to skip across the surface of the water like skimming stones towards the wall of the dam. They had promptly sunk and then exploded, thus breaching the walls.

"Barnes Wallis, the bomb's inventor, has made a smaller version of the bouncing bomb," said Chico.

I began to wonder where this was leading.

"This smaller version of the bomb, known as the Highball, has been tested not only on water but on land and specifically against railway tunnels," said Harpo.

The two spies extinguished their cigarettes and lit up two more before continuing. I glanced at James, who shot me a smile while we waited.

"The Ministry wants to see if these bombs will work against the fortress," said Chico finally. "By bouncing a bomb into this railway entrance here."

He pointed to the plan, where there was indeed a railway tunnel entrance. It seemed like a tall order, but I didn't like to say so. Instead, I picked up on a different point.

"So, it's an experiment, not a proper raid?"

"It's both," said Harpo. "An experiment in that we don't know if it will work. A proper raid in that, if it does work, then we'll at least have hampered the enemy's progress until we can figure out what to do next."

It sounded rather hit-and-miss, if I was honest.

"You want the Sirens to carry out this raid?" I asked, wanting to make sure I understood their intentions.

"Bingo," said Harpo.

"She's got it," said Chico.

"I have a few questions," I began.

"Fire away," said Harpo.

"I assume we'll get some kind of modified Mosquito to carry this bomb?"

"Yes, we will be getting two of them," said Henry, cutting in before Harpo could reply. He sounded as if he rather relished the prospect.

"And will the mission require special training?" I asked.

"It most certainly will, and that will be undertaken by the two crews flying the Highball Mosquitos," Henry replied.

"The initial testing of the Highball Mosquito bombs has been carried out by Six One Eight Squadron," said Chico. "The training usually takes around two months."

"However," added Harpo, "you will have two weeks."

"Two weeks!" I exclaimed hotly. "How are we supposed to cram two months' worth of training into two weeks?"

"We have every faith —" Chico began.

"And why can't Six One Eight Squadron do it, since they've done all this training?" I interrupted.

I looked over at James, whose expression was sympathetic, but I could tell I wasn't going to get any support from that quarter.

"They've been … ahem … reassigned to other duties presently, and so the Sirens have been assigned to do it," said Harpo, sounding apologetic.

"No doubt you've already agreed?" I said, directing the question at James.

"Well, we've tentatively said yes…" He trailed off.

I knew that tentatively meant unconditionally. In any case, we all knew that the Sirens had to carry out all missions given to us because of our unique position.

"All right," I said with a sigh of resignation. "Tell me more about the raid."

"The raid will include the rest of the squadron," said Henry. "They will bomb the facilities around the tunnel and help lay down suppressive fire on the ack-ack batteries."

"All right."

"Who do you want to fly the two Highball Mosquitos?" said Gloria, asking the obvious question.

I thought about it for a moment, but I had already made my decision when I had heard what the mission was.

"I'll take one of the planes," I said, flicking a glance at James.

"And the other?" said Gloria.

I couldn't use either of the radar crews, which ruled out Jennifer and Shelly, and their navigators, Susan and Pamela. Instead I picked the pilot I thought was the most reliable.

"Patricia will fly the second plane," I said.

"Excellent," said Harpo with satisfaction. "Perhaps we can set up a briefing for the whole squadron?"

"I'll get that in motion," said James.

It had been settled before I had walked into the room. However, I appreciated being briefed regardless.

"I assume the raid will take place two weeks after these Mosquitos arrive?" I asked as the meeting broke up.

"On the button," said Harpo.

"Precisely," said Chico.

James wasted no time in calling a briefing and we all assembled in the briefing room, Maria and I taking our usual seats at the front. James, Gloria, Henry and the Marx Brothers were already at the podium. There was an air of expectation in the room.

"I've asked you all here because we've been given new orders for an important mission," said James. "The codename for the mission is Operation Molecatcher which, as you will see, is aptly named. Our colleagues from Military Intelligence will give you more details."

Harpo, who had been casually smoking a cigarette, stubbed it out and stepped forward with Chico.

"This mission is top secret, like everything else we do, but even more so," he said. "You're about to be let in on something which is known only to a few, and so it must remain."

"First, let's take a look at the target," said Chico.

On his signal the lights were dimmed and the plan of the fortress I'd seen earlier appeared on the projection screen.

"This is the Mimoyecques Fortress," Chico continued. "It has a deadly purpose."

He went on to explain the intention behind the fortress, and there were audible gasps as he described the volume of ordnance which could rain down on London were the fortress to become operational.

"So, you see," said Harpo, when Chico had finished, "it is imperative that we take steps to prevent the fortress from being completed."

The lights came up again briefly.

"A new type of bomb has been designed by Barnes Wallis," Harpo continued, "who invented the bouncing bomb for the Dambusters raid. It's a smaller version which works on the same principle."

"We are now going to show you some top-secret film of this new bomb, known as the Highball, in action," said Chico.

The lights were dimmed again and I sat forward with interest.

The film showed a Mosquito flying low across an open area then dropping a round bomb, which bounced towards a concrete wall before hitting it square on. There was also footage of the bomb underneath the plane, before it was dropped and as it was released, to show how it worked.

"These were the first land-based experiments for a bomb that was meant primarily to be used on water," said Harpo. "They were a success, and subsequent experiments were tried on a railway tunnel. The aim was to get the bomb into the tunnel itself, which is no mean feat."

Another film was run, which showed a Mosquito dropping a bomb towards a railway tunnel. At least one of the attempts was successful and the bomb went inside. All of the bombs used were dummy bombs without explosives. Apparently, there was a clever method of detonation for when the bomb ended up where it was supposed to be.

"As you can see," said Chico as the lights came up again, "some training is necessary to achieve accuracy. However, the success of this mission is vital to the war effort. Jamming up the railway tunnel will certainly inconvenience Jerry for a while at least. If we can stop the works even for a brief time, it gives us a chance to work out a permanent solution to the threat posed by the fortress."

Henry stepped forward to go over the mission details.

"Two modified Mosquitos will be provided in order for us to carry out the mission," he said. "Two weeks of special training will then be carried out by the crews who are going to fly them."

A few glances were thrown in my direction, since everyone knew that I would have selected the crews.

"The two Mosquitos will be flown by FO Anna Nightingale with ASO Maria Preston as navigator, and SO Patricia Batley with ASO Connie Broadbent," Henry continued.

I felt SO Linda Harris's eyes upon me as he said this, but I didn't turn to look. Linda had been a thorn in my side on more than one occasion and had actively spoken out against my leadership.

"The entire squadron will carry out the raid," said Henry. "It will be led as usual by FO Nightingale as Flight Leader. The rest of the squadron will provide cover for the two Highball Mosquitos. That means bombing and strafing ack-ack and other defensive positions. Now, let's take a look at some recent reconnaissance photographs."

The lights were dimmed once more and aerial photographs were projected onto the screen. They showed extensive works being carried out at the site of the fortress. Henry pointed out the ack-ack positions and also where the entrance to the tunnel was. There was a railway track leading up to that entrance, thus providing a straight run in for the bouncing bomb.

"These photographs will be updated with new reconnaissance prior to the raid," said Henry. "The Mosquitos will carry two bouncing bombs each. This means we will have four chances of taking out the railway tunnel."

As the lights came up, James stepped forward. "That's all for now," he said. "As soon as the Highball Mosquitos arrive, training will begin. Time is of the essence. There will also be several full rehearsals of the raid with the entire squadron in order to ensure the success of the mission."

We were duly dismissed and I had just stood up when I saw Linda heading my way. Beside me, I could feel Maria starting to bristle. Linda was not her favourite person.

"Ma'am," said Linda, "I see you've already picked the crews for the bouncing bombs."

"Yes, I have," I replied. I wasn't entirely sure where this was leading, although I could make an educated guess.

"I would have liked to have been one of those crews," Linda continued, confirming my suspicions.

"I've already made my decision," I told her.

"You know, you could … change your mind. You are the Flight Leader, after all," she continued.

"I could…" I said, without finishing the sentence.

"We *could* be friends, put the past behind us," said Linda, meaningfully.

I considered her request. It was an olive branch of sorts. Was it better to have an enemy as an ally? I wondered about it briefly. Linda had certainly proven herself to be my enemy in the past. I thought of Churchill. What would he do? Appeasement didn't work, that was something he strongly believed.

Work from a position of strength, was his precept. I made up my mind.

"As I said, I've already made my choice."

A scowl crossed Linda's face. "You'll regret this, ma'am," she said in an even tone, before saluting and turning on her heel.

I put out an arm to prevent the inevitable response from Maria.

"Please, Boss, can't you let me? Just once?" she pleaded.

"No, Maria," I said, turning to her. "We can't rise to the bait, and you're too important to me and to this squadron."

Maria glowered at Linda's retreating back. "She's going to cause trouble, that one," she muttered.

"Then we'd best be prepared for it," I replied, with more confidence than I felt. What could Linda do, anyway, I wondered? However, there was something else Churchill said: *never underestimate your enemy*.

Later that evening in the house bar, there was some talk of the mission but for the most part discussion revolved around a Spitfire pilot from a nearby squadron.

"Have you heard about Jennifer's Spitfire pilot?" asked Pamela as I sipped my Coca-Cola. The beverage had been introduced by the Americans and seemed to be ever-present in all the forces' bars.

"He's *not* my Spitfire pilot," said Jennifer, glancing at Connie.

"Oh, he's a dreamboat," said Sandra in her Southern drawl. "I'll be happy to take him off your hands."

I was sure she could, considering her classic blonde bombshell looks.

"He's not *on* my hands," protested Jennifer.

"So, you say," Sandra persisted, shooting her a knowing look.

"For the last time…" Jennifer began, but it was too late. Connie got up from the table and walked out of the bar.

"Now look what you've gone and done," said Jennifer, getting up to rush after her.

"All right," I said, once Jennifer was out of earshot. "Tell me more about this Spitfire pilot."

"Well, he's quite tall," said Susan.

"And handsome," added Sandra.

"Does he have a name?" I asked.

"Pilot Officer William Runcorn," Patricia replied.

"It's not what you think," said Shelly, coming to Jennifer's defence. "William and Jennifer were just joking around. He was goading her, saying that his Spitfire was faster than her Mosquito."

"Of course, she said it wasn't," put in Lucy. "So William suggested they put it to the test —"

She broke off, suddenly aware that she had said too much.

"Put it to the test how?" I asked in a low voice.

Everyone at the table had suddenly gone very quiet. My suspicions were instantly aroused.

"If you lot won't tell me, then I'll just have to ask Jennifer myself."

After some hesitation, Lucy spoke up. "They were talking about … a race … between the Spitfire and the Mosquito. But I'm sure —"

I didn't let her finish. This was typical of Jennifer's impetuous nature.

"A race?" I interrupted, thoroughly fired up at the thought of Jennifer jeopardising the security of the Sirens. "What on earth is she thinking?"

"Please don't —" Shelly began.

"Don't what? Tell her that I forbid such a hare-brained scheme as a race?"

"I'm sure she won't do it, really. It was just banter," Shelly pleaded.

I stared at the others, who looked rather abashed. All except Maria, who took my side in almost every argument.

"Well then, you tell her," I said firmly. "Because I cannot answer for the consequences if this proposed race takes place. It just had better not. Understood?"

There was a chorus of "Yes, Boss" as I stood up. I was angry with Jennifer, and I needed to clear my head.

"Where are you going?" asked Sandra.

"Outside," I said grimly. "For some fresh air."

As I walked away from the table, I could hear them remonstrating with each other in forced whispers.

I went out into the formal gardens. The paths were lined with low hedges and the flowerbeds were still in bloom. It was still light, even though the days were growing shorter. Smoke curled upwards from a bonfire in the distance, where the garden crew had been cutting brush and burning it. It took me back to my parents' farm in Sussex, where life was less complicated.

I felt a light touch on my arm and turned to see Maria.

"Are you all right, Anna?" she asked.

"As all right as I can be when Jennifer is contemplating doing something to the detriment of this unit," I said irritably.

"Don't be so hard on her," said Maria, linking arms with me as we began to walk down one of the paths. "We all have different ways of escaping this war."

I sighed. "I wish she'd find something less foolhardy then."

Maria laughed. "I'm sure it's all talk. Jennifer knows how important this squadron is."

"I hope you're right," I said.

"Relax, Boss, we've got more important things to worry about."

"Like bouncing bombs," I said with a laugh, putting Jennifer's race firmly from my mind.

CHAPTER FOUR

I had little time to think about Jennifer, as the Highball Mosquitos arrived rather promptly. They had been borrowed from Six One Eight Squadron, since these were already fitted out for the bouncing bombs. Their insignia would be painted out and replaced with that of the Sirens.

Before we commenced any kind of in-flight training, however, we had to learn how to get the bombs to bounce and precisely hit the target. Since it was a specialised skill, I wondered who they would get to train us. Naturally, that person would have to be let in on the secret of the Sirens.

I was at breakfast when Judy appeared at our table.

"Wing Commander would like to see you, ma'am," she said.

It was becoming something of a familiar refrain. I looked up at her with my fork poised in mid-air and then down at my half-eaten breakfast. I was somewhat reluctant to leave it.

"After you've finished eating, ma'am, of course," she said, taking a seat at the table.

"You have been spending a lot of time with the Wing Commander lately, Boss," said Shelly slyly.

I shot her an enquiring glance. What did she know, I wondered?

"She's the Flight Leader, of course she would," said Maria, jumping into the breach protectively.

I smiled at her gratefully and continued eating.

"There's a lot of business to discuss with all the missions and so forth," added Judy diplomatically.

"Oh aye, business," Shelly continued, in spite of a quelling look from Maria.

Jennifer and Connie were sitting at the end of the table, sharing a cigarette. Jennifer handed the smoke to Connie.

"There's also minding your own business," Jennifer told Shelly firmly. "So, hush."

I polished off the last of my eggs and beans on toast and took a sip of my tea.

"Shall we go?" I asked Judy.

We walked together to James's office in companionable silence.

"Don't mind ASO Cartwright," said Judy as we reached the door.

"I'll try not to," I said with a smile.

I had managed to quash my qualms about my relationship with the CO of the Sirens. James didn't seem to worry at all, but he was mindful of my anxieties about making our relationship public, and my fear of possibly losing the role of Flight Leader — a role I'd worked hard for.

As I entered the office, I noticed that alongside James, Henry, Gloria and the Marx Brothers, there was another man in the room.

The newcomer was wearing civvies, had grey hair and wore glasses. He smiled as James came forward to introduce me.

"Anna, this is Barnes Wallis," he said. "Barnes, this is our Flight Leader, FO Anna Nightingale."

I shook hands with Wallis. He looked every inch the famous inventor we'd read about.

"I gather you'll be piloting one of the Highball Mosquitos," said Wallis.

"Yes, that's right."

I felt him appraising me, perhaps wondering if I was up to the job. I was determined to show him that I was more than competent to take on the bouncing bomb.

"Barnes is here to teach you how to drop the bombs," said James. "And there's no one better qualified, I'd say."

"May I say that it's a pleasure to make your acquaintance," said Wallis to me. "I've just been hearing about the Sirens from your colleagues, and it sounds as if you're doing some excellent work."

"I hope that we can live up to your expectations on this latest mission," I replied.

"You most assuredly will," said Henry, cutting in. "Just as the Sirens has on every mission they've flown."

Henry was a stalwart and would defend our reputation to the hilt.

"When do you want to start?" I asked Wallis.

"As soon as you're ready. We'll need to cover the theory and so forth first, before you try the Highball out in flight."

"We've an instruction room set aside for the purpose," Henry told him. "You can also use it as an office while you are here."

"Thank you, I'm much obliged to you," said Wallis.

"Why don't we have some tea before you begin?" suggested Gloria.

"A splendid idea," said James, picking up the phone to call his adjutant.

Maria, Patricia, Connie and I listened intently to Wallis as he explained the theory of the bouncing bomb. He illustrated everything clearly with diagrams on the board at the front of the instruction room.

"In order to drop the bomb correctly," he said, "you have to approach the target at exactly sixty feet. A bombsight has been rigged that will give you the correct distance to release it. You have to fly the plane at a ground speed of two hundred and thirty-two miles per hour, if possible. In practice, keep to between two thirty and two forty, but as close to the two thirty-two as you can."

The Highball Mosquitos provided had a bombardier position in the nose. The navigator needed to move forward and lie down during the bombing run, in order to guide the pilot into the target.

"So that's my job?" said Maria. "Releasing the bomb?"

"Yes," replied Wallis. "At exactly the right moment. That part is crucial to the success of the mission. The bomb will have backspin applied to it before it's released, as we've found this is the most effective spin to keep it bouncing."

"I can't believe it bounces on land," added Connie.

"It's surprising but very handy that it does," said Wallis with a smile. "Now, in order to maintain the correct height, the aircraft is fitted with two powerful spotlights, one in the front and one in the middle of the underside of the plane. These are calibrated so that when the two converge, you will be at exactly the right height. The navigator can observe these from the bombardier position."

There was another thing that was apparently different from the tests. Wallis outlined it for us.

"The tests we carried out had the bomb being bounced into the tunnel from just outside the entrance," he said. "However, because of the nature of the target, there's not enough time for the Mosquito to get clear without running into the hillside. So, it has to be dropped from further away, which does make the whole thing more challenging."

I exchanged glances with Maria; this was mostly on her. She gave me a wry smile. Even though this was an experimental mission, there was still a lot riding on its success. The safety of London, for one thing.

Wallis proved to be a quiet but effective teacher who answered all our questions and went over everything very thoroughly. After lunch, we were ready for a test run with dummy bombs.

Our usual range had been set up with a target on a flat field. In these first attempts, we'd get used to approaching it with one or two simulated runs before attempting to drop one of the dummy bombs.

We drove out to the airfield behind Hawberry in the back of one of the military trucks. Wallis went in a staff car with Henry to observe our progress at the range. They would be in radio communication with us through the Control tower.

Jennifer came with us, naturally, and sat at the back of the truck with Connie, sharing a cigarette. Whatever words they'd had over the Spitfire pilot seemed to have blown over.

"What do you reckon to this bouncing bomb lark then?" said Patricia. "Is it going to work?"

"I guess we'll find out soon enough," I replied.

I was a little apprehensive, considering we would be trying something new and there was a lot depending on getting it exactly right.

We arrived at the airfield to find the two Highball Mosquitos fuelled up and with the bombs loaded. Jennifer picked up on something right away.

"There are no guns," she said.

She was right. The guns had been replaced with the bombardier's position in the nosecone. So, the Mosquitos had no chance of defending themselves.

"We'll need a wingwoman," I said, thinking aloud. This would require another Mosquito to provide cover on the way in and the way back.

"I'll do it," said Jennifer immediately.

"We'll decide in due course," I responded. Jennifer would be flying one of the radar planes. I wasn't sure if flying cover would be the best use of the plane, besides which, they had fewer guns than the normal Mosquito due to carrying the radar in the nose.

"All right," she said with a shrug.

"Let's get to it," I said.

Leading Aircraft Woman Victoria Singleton was waiting by the planes. She was in charge of the team of mechanics. I had got to know her quite well after she'd been instrumental in discovering the sabotage to the planes a while back.

"All ready for you, ma'am," she informed me with a salute.

"Thanks, Victoria," I said, returning the salute. "Have you managed to get up to speed with these new bombs?"

"Yes, ma'am," she replied. "A mechanic who knows all about them has joined our crew."

I guessed this would be someone from Squadron Six One Eight. I also imagined that now they were part of the Sirens, they wouldn't be going back. That tended to be the way of it, in order to preserve secrecy.

"Excellent," I said. "Then I suppose there's nothing for it but to give it a go."

"Good luck," said Victoria as we climbed into the aircraft.

Maria secured the hatch. We strapped in. It was the first time we'd flown since ditching in the Channel. I shivered slightly at the recollection.

"Ready?" I asked Maria.

"Ready."

I fired up the engines and once these were turning over nicely, I radioed Control.

"Bluebird Leader requesting clearance," I said, using our usual codename. When on a mission this was changed to something different.

"You're clear to go, Bluebird Leader," said Control.

"Bluebird Two ready," said Patricia.

"Roger, let's go," I said.

I opened up the throttle and taxied down to the end of the runway. Once there, I cranked up the engines and released the brakes, and we barrelled down the runway. Soon we were airborne, and I felt a sense of exhilaration at being in flight once more.

Maria gave me the bearing and Patricia settled on my wing. It would take us a few minutes to fly to the range, and then we'd fly in for our simulated attack run. We didn't need to fly too low until we arrived at the airfield, so it didn't require the usual intensity of concentration when on a mission. That would come later.

"How are these spotlights going to work in daylight?" asked Maria.

"I don't know," I replied. "But apparently, they do."

"I guess we'll find out then," she said.

"In any case, it's highly likely the raid will be carried out at night," I told her, thinking aloud.

"Then how will I see the target properly to sight it?" she asked.

I didn't know, but I was sure these questions would be answered in due course.

"One thing at a time," I said, laughing. "Let's get the bomb-dropping right first."

Shortly afterwards the range came into view. I could see the target, which appeared to be a brightly coloured tarpaulin rigged up with some scaffolding.

"All right," I said to Maria. "Let's do this."

She unbuckled and slid down into the bombardier position.

"How is it?" I asked.

"Strange, but not too uncomfortable."

"Bluebird Two," I said over the radio, "we'll go around for a couple of practice runs, then we'll drop one bomb and then you follow. Then we'll go again. Give us time to see if the bomb hits the target."

"Wilco," said Patricia.

"Control, Bluebird Leader beginning the first practice run," I told them.

"Roger, Bluebird Leader," said Control. They would relay this to Henry and Wallis, observing the proceedings.

"All right, I am circling around for the bombing run," I told Maria.

"Roger. Here goes nothing," she replied.

I took the Mosquito in a wide arc and lined it up with the target, then started to drop down low.

"Spotlights on," said Maria. "Lower … lower … lower…"

I watched the altimeter at the same time as she guided me down.

"That's it, keep it there," she said. "Now, steady … no, left a bit … right a bit… That's it, we're lined up … steady…"

I made sure the speed was exactly where it needed to be at two hundred and thirty-two miles an hour.

"Steady," said Maria. "Almost there… That's it."

Instead of banking away, I zoomed over the target and came around for a second go. This time was easier, and I was able to get us at the right height a lot quicker. Maria sounded more confident too.

"Shall we try this for real?" I asked her as we went around again.

"Yes, why not? Let's give it a shot."

We came in for a third run and I kept the kite steady at the correct speed. Meanwhile, Maria quickly guided me down to the right height.

"Lower … a bit more … that's it… Keep it steady now…"

"It's all yours," I told her.

"Roger."

I waited patiently, imagining this would be a very different scenario when we were under fire. I would not be able to deviate from our course regardless, which made me even more determined to have a wingwoman for some form of protection.

"Bomb gone," said Maria as she released the first dummy Highball.

"Roger," I replied.

I banked away sharply as the bomb dropped, and then I turned tightly to watch it bouncing along the ground towards the target.

"Wow," said Maria. "It actually works."

Unfortunately, the bomb bounced right over the top of the target, which was disappointing.

"Oh dear," said Maria. "I must have misjudged it."

The bombsight had been constructed so that when the target was in the exact centre of the sight, we should be the right distance away. There was one set up in the classroom, which Wallis had used for instruction. Our first attempt illustrated that it wasn't as easy as we might have thought to bounce a bomb onto a target, let alone into a railway tunnel.

"Bluebird Two, your turn," I said, circling away from the target zone to give Patricia space for her attack.

"Wilco," said Patricia, bringing her Mosquito into line for her run. We were able to watch the whole procedure; she had three practice runs before Connie released their first bomb. It bounced along the ground and hit the target almost perfectly square.

"Bingo!" cried Connie triumphantly.

"First try too," said Maria, clearly trying to keep the disappointment out of her voice. I knew she would be happy for Connie, but frustrated that she hadn't managed to do the same.

Control came on the radio. "Blue Leader. The advice from Mr Wallis is to release the bomb a fraction sooner."

"Roger, Control," I said. "We're going around again."

I banked around the range and then, guided by Maria, dropped to the correct height for another run.

"Steady as she goes," said Maria as we approached the target. "I'm going to get it this time."

I kept the Mosquito as close to the right speed as I was able. The target was looming up in front of us.

"There she goes," said Maria, releasing the second dummy bomb.

We banked away to watch it bouncing along the ground in quite high arcs, but it still missed the target by a fraction. A fraction was all it would take to make the difference between success and failure.

"Damn it," said Maria in frustration.

"It's all right," I said. "You'll get it. Practice makes perfect."

"I had it dead on," said Maria. "I thought it was all beautifully lined up and it still missed."

She scrambled back up to her seat and strapped in. We banked around to watch Patricia line up for her second go and saw the bomb sail accurately to the target.

"Don't fret," I told Maria, seeing the look of exasperation on her face.

"I'm not fretting," she replied. "I'm just annoyed."

"You can do this."

"I bloody well hope so."

She was disappointed in herself. Maria was something of a perfectionist and could be her own worst enemy at times. However, her attention to detail also made her the best navigator in the Sirens.

"Bluebird Two, let's get back to base," I said.

"Roger," said Patricia and settled on my wing as Maria gave us a bearing for home.

"I can't understand why Patricia's bomb worked perfectly and mine didn't," said Maria.

"I'm sure Barnes will work it out," I replied, having every faith in the bomb's inventor.

We would have to wait while more dummy bombs were loaded up at the airfield. The practice ones we had just used would be fetched from the range. The dummy bombs were constructed from hardwood to ensure they could take the bangs and scrapes of practice bombing runs. At best we'd have one more go that afternoon.

We touched down at the airfield and taxied back to our standings. Henry, Wallis and Jennifer were waiting for us.

"What happened?" Wallis asked Maria.

"I'm not sure," Maria told him. "I lined it up exactly on the target. Just the way we went over it in the classroom. I even tried an earlier release like you said. It still missed."

Wallis looked pensive for a few moments before brightening up.

"Let me take a look at the bombsight," he said, before disappearing into the cockpit of the Mosquito.

"He's mightily impressed with you all," Henry told us.

"But I missed," protested Maria.

"By a fraction," said Patricia. "Come on, don't be so hard on yourself."

"Patricia is right. Give yourself a break," said Henry. "Barnes will sort out the problem, never fear. He has a brilliant mind."

"Well, that's for sure," said Connie. "Who on earth would have thought of a bouncing bomb in the first place?"

In the meantime, Victoria and some of the mechanics were loading the second lot of dummy bombs. A couple of trucks also left the hangars, presumably to pick up the bombs we'd already dropped.

Henry was interested to hear more about our first experience with the Highball. A few moments later, Wallis came up to us.

"The bombsight was a little off," he said. "I compared it to the other one and it was slightly out of kilter. I've adjusted it, so you should be good to go for your second practice."

He smiled broadly and Maria looked happier on hearing this.

"You see," I told her. "It wasn't you."

Once the dummy bombs were loaded up, we flew back to the range for a second go. This time we did better.

I lined up for the first practice run, watching the airspeed and altimeter as before.

"Steady," said Maria. "Steady … keep it steady… We're good … and bombs away."

I pulled away hard left just as I would need to do for the real thing. Maria was still able to observe with satisfaction the bomb bouncing along the ground and hitting the target.

"Yes!" she said. "We did it!"

Patricia had another turn and then we went again, then Patricia did her final run of the day. We all managed to hit the target and headed for Hawberry in a buoyant mood.

"See," said Maria. "That wasn't too hard."

"Let's hope it's as easy under fire," I replied.

We'd be heading into flak plus machine-gun fire, and not as fast as we might normally go. Something was niggling at me about the whole process. It seemed there was too little margin for error.

"Couldn't we drop the bomb a little closer?" I asked Wallis once we were back on the ground.

"The whole problem is that you've got to get the bounce right," he said. "Changing the distance changes the number of bounces. We've got the calculations right now and the bombsights. If we change it, we'll have to recalibrate, and there isn't the time."

"It still seems touch-and-go to me," I replied, even though I didn't want to cast a damper on the whole mission.

"That's what we're going to find out," said Wallis. "Just how possible it really is. It's a tactic that might get used again in other circumstances, and so the War Office is interested to know the outcome."

"You will, nevertheless, endeavour to destroy the tunnel entrance if you can," added Henry.

"Right…" I trailed off.

It didn't fill me with confidence. We were experimenting with ordnance and risking people's lives at the same time. The damage we might inflict on the fortress would be minimal if the bombs didn't go into the tunnel. Would it all be for nothing? I supposed these were the life-and-death decisions people like Churchill made every day. We just had to carry them out.

"Look at it this way," said Patricia as we headed back to Hawberry in the back of the truck. "We've got four chances. That's more than an even break."

"You're right," I said with a sigh.

"You worry too much, Boss," said Connie, flicking the ash from her cigarette out of the back of the truck.

"It's my job to worry and to try to keep this squadron alive on a mission," I told her.

"You can't do everything," said Maria. "We've all got our jobs to do. We *all* consider it our job to stay alive if we can."

She was right, of course, but I couldn't help how I felt.

I found James in his office and, as he poured us some tea, he echoed Maria's sentiments.

"A leader can only do so much," he said, handing me a cup. "Inspire, motivate, make the difficult decisions — but they can't be responsible for everyone's lives once the flak starts flying."

"Unless they do something stupid," I said obstinately, sipping my tea.

"But you won't," he continued, stirring sugar into his.

"I try not to."

"Do you think you've made any stupid decisions?" he asked with a raised eyebrow.

"Perhaps," I murmured, flicking him a teasing glance. "I fell in love with you, for a start."

"Personally, I think that's the best decision you've made to date," he replied.

I laughed and so did he. He understood me, perhaps more than anyone else ever had.

The mission was only two weeks away and we had a lot to do. The next day we were attempting to skim the bombs into a mock-up of a railway tunnel entrance.

"Think of it like playing croquet," said Wallis as he briefed us before practice.

"I've never played croquet," said Maria. "But I used to be a mean bowler with the lads we hung around with."

Wallis laughed. "It's not quite the same," he said. "And also, in croquet, you don't bounce the ball along the ground."

"If you played like my sister, you would," I told him, recalling happy times on the farmhouse lawn with Jennifer and my parents.

"Anyway," said Wallis, perhaps regretting his analogy, "we've made the tunnel entrance the approximate height of that of the fortress, based on the intelligence gathered. So, it's as realistic as we can get it."

"All right," I said. "Then we'd best have a go."

"Good luck!" Wallis called after us as we walked over to our Mosquitos. Shortly afterwards we were barrelling down the runway once more and heading for the range.

"Feeling confident?" I asked Maria.

"As I'll ever be."

"Better get ready then," I said as the range came into view. This was her cue to get down into the observation section.

I circled around for the practice bombing run and could clearly see the railway tunnel mock-up. This consisted of an arched plywood frame secured to the ground.

"Control, we're going for our first run," I said as Maria slipped into the forward bombardier position.

"Roger, Bluebird Leader."

Patricia would be circling the site, waiting for her turn. I dropped the kite to sixty feet as I lined up our approach.

"Spotlights on ... steady... That's good... Keep it steady," said Maria.

I watched the airspeed carefully and kept us in line with the target. Up ahead I could see the fake railway arch. I waited for Maria to drop the bomb.

"That's it, almost there… Damn … go again… I missed it… Damn it!" exclaimed Maria in annoyance.

"No matter," I replied. "Better to make a mistake now than on the mission."

We banked away without having released the bomb and then turned in again for another go.

I lined up the approach once more, dropped the airspeed and waited.

"Yes, steady … steady… We're dead-on target … and bombs away," said Maria.

I banked sharply while Maria let out a whoop. I craned my head around to see the bomb bouncing through the tunnel entrance.

"You did it!" I said to Maria.

"We did it!" she replied.

The radio burst into life. "Bluebird Leader, Wallis says well done. See if you can do it again," said Control.

"Wilco," I replied with a smile.

Patricia went next, but their bomb went slightly wide and missed the tunnel entrance. These were the margins we were playing with.

"I was out of line, Bluebird Leader. We'll do better next time," said Patricia as she banked her kite away.

"Don't worry, Bluebird Two," I told her. "That's why we're practising."

"I know," said Patricia. "But it's annoying just the same."

I turned the kite back for another run. Once again Maria got in a perfect shot. The dummy bomb bounced into the tunnel entrance just like the first one. She scrambled back up to her seat beside me, looking happy.

"Makes up for yesterday," she said.

"See, I knew you could do it," I told her.

Patricia went next and this time her bomb also went into the tunnel. Well satisfied, we returned to base. Henry and Wallis were waiting.

"Good work," said Wallis. "You're getting the hang of it already."

"We're getting there, for sure," I replied. "I'll feel better once we've had a few more successful goes."

"We'll get as many as we can in today," said Henry. "You've got to start flying with the full squadron, to get them used to the mission."

"How are we going to manage to see the target at night?" asked Maria.

"We've thought of that," said Henry. "You'll be dropping some parachute flares for your bombing run after you've tried to neutralise the ack-ack."

"What about the smoke from the bombs obscuring the target?" I asked.

"It could be an issue," said Henry. "We think you might need a short delay between the first attack and your bombing runs, to allow some of the smoke to disperse."

That sounded dangerous to me. Hanging around the target zone was always a hazardous endeavour. It gave the enemy time to scramble aircraft and so forth.

"Much of the ack-ack is on top of the hill," Henry added. "So, you'll be attacking those positions first. The smoke will be higher than you, and it will obscure you from view."

"We should discuss tactics properly," I told him. "I've a few ideas myself."

"We should, and we will do so later on with James and Gloria. And, of course, Barnes here."

I wanted to be sure that the bombing runs had adequate cover. Each Highball Mosquito needed at least one Mosquito, preferably two, one on each wing, to lay down suppressive fire. We had eighteen planes in the squadron now, and I decided we were going to need all of them at this rate.

"All right," I said. "Looks like the next set of bombs has been loaded, so I suppose we should go again."

"Practice makes perfect," said Maria.

"It does indeed," agreed Wallis.

CHAPTER FIVE

We had a council of war in James's office. Present were myself, Maria, Patricia, Connie, James, Henry, Gloria, Wallis, and the Marx Brothers. After some discussion, it was decided that the squadron would attack in groups of six. The first six planes would drop their ordnance on the hill above the tunnel entrance in order to try and neutralise the ack-ack.

"They can't drop too near to the tunnel," said Henry. "Otherwise it will collapse the entrance, and then the whole point of the mission will be lost."

There was a flat area above the tunnel forming a kind of ridge. The ack-ack positions were in that area, giving them a commanding view of the countryside. There were earthworks and various work vehicles at the top of the hill.

"It's the ack-ack here which threatens our bombing run," I said, pointing at the positions on the reconnaissance photographs.

"The ack-ack on the other side of the hill and further up is probably less of a threat," agreed Henry.

"All right," I said. "So, directly after the first bombing run, we'll begin the main attack."

"Yes," said James. "And in order to see the target, you'll need to have one or more parachute flares dropped from a high enough altitude."

"For each run?" said Maria.

"Very possibly, yes," he said.

We couldn't know for sure until we were going into the target. The flare would obviously give Jerry visibility, too, which might work against us.

"You'll start your run directly after the flare with one Mosquito on either side to cover you. They will strafe the area as you go in," said Henry.

"How many runs do we need?" I asked.

"As many as it takes to get one in the tunnel," said Wallis. "One should be enough to at least cause a cave-in and delay the construction for a while."

"There's no need to put yourself or the squadron in the line of fire for any longer than necessary once you've succeeded," said James. "The second wave of six can drop their ordnance in front of the entrance, and then you can all get the hell out of there."

It was settled. We'd get four goes at the tunnel. As soon as one bomb had gone in, we would be gone. James was right. The longer we stayed, the higher the chance of getting shot down.

"We can brief the rest of the squadron in the morning and then begin practice," I said.

"Are we going to try it with live ordnance?" Patricia asked.

"No," said Henry. "We are going to take it on faith that the Highballs will work. Barnes has assured us that this will be the case."

Wallis nodded. "They have been tested enough to warrant us having sufficient confidence in them."

"You've all had plenty of practice dropping bombs for real," added James. "So there's no need to waste ammunition."

"All right," I agreed.

"It all sounds splendid," said Harpo, stubbing out his cigarette.

"Indeed," said Chico.

The two of them had been listening intently to what was being said, despite having assumed an air of studied nonchalance. I was glad that they didn't add the rider that it would be a 'walk in the park'. We all knew that it was a dangerous mission, like every one we'd flown before, but possibly even more so.

The following day, I briefed the squadron, along with James, Henry, Gloria and Wallis. The mission was all about timing, and that had to be spot on.

"I will lead the flight to the target," I said. "Once there, the three groups, Alpha, Beta and Gamma, will split. Alpha will carry out an immediate bombing run above the hillside, then rendezvous away from the target to wait. One plane from Beta will drop flares then retreat to a different rendezvous point and wait. In the meantime, Gamma will attempt the Highball run. As soon as a successful run is made, Beta will bomb the entrance to the tunnel area. Then we'll all get out. Any questions?"

Linda raised her hand. "What if all of the Highballs miss?" she asked, holding my gaze.

"Then we still drop what ordnance we can and get out," I said flatly. "It will be disappointing, but those are the fortunes of war."

"I suppose you'd better not miss then," she replied.

There were one or two sniggers at this barbed remark. James responded immediately, for which I was grateful.

"All the practice in the world cannot completely prepare you for the real thing," he said. "You should all know by now that anything can go wrong on a mission, no matter how well prepared you might be. If the Highballs miss, it will prove one thing: that perhaps using them against railway tunnels isn't going to work."

"We can't know if they work for sure," added Wallis. "I invented them, and even I don't know. Using them in action is the only way we're ever going to find out. The Wing Commander is right. All the practice in the world is no substitute for the real thing. The Dambusters raid is an example of everything pretty much going right. It could have easily gone disastrously wrong too. We were lucky, and there's always an element of luck with these things."

"Any other questions?" I asked the squadron. Nobody said anything. "All right then, let's get to the details and then we'll carry out some dummy runs today to get the timing correct."

Shortly afterwards, everyone knew which group they were in and where they were supposed to be. We'd have one final briefing before the mission itself, when mission sheets would be issued with codenames, timings, and bearings for the navigators, and there would be time to study the reconnaissance photographs, but for now it was time to put the theory into practice.

On the way to the airfield, Maria was particularly scathing about Linda.

"What did she have to go and ask a question like that for?" she said.

"I suppose it's a reasonable question to ask," I replied.

"It was a stupid question," said Shelly. "The answer was obvious."

"James certainly told her," said Jennifer with a smile.

"Never mind Linda," I said. "Let's get our minds back on the job."

I knew that at some point I would have to deal with Linda, but now wasn't the time. She'd do her job regardless and I was counting on that.

We had spent some time mapping out positions for each group, where to wait and so forth. Jennifer was to lead Alpha on the first bombing run. Susan was to lead Beta to drop the flares and the final bombing run. I was leading Gamma. On my wings would be Sandra, whose navigator was ASO Lucy Morgan, and SO Dorothy Farmer, whose navigator was ASO Diana Fletcher. On Patricia's wings would be SO Molly Chingford with ASO Eileen Rutherford, and SO Carol Davies with ASO Loretta Harding.

At the airfield, I gathered everyone together.

"All right," I said. "You all know what you have to do and where you are supposed to be. Once we take off, form up on me until I give the order to disperse. Then form your groups and wait for the order to attack. Once that's given, we need to go into action. Getting the timing right is essential. Got it?" There were murmurs of agreement. "Good. Then let's get to it."

We headed for our respective Mosquitos and strapped in.

"Shall we give it a go?" I asked Maria.

"Let's do it," she replied with a smile.

I fired up the engines. When everyone was ready, I requested clearance from Control. Shortly afterwards we were airborne.

We flew low to the target in formation, Gamma leading. As we approached the range I ordered the split.

"Alpha attack, Beta to hold, Gamma to hold," I said as we banked away to our respective waiting areas. I had kept these close together so that I could observe what was going on. Henry was up in the replacement Spitfire to get an aerial view of the practice. James, Gloria, Wallis and the Marx Brothers were observing from the range.

Alpha had swooped in for their mock bombing run.

"Bombs away," said Jennifer, once they were over their designated target zone. These had been marked out on the range for clarity.

"Beta drop the firework," I said, referring to the flare.

Linda, who was part of that group, flew over the target zone to simulate releasing the parachute flair.

"Firework gone," said Linda.

"Bluebird Two, I'm going in," I said to Patricia.

I turned rapidly onto the approach, dropping to sixty feet while Maria slipped into the bombardier's position. Sandra and Dorothy were on each of my wings, flying close. On the mission, they would strafe the target as we approached.

"Steady," said Maria. "Steady … that's it… Bombs away."

The dummy bomb released and bounced towards the tunnel. It was a fraction off and flew past the side of it.

"Damn it," Maria said.

"Bluebird Two, your turn," I said without missing a beat. Although I might have to call in another flare on the night.

Patricia approached the target perfectly, and the bomb bounced nicely into the tunnel entrance.

"Bingo," said Patricia triumphantly.

Since it was a practice run, we had another go each and this time our bomb went in, and Patricia's went slightly wide.

"Bluebirds on me, return to base," I said.

We'd discuss what happened and then have another go.

"Not quite as easy as it looks when you're under pressure," Maria observed as we flew back to the airfield.

"And we'll be under fire too," I said.

We exchanged glances. We both knew that regardless of how much practice we did, on the night of the mission it might all turn out to be very different.

The days passed rapidly until the bombing runs became routine. We were getting close to the mission date. It just remained for us to practise at night using actual parachute flares. After the final daytime practice run, I gave the order to form up and return to base.

As we landed and taxied to our standings, I noticed that Jennifer's plane had not landed with the rest.

"Where are Jennifer and Shelly?" I asked Maria.

She looked at me and shrugged. "Search me," she said.

I immediately started to worry. Jennifer hadn't radioed in. Had something happened to her? The rest of the squadron were climbing into the back of the waiting trucks to return to Hawberry.

"Connie!" I called. It seemed odd that she would leave without Jennifer. The two of them were inseparable. Also, if Jennifer was missing, surely she would be the first to tell me.

Connie ran over, inevitably followed by the rest of the gang.

"Connie," I said, "where are Jennifer and Shelly?"

Connie dropped her gaze to avoid looking at me. I wasn't having it.

"You might as well tell me, Connie," I said. "I'm going to find out in the end."

"Their plane dropped out of formation, Boss."

"What?" I exclaimed. "What happened?"

"She's probably gone to race that Spitfire pilot," interjected Lucy. "They were talking in the pub again, the other night. He's been goading her for days."

"What?" I repeated, trying to quell the rising fury in my breast. "You all knew about this?"

"We didn't know, exactly. We didn't think she'd actually do it," said Sandra, trying to mitigate the situation.

"Did *you* know?" I said, turning to Maria.

Maria shook her head firmly. I believed her. She would have told me if she'd known, I was sure of it.

"Connie?" I said again.

Connie finally looked at me. "Jennifer wasn't going to do it, I swear. Then William bet her ten pounds… Jennifer said she's never one to lose a bet…" She trailed off with a guilty expression.

"You didn't think to bring this to me?" I began, but I knew her loyalty would lie first with Jennifer. "Oh, never mind. Where is this race taking place?"

"They're racing to Birling Gap from Cambridge," said Connie. "That's the bet."

That was all I needed to know. "All right," I said. "Come on, Maria. We're going after them."

"We're coming too," said Sandra at once.

"No, you're not," I said. "How will it look if we all turn up? We'll look like a squadron — exactly what we're trying to conceal. Now, all of you, go back to Hawberry and say nothing about this to anybody. Is that clear?"

Nobody spoke, so I took their silence for assent.

Reluctantly the others turned away to the waiting trucks. Without another word, I walked over to our usual Mosquito, which had been sitting idle for a while. Victoria was nearby, supervising the loading of more dummy bombs onto the Highball Mosquitos.

"Is this one fuelled up and ready?" I asked her, pointing to my kite.

"Always," she said, smiling.

"Great, I just need to take it up," I told her.

"You're the boss," she replied.

Maria and I climbed into the cockpit and strapped in. I fired up the engines.

"Bluebird Leader requesting clearance," I said to Control.

"Roger, Bluebird Leader, you're clear," replied Control.

I knew they wouldn't question it if I wanted to take up one of the Mosquitos. I taxied to the end of the runway and opened up the throttle, and we shot off down the runway a little faster than normal.

"Easy, tiger," said Maria, noting my barely suppressed fury. "Can we at least end this escapade in one piece?"

I sighed. "Yes, all right."

Maria gave me the bearing for Birling Gap. The chances of catching Jennifer were slim — she had a head start and we didn't know which route she was flying. However, I needed to do something other than sitting helplessly, seething whilst waiting for her to come back.

We flew rapidly at a reasonable height out towards Kent. We crossed the Thames at Gravesend and set a course for Birling Gap. The Gap was a cliff and beach close to Beachy Head — an easy run over the Sussex Downs.

We flew in silence while I wondered what on earth I was to do. Jennifer had crossed the line. I hoped at least to make her see sense. As for any consequences, I knew I would have to talk to James. This close to the mission, I could hardly stand her down — a fact she had probably counted on.

"We're nearly there, Boss," said Maria.

We could see the shimmer of the English Channel in the sun. It was hard to see if there were any other planes around.

"Should have brought a radar plane," I said.

Hindsight was a wonderful thing. I quashed my annoyance and scanned the skies. We moved closer to Birling, but there was no sign of Jennifer.

I sighed. "I suppose we'd better turn back."

"All right," Maria began and then pointed. "Wait ... over there ... is that them?"

I turned in the direction she was pointing and sure enough, there was a Mosquito and a Spitfire. They appeared to be flying in loops. I was about to bring Jennifer back down to earth.

"Bluebird Four," I said over the radio while taking us closer. "Bluebird Four, this is Bluebird Leader."

There was no response from Jennifer, but that was because she was probably on a different frequency. The Sirens had our own reserved channel for comms. I hoped she would spot us as we approached them.

"How close do you want to get?" Maria asked.

"Not close enough to accidentally get hit," I replied, starting to circle around.

Suddenly, the radio crackled to life.

"Anna?" Jennifer said.

"Bluebird Four," I said, maintaining protocol. "Cease whatever it is you're doing and return to base immediately."

Jennifer didn't answer right away, but I saw her Mosquito level off.

"That's an order, Bluebird Four," I told her.

"Roger, Bluebird Leader," said Jennifer at length.

"Let's go," I said, turning northwards.

Jennifer settled her plane on my wing. Maria gave out a bearing for home. The Spitfire flew across our boughs, dipping his wings before flying off in a different direction.

"Think carefully," advised Maria, "about what you're going to say when we get back to base."

My initial worry at Jennifer's absence had been replaced by anger. All our lives Jennifer had been cutting up a lark and I'd played along with it. In wartime, I had hoped she had grown out of it. I was furious to discover that she hadn't.

"Perhaps she thought you wouldn't find out," said Maria, reading my thoughts.

"That doesn't make it any better," I replied. "Because then everyone would have known except me, and I would have looked like a fool."

"I would have told you," said Maria. "As soon as I knew."

"Thank you," I said and shot her a grateful smile.

The trip back to Hawberry helped me to calm down. I felt a sense of relief that nothing bad had happened to Jennifer and Shelly, which did a lot to mitigate my wrath.

We landed and taxied to our standing. I jumped down from the Mosquito, along with Maria. Then we waited for Jennifer and Shelly to join us. When we were all standing together, I fixed them with a hard stare.

"I'm not going to lecture you about what you've just done," I began in an even tone. "Because I'm pretty sure you know it was wrong, otherwise you wouldn't have done it in secret."

When Jennifer didn't respond, I asked, "So, did you win?"

"Of course I did. The result was never in doubt," she said.

"And what was all that?" I continued. "Looping the loop when we turned up?"

"It was just a bit of fun, Anna. We were pretending to have a dogfight."

She didn't seem in the least contrite. I tried to curb my annoyance and keep my voice level. "Why did you do it, Jenny? At least tell me that?"

Jennifer shrugged. "You know I could never refuse a dare, Anna, particularly when there's money involved."

"So all this for a ten-pound bet?" I said, firing up. "You need to grow up and start acting like an officer in the RAF."

"I do my job and I do it well," Jennifer said hotly. "You can't blame me for letting off a bit of steam."

I shook my head. This wasn't the response I had expected from her. She wasn't taking into account all of the protocols she had broken or how irresponsible she had been.

"Well, maybe you can let off steam back at the farm," I said.

Her eyes widened. "Are you threatening to throw me out of the Sirens?" she asked.

I didn't mean it, of course, but I was blazing mad at that moment. "I'm tempted. And you're pushing it, just because you're my sister," I continued.

"And you're getting too bloody big for your boots, Miss Flight Leader," she flung back at me.

I was flabbergasted. Even Shelly, who was standing beside her and keeping quiet, looked shocked.

"What did you say?" I asked.

"You heard me! You're always throwing your weight around, ordering everybody about."

"That's my job, in case you didn't know!" I shouted.

Jennifer, however, was in full flow. "You've changed. You're not the sister I once knew."

I was hurt and angry almost beyond words. "How could you say that? If I've changed, then so have you, and not for the better."

She shrugged as if she didn't care. Deep down I knew she would be regretting every word, but that didn't help.

"Well, anyway, do your worst, whatever it is. Get it over with."

I hesitated, because I didn't really know what to do. "I … I haven't decided," I said.

"Let me know when you do," said Jennifer, turning to go.

I had had enough. She wasn't just going to walk away from me like that. I could pull rank when I had to, and I did.

"Stand to attention!" I shouted in my best parade ground voice. "You are *not* dismissed."

Jennifer automatically complied. She stared back at me with defiance. We were both angry but at the same time, all of the training and drill was now part of our make-up.

I saluted her very smartly. "Now you are dismissed," I said quietly.

Jennifer and Shelly returned the salute without another word. As I watched them go, I felt a touch on my arm. It was Maria.

"Want to talk about it?" she asked quietly.

"What is there to say?" I replied.

"Well, first of all, it's not true, what she said. You're not too big for your boots. You have an enormous amount of respect in the squadron."

"Not from Jennifer, obviously," I said bitterly.

"She's just hitting out at you because she knows she's in the wrong. It takes a bigger person to admit it."

I sighed. What Maria said was true, but knowing it didn't make it any better.

"What am I supposed to do with her?"

"Whatever you decide," said Maria with her usual pragmatism, "you know you can't leave it like that."

This was also true. Military discipline had to be adhered to. Jennifer had transgressed standing orders with her behaviour.

"We haven't fallen out for years and now this," I said, sniffing back a tear. I was determined not to cry.

Maria smiled in understanding and put an arm around my shoulder.

"She'll come around. You'll see. In the meantime, perhaps ask James what he thinks you should do."

"I want to handle it myself," I said quietly.

"Sometimes you need another voice, a voice of reason," she said, smiling.

She was right. In any case, James needed to know. This was the kind of thing that would get out in the squadron.

"Yes, all right."

"Come on, let's get back to Hawberry," she said.

As I was turning to go, Victoria appeared from one of the hangars. No doubt she'd heard the entire fracas. It was loud enough.

"Victoria?" I asked as she flicked a salute.

"I just want you to know, ma'am, that you have the utmost respect from me and from all of the ground crew for the job you do," she told me.

"Thank you. I appreciate it."

"Chin up, ma'am," she said.

"Told you," said Maria as we watched her walk back to the hangar.

"Yes," I said as we walked over to the truck that was patiently waiting. "You always do."

Back at Hawberry, I found James alone in his office. He got up at once when he saw my expression.

"Anna, what's happened?" he asked, leading me to the sofa. "Didn't the practice go well? According to Henry, it's looking pretty good."

"It's not the practice," I told him with a sigh. "It's Jennifer."

James took my hand in his and held it as we sat down together. He listened patiently and without comment until I had finished.

"I see," he said at length.

"Meaning?"

"Well, she's obviously disobeyed orders…" he began.

"I know. And I need to make an example of her. I can't just let her off because she's my sister," I told him.

"I understand," he said. "But Jennifer is still one of our best pilots, and the mission is almost upon us."

"I am aware of this."

"So what do you want to do about it?"

"I don't know, James," I said, a little exasperated.

"All right, well … what do you *suggest* we do?" I guessed this was the burden of command. It should be up to me, I supposed, although in the past James had dealt with breaches of discipline.

"A court-martial is how I feel right now!" I said crossly.

"I'd advise against it," he said with a trace of amusement.

"Don't make fun of me, James."

"I'm not, darling, but perhaps something less … severe?"

"She's already had to apologise once to the whole squadron. So a fat lot of good it will do making her do it again," I said, thinking out loud. "I can't stand her down because of the mission, but nor can I allow her behaviour to go unchecked."

"Drill?" James suggested lightly.

"Doesn't seem quite enough," I mused.

"Well, why don't you think on it and exercise your authority after the mission is over," he said gently. "Tell her that the consequences are deferred until then."

"All right."

A thought had crossed my mind. Perhaps I did need to stand Jennifer down or even send her home for a week or two. It might give her cause to think. In the meantime, we at least needed to remain on good terms until the mission was completed.

"Tea?" James suggested with a smile.

A cup of tea helped soothe my nerves, and afterwards I returned to my room to try and make it up with Jennifer. But when I arrived, she wasn't there. There was only Maria.

"Hi," she said, sitting at ease on Jennifer's bed.

"Where's Jennifer?" I asked.

"She's gone to bunk up in Connie's room."

"Oh, for goodness' sake!" I said, annoyed all over again. "I came here to make it up with her and now she does this!"

"Leave it, is my advice," Maria said. "Anyway, what did James say?"

I told her what had transpired and that I'd elected to leave any disciplinary action until after the mission was over.

"Very wise," said Maria.

At the back of my mind was the thought that one of us might not return from the mission. The notion that Jennifer and I might part on bad terms was unbearable, but I set it aside. There was a job to do. I had to focus on that. I was the Flight Leader, and I was determined to live up to the role I'd been given.

CHAPTER SIX

For the next two days, things were a little strained between Jennifer and I. She was punctilious to a point which served to infuriate me. The rest of the gang were uncomfortable too, I could tell. The talk at mealtimes was subdued and Jennifer said very little, sitting at the end of the table with Connie and sharing a cigarette.

Two nights before the mission, I briefed everyone about the night practice before we headed out to the airfield in the trucks.

"Do you think it will go okay?" asked Patricia as we trundled down the track.

"It should be fine," I replied. "We've not used the parachute flares before, but apart from that, we've done plenty of night missions."

The truck came to a halt. We jumped down and headed for the Mosquitos. As I walked, I noticed Sandra at my elbow.

"Boss," she said. "Nobody blames you for … you know. Jennifer was in the wrong."

"Thanks," I said.

"It's just a bit … awkward. That's why everyone is so quiet."

"I know, but thank you," I told her. "Let's get this practice done."

"You got it, Boss. We'll be there on your wing, watching your back."

I smiled and we carried on to our respective planes. Maria and I strapped in and I fired up the engines. Soon we were airborne. The practice proceeded satisfactorily and it was soon time for the first parachute flair.

"Firework dropped," said Linda, as I lined up the Mosquito for the approach.

The flare lit up the approach nicely and we dropped to sixty feet with our escort. Maria slipped into the bombardier position.

"Visibility excellent," she said as we headed towards the target. "Bombs away…"

The Highball bounced nicely into the tunnel entrance. I banked away sharply.

"Yes!" said Maria triumphantly.

"If that happens on the night," I said, "then we can all go home early."

We went through the motions of dropping the other three bombs. More parachute flares were needed as each one only lasted a few minutes. Then it was time to wrap up the exercise.

"Let's hope it doesn't take four attempts," said Maria as we headed back to the airfield.

"I agree. Because one thing we haven't thought of is that the bombs will detonate even if they miss," I said.

There was nothing we could do about it. Smoke might obscure the target, or the bomb might obstruct the entrance even if it didn't go in. I would have to make decisions on the fly — that was all I could do.

"Also, those parachute flares work both ways," said Maria. "If we can see them, then they can see us."

I had thought of this too. It couldn't be helped.

"Let's hope that our wingwomen can keep their heads down then," I replied.

"One more night," said Maria. "And then we're doing it for real."

On that sobering thought, I landed the plane. The second practice went as well as the first and the banter in the crew was back to normal, though Jennifer was still barely talking to me, which I hated more than anything. When we were younger, we could never stay angry with each other for long. This was different, and I wondered if things would ever be the same between us.

I was on the way to my room when Linda suddenly appeared in the corridor. I stopped, a little startled, wondering what she wanted. She flicked me a lazy salute. I collected myself and returned the salute.

"Can I help you, Section Officer Harris?"

"Have you thought any more about our last conversation, ma'am?" she asked.

"Should I have?"

"I think you should," said Linda. "Particularly since you can't control some members of your squadron."

I knew exactly what she was alluding to, but wasn't going to be drawn on the subject.

"How I choose to run the squadron is my business and the Wing Commander's," I told her.

"Easy to say when your sister is involved, isn't it? No doubt you're going to turn a blind eye."

I knew she was goading me and I ignored this comment with difficulty.

"Have you actually got anything important to say to me, Section Officer Harris?" I asked icily.

"I'm keeping notes, ma'am. I told you you'd regret not accepting my offer, and you will," she said.

I could hear the menace behind her words. However, I was determined not to engage with her on the subject.

"Dismissed, Section Officer," I told her.

She smiled, saluted and walked away. I stared after her. What was she intending to do? It was the last thing I needed, to be worrying about a fifth columnist in the ranks the night before a mission. I wasn't sure what I could do about it anyway.

I put it from my mind to deal with at a later date. Now was not the time. I went to bed on my own, as Jennifer was still sleeping in Connie's room. As I closed my eyes, I realised how lonely a leadership role could be. In the end, I gave up trying to sleep. I put on my dressing gown and made my way silently to James's room.

The following afternoon we held a final briefing. I was on the podium along with James, Gloria, Barnes and the Marx Brothers. Final mission orders would be given along with up-to-date reconnaissance. I spoke first.

"This is it, Sirens," I said. "Mission day is here. We've practised and I won't say we're perfect, but we're as near as, damn it. Nothing can prepare us for doing this under fire and in combat conditions, but if we all carry out our assigned roles to the best of our ability, then hopefully we'll all come home safe and sound. On this mission, communication is key. I need to be informed at all times of anything that happens. In the event that I get shot down, Section Officer Batley will take over."

I glanced at Jennifer. She was stony-faced. Ordinarily, I would have named her as the second-in-command. After her escapade, however, I didn't feel that I could. Patricia was the logical choice, since she was flying the other Highball Mosquito.

"Good luck, everyone. Let's make Operation Molecatcher a success."

Henry stepped forward and motioned for the lights to be dimmed. "Here are the up-to-date photographs of the site," he said. "And the flight path you will take to get to the fortress…"

He pointed out the various gun batteries and so forth; we would spend some time studying these. When he'd finished, he said a few words of encouragement.

"Sirens," he said, "in terms of complexity, this is probably your most difficult mission to date. The element of surprise should be with you, however, so make the most of that. I just want to wish you good luck and Godspeed. I'm sure you will acquit yourselves well, just as you always have. Most importantly, make sure you do your damnedest to come back."

The Marx Brothers wished us well and then the briefing was over. Most of the squadron remained to go over the flight plans and review the reconnaissance photographs. At the hangars, the ground crew would be arming the planes and loading up the Highballs.

There wasn't the usual tension before a mission. Perhaps it was down to all the practice, but I felt more confident going into this mission than I had before any other.

"Are we taking bets on the success of this mission?" asked Shelly as we made our way to the dining room.

"I think we've had enough bets for the time being, don't you?" I said as we sat down at our usual table.

I glanced at Jennifer, who looked away.

"Well, I think it will go just fine," said Sandra, who was always a fount of optimism.

"Seconded," said Lucy.

"Thirded," said Susan.

We all laughed. Humour always helped ease the tension before a mission. We all knew things could go wrong and people could die. There was no sense in dwelling on it.

"All right then," said Shelly, raising her mug of tea. "Here's to a successful mission."

Later that night, I was in my room getting ready. I had said goodbye to James earlier. The memory of our last kiss still lingered.

I had just pulled on my flying suit and the sheepskin jacket when the door opened. It was Jennifer.

For a moment we just stared at each other, and then she was in my arms.

"Anna, I'm so sorry," she said tearfully.

I embraced her, feeling a rush of gladness. "Jenny, I've missed you," I told her.

We held each other for a long time, and then eventually she pulled away.

"I'm sorry, Anna, for being so distant. You were right. I shouldn't have done what I did."

I smiled and shook my head. "Jenny, what are you like? It's been awful with you not speaking to me. I hated every moment of it," I said quietly.

"I know. Anna, I didn't mean those horrible things I said to you. Of course, you're the best leader. And the very best sister."

We hugged again tightly, reconciled at last.

"I couldn't let you go on the mission thinking I hated you, Anna," she said at length.

"I never thought that. But I was angry with you for a while."

She laughed. "I don't blame you. I was perfectly horrid and selfish. I see that now."

"Never mind that. We'll discuss it properly after the mission," I said.

She caught the meaning in my words. She knew that as Flight Leader, I couldn't let it pass.

She nodded. "All right."

There was a knock at the door and Maria came in.

"Made it up, have you?" she asked with a smile.

"Yes," said Jennifer.

"Well then, come on, you two," Maria continued. "We've got a mission to fly."

CHAPTER SEVEN

The mood in the truck was buoyant. Now that the awkwardness between me and Jennifer was gone, the camaraderie was back.

"Heigh-ho, heigh-ho, it's off to bomb we go," sang Shelly.

We all laughed. We'd recently watched a showing of *Snow White and the Seven Dwarfs* in the briefing hall at Hawberry, which sometimes doubled as a cinema.

All too soon, the truck rolled to a halt at the airfield. We jumped down from the back and everyone assembled around me.

"All right, Sirens," I said. "You know what we have to do. So, let's get to it!"

There were a few whoops and cheers and then we dispersed to our various planes. I took the opportunity to have a quick look underneath our Mosquito. I was curious, as I had never seen a real Highball bomb.

The bomb was spherical with flattened sides where it was secured to the aircraft in the open bomb bay of the Mosquito. There were no doors due to the odd shape of the bomb itself. The clamps on each side of the bomb would impart the backspin before releasing it, and that helped it to bounce correctly.

Maria joined me. She kissed two fingers and then pressed them to the side of one of the bombs. "For luck," she said.

We climbed up into the Mosquito, strapped in and then I fired up the engines. Once these were purring nicely, I radioed Control.

"Control, this is Harrier Leader requesting clearance," I said.

Harriers had been chosen as our codename, apparently because they hunted moles.

"Roger, Harrier Leader. You're clear," said Control.

"Harriers, check in," I said and waited for the pilots to respond. One by one they answered.

"Harrier Two ready."

"Harrier Three ready."

Once all seventeen had acknowledged they were ready, I gave the flight the order to leave.

"Harriers, let's do this."

I steered the Mosquito out from the standing and headed for the end of the runway, followed by the others. Once there, I pulled to a stop and began to wind up the engines for take-off. I let off the brakes and we barrelled down the runway. Moments later we were airborne. The night was reasonably still and clear. The stars were out, and so was the moon. It was a perfect night for the attack. I circled the base, waiting for the flight to join me. Once everyone was in the air, it was time.

"Harriers, three groups in close formation. Gamma on me, low level," I said.

"Alpha on me," said Jennifer.

"Beta on me," said Susan.

I checked my wings for the others and seeing their black shapes in position, I dropped down low to hedge-hopping height.

Maria gave out the bearing and we were away.

The monochrome landscape flashed by beneath us, a patchwork of white and grey fields, along with the occasional house and town. The route took us down past Cambridge, to Gravesend, and then through Kent towards Dover.

Maria, alert for obstacles, called them out to me.

"Lines."

"Seen it."

"House."

"Got it."

"Hedge and … trees."

"Got them."

The time seemed to pass quickly, and soon we were over the Thames. The ink-black water gleamed in the moonlight. We turned east, heading past Chatham and down to Dover. The flight was uneventful, and soon we left Ashford behind us. The town was in darkness due to blackout regulations.

"Not far from the coast now," said Maria as she gave us a new bearing.

"Then the fun begins," I quipped.

"Nervous?" she asked.

"A little," I replied truthfully. I didn't feel entirely confident because there were always unknown factors on a mission.

"It'll be fine, Boss, you'll see," she said.

I glanced at Maria. She gave me a reassuring smile.

"Here's the coastline now."

The land ended abruptly. The Channel stretched out beyond it. I shivered at the memory of ditching in that icy water.

"Alpha and Beta, are you with us?" I said in one final check before we left the shores of Blighty.

"Roger," said Jennifer.

"Roger," said Susan.

I had not replaced Jennifer as the leader of the Alpha team. It did not make sense to do so, considering all the rehearsals we had done.

"Here we go," I said, flicking off the navigation lights.

It was now a straight run, skimming the waves and watching out for shipping. We would make landfall west of Calais, near a town called Wissant. From there it was a short hop to the Mimoyecques Fortress.

The Channel was a little choppy with a light offshore breeze, but nothing to worry us. The moon lit our way, glinting off the water. We flew fast and low to avoid radar detection by the Germans. We wouldn't be easy to spot. Even if we were seen from the ground, we'd be long gone before the ground defences could react.

I played the mission through in my mind as we flew, ensuring I knew every detail of what we had to do. We had to rely on each group playing their part.

"Beach dead ahead," said Maria, cutting into my thoughts.

Sure enough, a strip of white sand loomed ahead of us. I turned my attention back to the terrain as the coast slid under us. Just as rapidly, the beach was gone. We were once more over fields and countryside. This time, however, we were flying over hostile territory.

"House," said Maria.

"Seen it."

"Lines."

"Got them."

My heart began to race with the anticipation of what was to come.

A few moments later, Maria said, "Get ready to split."

It was our cue. The mission was upon us. All those hours of rehearsal came down to this moment. Gammas would go to a holding pattern and wait for Alpha to drop their ordnance. Then Linda from Beta group would go in and drop the first flare.

"Now," said Maria.

"Harriers, split. Gamma to hold, Beta to hold. Alpha, start the Circus Show," I said. The Circus Show was the codename for the target.

"Wilco," came back the responses. Maria gave a new bearing for Gamma. I led my group to the west of the fortress, where we began to circle around. Beta went east and did the same.

"Alphas starting the show," said Jennifer.

I listened intently while glancing over to where the fortress would be. When the ordnance went off, we ought to see the explosions.

"Alphas, attack formation," said Jennifer.

This was it. I glanced at Maria as the tension mounted. In a few moments, we'd be going in ourselves.

"Bombs away," said Jennifer at last. "Alpha to hold."

Seconds later the sky lit up with multiple explosions from Alpha's bombs. There was no time to enjoy the spectacle.

"Beta, drop Firework one," I said. "Harrier Leader going in, escort on me."

I split from the formation with Sandra and Dorothy on my wings, just as we'd rehearsed. Maria gave me a bearing and I headed for the spot where we would begin the run. We'd timed it over and over again. My heart began thumping just as it always did when we went on the attack for real.

"Firework dropped," said Linda as we made the turn for the attack run. "Returning to Beta."

"Here we go," said Maria, slipping out of her harness and sliding down into the bombardier's position.

"Good luck," I called after her.

We were now on the approach to the tunnel. I dropped the kite to sixty feet. Maria would check our height using the spotlights. I kept an eye on the speed. So far it was going like clockwork, just as we had practised.

"That's good," said Maria. "Keep it steady … steady…"

The parachute flare had lit up the target. I could see some fires still burning on the hillside from the bombs. Hopefully, they had taken out the ack-ack. At least we weren't under fire, which was a good sign. My heart was in my mouth as the target loomed closer.

"Keep going," said Maria. "All good. Steady now… Almost there…"

Suddenly the blinding beam of a searchlight hit us square on. Tracers streamed out of the darkness from a machine-gun post. The searchlight was positioned on the ground near the tunnel, something we hadn't accounted for.

"Incoming fire!" shouted Dorothy.

"I can't see a thing! I can't see!" called Maria frantically.

I kept going, but I was ready to abort at any second. Without hesitation, Sandra and Dorothy's planes opened up with cannon bursts. They scored a hit on the machine-gun. It stopped abruptly, but we still had the searchlight directly on us. It was hard to see anything at all, and the tunnel was getting ever closer.

"It's no good," said Maria. "I can't see… We're going to have to…"

She didn't finish, because the searchlight went out as suddenly as it had come on. Sandra or Dorothy must have hit it. I still had the afterimage in front of my eyes, but at least I could now see where we were going. Was it too late? Would we have to try again? I waited tensely for Maria's call.

"Bomb released," said Maria to my immense relief.

I banked sharp left, since we were now very close to the limestone cliffside. Maria would be watching the bomb going in.

"Damn," she said in annoyance. "It missed."

The parachute flare went out, plunging the fortress into darkness once more. There was no time to waste; Patricia would have to try next.

"Harrier Four, your turn," I said. "Beta, drop Firework two."

Maria gave us a bearing, taking us back to the holding point while we waited for Patricia to have a go. At least we'd stopped the searchlight; it wouldn't be a problem for her. A tremendous explosion from the fortress indicated that our bomb had gone off. It was hard to see, because we were on the other side of the hill. I hoped that the smoke wouldn't obscure the target.

"Damn that bloody searchlight," said Maria in exasperation.

"You'll get it next time," I said. "*If* you need to."

"Firework dropped," said SO Judith Ellington, who was part of the Beta group and flying Harrier Five. We had two planes loaded with parachute flares.

"I'm going in," said Patricia. "Escorts, give me immediate fire cover."

I grinned. She was sharp. After our experience, Patricia's team would go in with their guns blazing. Agonising seconds passed while we waited for a result.

"Bombs away," said Connie. "And … it's missed."

"Damn it," I said under my breath, then, "Beta, drop Firework three. We're going again."

"I'll get it this time, Boss," said Maria from her forward position.

The Germans would surely have cottoned on by now as to what we were up to. We needed one successful Highball before they came after us. Another explosion went off as the second Highball exploded. At least this would distract the enemy.

"Firework gone," said Linda, who had dropped another flare.

We were in position for our second attack run. I took the Mosquito down to attack height once more, easing up on the throttle until it was at the correct speed. There was smoke drifting across the target area as we flew in.

"Escort, suppressive fire," I said to Sandra and Dorothy.

"Roger."

Tracers erupted from their planes as I kept ours steady, hoping Maria could see well enough to release the final bomb. It seemed pretty clear in spite of the smoke.

"Steady," she said. "This is good… Keep it steady."

"Incoming," said Sandra as more tracers headed in our direction. They zinged past the cockpit from somewhere up on the hill. "I'll take it," she went on, splitting out of formation to attack the machine-gun position.

I didn't argue. It was her job. Ours was to stay on target.

"Yes, steady, nearly there… We've got it… Bombs away," said Maria.

There was a note of triumph in her voice as I banked away from the target with Dorothy on my wing and Sandra catching us up.

"Yes! It's gone in! Woohoo!" cried Maria triumphantly.

We had done it. All that remained was a final bombing run over the general tunnel area.

"Beta, attack," I said, giving the order.

We flew back to our holding position and waited.

"Beta, attack formation," said Susan, and then shortly afterwards, "Bombs away."

The sky was lit up by further explosions. It was time to go. We couldn't know if the Highball had worked or not, but if it had gone into the tunnel then that was all that mattered. We'd done our job. I wasn't going to waste another second hanging around.

"Harriers, let's get the hell out of here," I said.

I opened up the throttle and we headed to the rendezvous point. I eased back, waiting for the others to catch up.

"Alpha on station," said Jennifer.

"Beta on station," said Susan.

"Harriers, close formation, low level, let's go," I told them.

Then we were away. We still had to get out of France. I hoped the Germans hadn't had time to scramble any night fighters. This hope proved to be in vain.

Minutes into our flight away from the fortress, Pamela piped up.

"Radar contact, coming our way. One, possibly two."

"Confirmed," said Shelly.

I reacted at once. "Roger. Harriers, full throttle."

The flight immediately sped up in unison. We would try to outrun the enemy fighters and hope for the best. It all depended on whether they were behind us or on an interception course. The ground flashed by beneath us, taking nearly all of my attention.

"House!" yelled Maria.

"Got it."

"Lines, lines, lines."

"Seen them."

The news from the radar planes was cold comfort.

"Contact still closing," said Shelly.

"Confirmed," said Pamela.

I swore softly under my breath. Maria was back in her usual position and navigating.

"Not far to the coast," she said.

"Let's hope we can make it," I replied, concentrating fully on the terrain in front. However, it seemed our luck was about to run out.

"Still closing," said Pamela. "They're nearly on us."

"There they are. Bandits at nine o'clock!" shouted Sandra.

I flicked a glance to the side and could just make out the outline of two planes heading in our direction. They were Messerschmitt Bf 110s, German night fighters. Before I could react, a stream of tracers shot past the canopy. We were out of options. There was nothing for it but to fight back.

"Beta, Alpha, break, break," I said. "Attack."

Behind me, the Mosquitos split out of formation and turned to attack the fighters. I had hoped to avoid a dogfight, but it was our only choice. I could do nothing to help, as neither I nor Patricia had any guns.

The radio was suddenly alive with chatter.

"On your left, your left, take him."

"Fire, fire!"

"Missed, damn it."

"Look out!"

I looked at Maria. We both knew we had to keep going. Sandra, on our wing, started chafing.

"Permission to break," she said.

"Denied," I told her. "Escorts, stay close. We keep going."

Without them, we were sitting ducks. Behind me, the fight raged on, and then came the words I didn't want to hear.

"We're hit, we're hit. Going down."

It was SO Alice Rowe and ASO Carolyn Edwards from Beta group.

"Goodbye, Sirens. I'm pulling the pin," said Alice.

She meant the grenade. They had no choice. A fireball lit up the sky as their plane exploded. Then one of the Bf 110s also went down.

"Got the Jerry," said Jennifer triumphantly.

That left one enemy fighter. I wondered where it was.

"Harrier Leader, he's on your tail," yelled Susan as tracers shot past the canopy yet again.

"Break, Gamma, break," I said, banking sharply.

"Damn right I'm going to break," said Sandra grimly. "And then I'm going to break his goddamn butt."

Her plane flicked right and then turned sharply. I started to zig-zag to try and throw the German off.

"He's still there," said Maria as more tracers slid past the wing.

"Don't worry, Boss. I'm coming," said Sandra.

"Yes," said Maria. "There she is!"

I couldn't look because I was flying the plane, but Maria gave me a running commentary.

"She's firing … and another burst… She's hit it… Yes!"

"Bandit is going down," said Sandra. "Just like I said."

Out of the corner of my eye, I saw the enemy plane drop to earth.

"Thanks, Sandra," I said.

"Nobody messes with the Boss," she shot back. "Not on my watch."

I had to laugh, and so did Maria. There was still an urgent question I needed to ask.

"Radars, are there any more bandits?"

"Negative," said Shelly.

"Confirmed," said Pamela.

This was the news I wanted to hear. However, more fighters would probably be scrambled. We needed to be elsewhere, and fast. The squadron had dispersed somewhat due to the dogfight. I had to get us back together.

"Harriers, form up. We need to get out of here," I said as Maria gave out a new bearing.

I dropped down low once more and throttled up once the others had settled on my wings.

"We're nearly at the coast," said Maria.

"Thank goodness for that," I said with relief. The white sand of the beach flashed beneath us, and then we were over the black water of the Channel once more. It didn't mean we were out of danger, but every mile we put between us and France would bring us closer to safety.

We flew rapidly over the Channel as low as we could go. I didn't let up on the throttle, wanting to get as far from enemy territory as possible, in the shortest amount of time. Halfway across, I received some more unwelcome news.

"Radar contact behind us," said Shelly.

"Confirmed," said Pamela.

"How many?" I asked them. "And how far?"

"Many," said Shelly. "Possibly a squadron."

"They are several minutes away, though," said Pamela.

I looked at Maria in exasperation. "What else can go wrong?" I said bitterly.

"Well, that many might indicate Focke-Wulfs," said Maria.

We knew that the enemy sometimes flew these fighters at night. It would be bad news if they caught up with us. There was no possibility of turning to fight. We'd be decimated by the highly manoeuvrable planes. On the plus side, we had a head start on them, and I knew we could go faster than they could.

"Harriers, keep going at full throttle. We'll aim to outrun them," I said. "Radars, keep me posted."

"Wilco," came the response.

I radioed ahead to Control with our position. We rarely requested help, but this time I felt it was politic to do so.

"Control, we're being chased by a bandit squadron, likely 190s. Possible assistance needed," I said.

"Roger, Harrier Leader. We'll send support," said Control.

Maria gave them our bearing and heading so that if they scrambled some support, they would know where to go. Meanwhile, we streaked across the water as fast as we could go. After a few moments, I checked in again.

"Radars, where are the bandits?" I asked Shelly and Pamela.

"A little closer, but not by much," said Shelly.

"Confirmed," said Pamela.

"We keep going, Harriers," I said to the squadron. "It's all we can do."

"Looks like we kicked the hornets' nest one too many times," said Maria with a small laugh.

"Let's hope we don't get stung," I replied.

"We already have, remember?" Maria added softly.

I had not forgotten. We had lost a plane, a good pilot and navigator. I consoled myself with the thought that we were lucky it wasn't more. We'd had the element of surprise on our side, but after we'd hit their tunnel and their fortress, the Jerries wanted revenge. Perhaps the size of the response reflected the importance of the target.

In the distance, I began to make out the English coastline — the faint gleam of the white cliffs at Beachy Head.

"The bandits are still following us," said Pamela.

"They're not gaining, though," said Shelly.

Out of the darkness, some black shapes appeared. I could see the flare from their exhausts. The next moment, a squadron of Hurricanes roared over the top of us.

"There goes the cavalry," said Dorothy.

I breathed a sigh of relief, knowing we wouldn't be chased all the way back to Hawberry Hall. You could never tell what the enemy might do, and I didn't want to test their mettle that far.

I kept the squadron at full speed until we were well over Blighty. Then I gave the order to throttle back. There was no need to use up fuel unnecessarily, and it was far more taxing flying low-level at breakneck pace.

The journey back to the airfield was uneventful, and soon the familiar landmarks came into view.

"Control, this is Harrier Leader requesting permission to land," I said.

"Roger, Harrier Leader, permission granted," said Control.

As the landing lights came on down the sides of the runway, I took the Mosquito down. The wheels touched the ground and I taxied to the standing. Once I had brought the plane to a stop, I killed the engines.

"That was quite a mission," I said to Maria as we unstrapped.

"It was certainly hairy at times," she agreed.

"But I think we succeeded, in spite of everything."

"Yes, we did. The bomb went in, and that's mission accomplished."

We climbed down from our plane in a buoyant mood and made our way to the waiting trucks. There would be some much-needed refreshments in the dining room. I would have to break the sad news to James regarding the loss of Alice and Carolyn. I was only glad that we hadn't lost more.

"We live to fight another day," said Maria, divining my thoughts.

I linked my arm through hers and smiled. "Yes, indeed we do … and amen to that."

CHAPTER EIGHT

The following morning, after breakfast, James held a debrief in his office. Maria, Patricia, Connie and I sat around the table with James, Henry, Gloria, the Marx Brothers and Wallis. The Marx Brothers were smoking cigarettes as usual. They spoke first, as they evidently had up-to-date information.

"You will be pleased to hear that our intelligence reports indicate the mission was a success," began Harpo.

"The railway tunnel entrance was caved in by the bomb, although we don't know how far in it went. That will, at least, slow down the progress of the Germans. In the meantime, ideas are being kicked around at the War Office as to how we can cause more permanent damage to the fortress," said Chico.

"I am glad," I said. "Our efforts were not wasted."

"Nothing is ever wasted," put in Wallis with a smile. "You tried the bombs out in anger and that was incredibly important, regardless of the outcome."

"We'll be getting reconnaissance photographs to assess the damage overall," Henry added. "We'll be able to see more from those, at least on the surface."

"How did the Highballs actually work in practice?" asked Wallis, who was naturally anxious to know.

I let Maria and Connie tell him, since they were the bombardiers.

"It wasn't easy under fire," said Maria. "The parachute flares helped, but then we had the searchlight problem."

"I agree," said Connie. "Practice is one thing, but going in under fire is quite another."

"But you did it," said James, who liked to emphasise the positive when he could.

We went on to tell them about the bombing runs in more detail and the fact that it had taken three goes to get a bomb into the tunnel.

"So, really it was a twenty-five to thirty per cent chance," said Wallis when we had finished. "Not great odds."

"Do you feel you've got something useful from this mission?" Gloria asked him.

"Yes," he replied. "Everything is useful when it's carried out for real. That's the thing we simply cannot simulate. Whether the powers that be will want to continue with the Highball project remains to be seen, but I'm very thankful to you all for testing these bombs out."

Patricia shrugged. "Orders are orders."

She was right, of course. We did our duty regardless of whether we thought it was worthwhile or not. It was better, though, to feel that there was some point to it.

"I'm glad you came back safely," said James. He shot me a meaningful glance.

"All except Alice and Carolyn," Gloria reminded him.

"Sadly," said James. "We will make arrangements for a joint funeral service."

The bodies couldn't be recovered, naturally, but two coffins would be provided, filled with appropriate ballast. It would be put about that they died transporting a plane and ran into trouble. There was a known risk factor for transport pilots, and some had already died in service. So, nobody would question it. But I knew James would feel the loss keenly.

"We also had that trouble with Me 110s on the way home," I said.

"Indeed. Your team did well to shoot them down," said Henry. "Hopefully the next mission won't be so fraught."

I smiled but didn't entirely believe it. It seemed that we were being called upon to handle more complex missions of late. It was highly likely we would again.

"If there's nothing else?" said James, glancing around the table.

"What happens to the Highball Mosquitos?" I asked him.

"They'll be returned to Squadron Six One Eight," he said. "They're not much use to us, since they are entirely adapted for carrying Highball bombs."

"I'm not keen on flying a plane with no guns, anyway," said Patricia.

James laughed. "Duly noted."

The meeting broke up. I remained behind at James's request. When the others had gone, he pulled me into an embrace.

"I'm glad you came home safely."

I smiled and showed him how glad I was to *be* home. It was strange to call Hawberry home, but that was how it felt. I supposed that if you loved someone then, as they say, home is where the heart is.

After a few moments, James led me to the sofa.

"Have you decided anything about Jennifer?" he said.

I hesitated. I had thought about it a lot and had reluctantly come to a decision.

"Now the mission is over," I said, "I think she should be stood down … for at least two weeks. Shelly, too, because she was complicit."

"All right," said James. "You're the boss. When do you want to tell her?"

"As soon as possible, I suppose," I said. "Get it over with."

There was no time like the present. The longer I put it off, the more it would seem to be a pointless action. I didn't know if Jennifer would hate me, but I felt I had no option. If I did nothing, then it would reflect badly on me as Flight Leader.

"I'll send Judy to fetch them now," James said. "And we also need to inform Gloria."

Shortly afterwards, I was standing with James and Gloria when Judy ushered Jennifer and Shelly into James's office. They saluted and stopped in front of us. I could see the question in Jennifer's eyes. She probably knew what was coming, so I didn't beat around the bush.

"Jenny," I said, "I'm sending you home."

I saw her lip tremble as she fought to control her emotions. I hurried to explain my intentions so that she would realise it wasn't for good, and that she wasn't being kicked out of the Sirens.

"I'm standing you down for two weeks because you disobeyed orders and indulged in a race which could have jeopardised this squadron and risked our real purpose becoming known. I think it's better that you don't remain on the base for that period, and that's why I'm sending you home."

Jennifer said nothing, but I could see the hurt in her eyes.

"And me?" asked Shelly quietly. She probably knew that she wasn't going to escape some kind of punishment. She was correct in that assumption.

"I'm sending you home too. I'm standing you down for two weeks. You were complicit in the race."

I let that sink in, but Shelly didn't respond.

"I'm sorry, Jenny, Shelly. You know I have no choice," I continued, trying to mitigate the punishment as best I could.

After a long moment, Jennifer finally spoke. "I know. It's my fault, I deserve it," she said.

I watched a solitary tear run down her cheek. I felt as if my heart would break. She held her composure admirably, however. At that moment, I was as proud of her as I had ever been.

"When do we have to go?" she asked.

"Today," I said. "When you come back, we can put all of this behind us, all right?"

"All right," she said. She thought for a moment and added, "What should we tell the others?"

"The truth," I replied. "Tell them that you've been stood down and sent home for two weeks."

Jennifer swallowed hard. This wasn't easy for her, I could tell.

"Is there … anything else?" she asked me.

"No. Unless there's anything you want to say, you're dismissed. I'll come and see you off shortly."

"Ma'am," she said, a little stiffly.

The two of them saluted and walked out of the room with their heads held high. I knew Jennifer was upset but it couldn't be helped. Shelly would take it in her stride. She was far more insouciant. I was sure that part of Jennifer's chagrin would stem from having to leave Connie for two weeks.

"You did well," said James after they had gone.

I breathed a sigh of relief. "Thanks."

"It can't have been easy for you," said Gloria sympathetically.

"No, it wasn't."

"Sometimes you have to do things you don't like when you lead," said Gloria. "We've all been there, I assure you."

"It was for the best," said James. "It will send the right message to the rest of the squadron."

"Yes," I agreed.

My mind immediately went to Linda. I didn't suppose it would satisfy her in the least. She was a thorn in my side that was not about to go away any time soon.

"I'd suggest having a stiff drink," said James, "but I know you don't indulge."

I laughed. "I'll take a cup of tea if it's on offer."

"Tea, we can always do," said James with a smile.

I returned to my room to discover the usual gang assembled while Jennifer was in the process of packing a small suitcase. I had heard the sound of several voices through the door, but as I entered, there was a sudden awkward silence. I caught a stricken look from Connie. I looked from one person to another, expecting someone to at least attempt to remonstrate with me. However, it didn't happen. Instead, Jennifer stopped packing and looked around the room.

"If anyone thinks they've got something to say to Anna, they can stow it," she said firmly. "I deserved this. I have accepted the consequences of my actions. You should too."

This made me wonder if there had been some dissenting voices. It was probably better not to know.

"Well," said Susan, quickly standing up, "I think we'd better leave these two to their goodbyes."

"Yes, absolutely," said Sandra, following suit. "Sorry, Boss, we'll get out of your way, pronto."

Each of them hugged Jennifer in turn and left the room. Maria was the last to leave.

"See you in two weeks," she said as she embraced Jennifer. "We'll miss you."

Then Jennifer and I were alone.

"Jenny…" I began.

"Don't say anything," she begged me. "Please, Anna. I know that you had to do it. I know what I did was wrong."

"Oh, Jenny, I'm so sorry," I said softly.

Then she was in my arms. Her shoulders shook briefly as she shed the tears she had been holding in.

"Don't be sorry," said Jennifer. "I deserve it. I know I've pushed the boundaries and sometimes taken you for granted."

She pulled out of my embrace. I fished a hanky from my pocket and gently wiped her tear-streaked face, just as I had done many times when we were younger.

"I didn't mean to cry, damn it," she said.

"It's all right," I replied. "Anyway, you'll give my love to Daddy and Mummy, won't you?"

"Of course, I will," said Jennifer.

"What will you tell them?" I asked her.

"I'll say that I've been given some leave. I'll make up a whole bunch of stories about transporting planes. Enough to keep Daddy happy."

We both laughed, knowing our parents could never be told the reality of our life in the Sirens.

"I'll take the car," she said. "I invited Shelly to stay with me."

"Good idea. She'll keep you company," I said.

"Yes, because I won't have you … or … Connie," said Jennifer with a wry smile.

"Is Connie very upset?"

"She understands. She doesn't hate you, but I suppose she's a little mad at you. She's even madder at me, so I wouldn't worry," said Jennifer with a laugh.

"I'll take that," I said, laughing too.

We stood holding hands for a long moment and then Jennifer hugged me once more.

"I'd better go. No sense in hanging around."

"No."

"Don't die while I'm gone," she said.

"I'll try not to."

She dropped a kiss on my cheek, picked up her suitcase and left the room. I stood there for a long moment without moving. It seemed, just then, like the hardest thing I'd ever done.

Maria came back into the room shortly afterwards.

"Chin up, chuck," she said, taking in my expression. "You did what you had to do and I'm proud of you."

I could always rely on Maria to be pragmatic.

"Life goes on. We'll have more missions to fly," she continued.

"And we're one radar plane down," I replied, forcing my mind back to practical matters.

"There is that."

Since it was nearly lunchtime, we went downstairs to eat. I got myself a portion of ham, mashed potatoes, peas and carrots with gravy, then sat at our usual table. After a minute or two of eating in silence, I'd had enough.

"Look," I said, "if you all think I'm some kind of ogre, then let's get it out in the open. I'm damned if I'll sit here eating every meal like this."

"We don't think that," said Patricia at once.

"No, we don't," said Pamela.

"It's just a shame —" Sandra began.

"What's done is done," said Connie, cutting in. "I told Jennifer not to do it and she didn't listen. So, here we are." She angrily stubbed out her half-smoked cigarette into an ashtray, pushed away her plate and stood up. "I'm going for some fresh air," she announced.

I watched her leave the dining room and decided that we needed something to distract us from these internal problems.

"Boss," said Sandra, "you had no choice. We all respect you for that."

I smiled at her gratefully and resumed eating my lunch.

As it happened, we did have something to distract us: the funeral of Alice and Carolyn, who were killed in action on the fortress raid. This was not our first squadron funeral, nor would it be our last. On this occasion, neither of their families had elected to come, instead holding their own private memorial services. Unfortunately, the coffins could not be released to them because there were no bodies inside them.

In any case, James insisted that burials would take place on-site for all Sirens killed in action or otherwise. It was the only way to preserve our security. As always, the two coffins, each draped with a Union Jack, were each placed on a gun carriage, to be processed to the chapel in the grounds of Hawberry Hall.

The chaplain led the funeral procession. He was dressed in uniform but wearing a priest's dog collar. Behind him, I led the Sirens in two marching columns. James, Henry, Gloria, the Marx Brothers and various other base personnel followed behind the gun carriages.

Every Siren marched with a rifle in the crook of their left arm, with the butt pointing upwards and the barrel pointing behind them to the ground. It was the traditional manner of carrying them for service funerals. It was somewhat unusual for WAAFs to bear arms. However, the Sirens were not a normal WAAF unit and were exempt from these restrictions.

Sergeant Wallace gave the orders to the funeral procession when we were all assembled.

"Funeral parade, forward march!" ordered Sergeant Wallace.

We marched forward in slow time until we arrived at the small chapel. Thankfully, this was not too far. Slow-time marching was quite taxing to keep up for long periods.

At this point, the order came to "Form up!" and we formed a guard of honour on either side of the path to the chapel entrance, presenting our rifles in salute while the coffins were carried up the path and inside for the service. We all filed in afterwards and took our seats. The chapel organ was playing something appropriately mournful.

The chaplain began the service and talked about Alice and Carolyn as if he knew them. I was aware, of course, that this wasn't the case. Many of us never saw the chaplain from one day to another, unless we felt the need.

Afterwards, James stepped up to the lectern to speak. I already knew that I would be expected to say something, and this time I was prepared. I had not really known Alice or Carolyn. It was impossible to know everyone in a thirty-six-crew squadron well. It didn't stop me feeling their loss, however.

"We are gathered here to mourn the tragic loss of Section Officer Alice Rowe and Assistant Section Officer Carolyn Edwards," said James. "These two brave women were killed in action carrying out the duty given to every member of the Sirens. We know that they did so to the best of their abilities, and with the diligence and fortitude we have come to expect from this squadron. Alice and Carolyn made us proud, and they will be sorely missed."

As James stepped down, I got up from my seat and walked over to take my turn. James shot me a reassuring smile. As their family were not present, I could at least be honest about the circumstances of Alice and Carolyn's deaths.

"Alice and Carolyn were two stalwart members of this squadron. They were in the thick of it, defending the squadron against an enemy fighter when they were shot down following a difficult but successful action in France. Alice carried out her sworn duty to the last in that regard."

I paused. Everyone knew what I meant without me spelling it out. She had used the grenade we had each been provided with to preserve the secret of the Sirens.

"Those final moments and that duty took a tremendous amount of courage. Courage I hope we would all show in the same circumstances. While I might be the Flight Leader, we each lead by example. Alice and Carolyn certainly did that. Let us hope that we will be as resolute as they were if the time comes."

It was a timely warning that none of us knew if or when that occasion might arise — the moment when we would have to make a life or death decision for ourselves.

"We are Sirens, until death us do part or at least until the war ends, whichever may come sooner. Thus, we honour our fallen comrades. We will remember them long after the drums of war are silent. Thank you."

I resumed my seat and James looked on approvingly.

"The coffins will now proceed to the graveside, where I will administer the last rites," said the chaplain.

"Guard of Honour, form up!" ordered Sergeant Wallace.

We lined up in two columns and preceded the coffins out of the chapel, then on to the graveyard. Each coffin was lowered into the ground and honoured with a gun salute consisting of six salvos. The flags from the coffins were carefully folded and would be sent to the families.

Following the ceremony, we were dismissed and began to disperse. I remained at the graveside for a few moments, along with Maria and Sandra.

Linda sauntered up and saluted casually. "Your sister is not here, I see," she said.

"You know exactly where she is," Maria snapped, firing up immediately.

"Oh yes, that's right. You sent her home. Well done, ma'am. I didn't know you had it in you."

"Dismissed, Section Officer Harris," I said quietly, knowing she had nothing useful to say to me. It was simply another opportunity to taunt me whilst staying just within the lines of protocol.

Linda flicked another lazy salute and wandered away.

"What did she want to go and bring that up for?" growled Maria.

"I suppose she's trying to bait me," I said.

"What?" exclaimed Maria.

"It's not the first time," I said.

"Boss!" said Sandra, looking shocked.

I realised I had said too much, but now the cat was out of the bag I'd have to tell them. "Look, I'll explain later, all right?" I said.

James came up to us at that moment. The other two saluted him and then left us alone.

"Was Harris bothering you?" he asked without preamble.

"Oh goodness," I said, rolling my eyes. "Was it that obvious?"

"It was rather. What's she been saying?" he asked.

I sighed. There was nothing for it. He would get the truth out of me one way or another.

"I'll tell you, but not here," I said.

"All right. But if she is becoming a problem, I need to know." Then he changed the subject. "Great speech, by the way."

"Oh, you know," I replied, blushing. "I had a bit of time to work on it this time."

"I'm sure Churchill would be impressed."

"No, surely not," I said, laughing, but was flattered just the same.

"Anyway, let's join the others, shall we?" he said.

It was traditional to hold a wake in the dining room, where refreshments were served. It was primarily for the families, and although they were not present, James still felt it politic to hold one for the Sirens.

We slipped into the dining room and then lost each other in the throng. I took the opportunity to talk to some of the Sirens that I didn't know so well, plus the ground crew and other personnel. It was noticeable that James was treating me like a senior member of the squadron. I took it as a sign of trust.

Later on in James's office, we talked about Linda over a cup of tea. Tea seemed to be becoming our thing, rather like an established couple. I pushed the thought away as I told him what Linda had said. He looked pensive.

"I should have said something to you before," I confessed. "I thought I could handle it myself."

"There's no chance I would accept her being second-in-command," he said. "So, she's on a hiding to nothing if she thinks she can coerce you."

"I have no intention of acceding to her demands in any case," I replied.

For once, he looked quite serious. "The question is, how long do we let this go on for?"

"I don't know. She's performing well enough on missions. It's also her word against mine. If challenged, she would simply deny it."

He took a sip of his tea.

"What could we do about her anyway?" I asked him. "Kick her out of the Sirens?"

"I'd rather she was given a different assignment," he said after some thought.

"Maybe she could be sent to Europe as a spy…"

"It's not a bad idea — she has the right qualities to do it," James said with a laugh. "But I think the Marx Brothers would naysay it because she knows too much about the Sirens. If she was captured…"

He trailed off, because we both knew what the consequences of that would be. Our cover would be blown with the Germans for one thing.

We turned our attention to other topics, since neither of us had a solution. I suspected that Linda would eventually force our hand.

"Anyway," said James at length, "have you given any more thought to what we talked about a while ago?"

"What did we talk about?" I said, prevaricating.

"Marriage," he said lightly. "We talked about marriage, or at least getting engaged."

"And I said you haven't asked me," I shot back.

"You can't blame me for wanting to know how such a proposal might be received," he said, sounding a little aggrieved.

"I do love you, James," I said, wanting to reassure him.

"I love you too, Anna, and well … you know how I feel."

He smiled. I reached out my hand and he took it.

"It's not that I don't want to marry you one day, James," I began.

"Then what is it?"

"I don't know," I said, unable to fathom my own feelings.

"What shall we do with you, Flight Officer Nightingale?" he said, setting down his cup.

I shrugged helplessly as he took me into his arms, thus ending the conversation about marriage for the moment.

The best part of a week passed without further incident or any cause to think about Linda.

Maria and Sandra had been incandescent when I told them about what had occurred.

"Please," I said to them, "don't do anything to make matters worse. I will figure it out, with James."

"All right, Boss," said Sandra. "But if I hear her saying anything…"

She trailed off with an ominous expression on her face. Luckily, Linda had kept out of my way.

It was strange being without Jennifer. She would no doubt concoct some plausible story for our parents as to why she was on leave. I wondered how they were getting on. In a way I envied Jennifer. I had not seen my mother or father since I had joined the Sirens, talking only sporadically with them on the phone.

Each night, I returned to my room in the early hours to an empty bed after visiting James. I had become so used to finding Jennifer there. I tried not to feel regretful about what had transpired; I knew I had had no choice.

One afternoon not long after lunch, a briefing was called. This was unusual, and there was something of a buzz in the briefing room as we all assembled.

"I wonder what's going on?" said Connie.

"Is it a mission?" put in Pamela.

Before anyone could offer further conjecture, Gloria arrived in the room along with James, Henry and the Marx Brothers.

"Attention!" said Gloria.

We all stood up and waited until James said, "At ease, everyone."

When we were seated once more, James stepped forward to speak. His expression was grim.

"A situation has developed in Northern France," he said. "A number of Resistance fighters have been surrounded by the Germans with no hope of escape. The Sirens have been asked to provide air cover in order to give them a chance to get out before they are completely decimated."

A hush came over the room. The war had a habit of disrupting daily routine and springing surprises like this. The Marx Brothers stepped forward after stubbing out their cigarettes.

"British Intelligence has received a coded distress call from a group of Resistance fighters known to us in France. They had gathered their compatriots together in order to carry out an insurgency operation when they were trapped by German forces," said Harpo.

"It seems that one of their number may have betrayed them," said Chico. "But no matter how it came about, they are in a perilous situation. They've requested help and the Sirens have been asked to give it to them."

Henry motioned for the lights to be dimmed. A photograph of a walled farmhouse sitting in a field was projected onto the screen.

"This farmhouse, situated east of a town called Guînes and near a large forest, is the current location of the Resistance fighters. They are surrounded on all sides by German infantry. So far, they have not deployed artillery, presumably in the hope of starving the Resistance out and capturing them alive."

He paused and Harpo said, "They could easily wipe out the fighters, but members of the Resistance are more valuable to the Gestapo alive than dead, for obvious reasons. So far, they've taken a softly-softly approach in order to try and force the surrender of the people in the farmhouse."

"However, we know that within a short period of time, the Germans will run out of patience," added Chico.

"That is why," said Henry, "you will launch an air attack tonight, causing enough of a distraction and killing enough of the surrounding forces to give the Resistance fighters a chance to break free." He indicated the area between the farmhouse and the forest. "You need to concentrate your firepower here so that they can make a run for the forest. Once in the woods, they will be able to disperse and hopefully evade the Jerries."

James stepped forward again. "I know this isn't what you're used to," he said. "You'll have very little time to prepare for the mission. You won't get a chance to practice. You'll have to fly in, do the job and get out. We will all just have to hope it will be enough."

"And if it's not, sir?" piped up Susan.

"Then at least we will have tried," said James. "That is all we can do."

Henry went on to outline the plan of attack. "You will be leaving very shortly after dark. Your route will take you east of London and you'll cross the Channel at Dymchurch. From there it's a straight run over to Wissant, with which you're no doubt familiar…"

There were a few chuckles at this. It was where we'd crossed on the last mission.

"You will proceed west of the fortress and towards the farmhouse. Once there, you'll carry out a bombing and strafing strike on the Germans. Then you'll head home."

"We're sending twelve planes," said James. "We think that's enough. It's not reported to be a large German force, and it gives you a chance to attack them on all sides."

"It's a small target, sir," I said. "Is there an easy way we can identify it?"

Attacking an airbase was one thing. A farmhouse in the middle of nowhere was quite another.

"It's difficult, I know," said James. "Which is why you will give Control a codeword when you are close enough to the target. This will be relayed to the Resistance fighters, and they will set off a flare marking the target."

I nodded. "Thank you," I said.

"Let's get down to more detailed planning," said Henry. "Flight Officer Nightingale will be leading the flight as usual. We will post a list of those crews going on the mission shortly."

I was glad to hear him say that. I would be consulted on the final choice. We all spent another hour going over the mission in more detail, studying the route and the layout of the land around the farmhouse.

In essence, it was straightforward. We'd fly in and attack the farmhouse from the east. The flight would split into four groups of three. The front group would fly over the farmhouse and attack the German positions from there. The left and right groups would drop ordnance on either side of the farmhouse. The rear group would drop ordnance to the east. Thus, we'd cover all four sides. We'd regroup and strafe the west side — the area that the Resistance wanted to escape through. After that, they were on their own.

With the briefing over, I sat down with James, Henry, Gloria and the Marx Brothers to decide on the mission team.

"Along with me, I would like Susan, Patrica and Sandra," I began, rattling off the names of my usual gang. It was a shame that Jennifer wasn't part of it, but two radar planes weren't necessary in my estimation.

I then gave them the names of the other eight crew members I wanted. I deliberately excluded Linda.

"You're happy with your selection?" James asked when I'd finished.

"Yes," I said. "I'm happy enough."

The mission crews were posted on the board at the back of the briefing room before dinner. The room also doubled as a mission room when we were undertaking missions. It was the one place where we could find all the notices and assignments pertinent to our squadron. In the dining room at lunch, everyone knew who was going and who wasn't.

"I wasn't expecting a mission like that out of the blue," said Susan, cutting into the meat on her plate.

Lunch consisted of corned beef, boiled potatoes, cabbage and some gravy. Since we were used to the varied fare, we didn't complain.

"It's a good sign," I replied.

"How so?" said Patricia.

Maria answered for me, cottoning on to my line of thinking. "It shows we're now a trusted squadron. They're not giving missions like this to just anybody, not where the outcome is so important."

"I suppose you're right," said Pamela. "The Resistance is our only insurgency operation on the ground in enemy territory. Thus, it can harry the enemy in ways that our Allied forces cannot."

"Sounds like you've been reading a military textbook," said Connie drily.

"And who says I haven't?" said Pamela.

"I can think of better things to read," Connie shot back.

"Like your trashy pulp fiction magazines?" came the sarcastic response.

"They're not trashy! You take that back," said Connie.

I decided to intervene. Connie had been decidedly tetchy in Jennifer's absence.

"Enough, the two of you. We've a mission to fly," I said as sternly as I could.

"Fine," said Connie, lighting up a cigarette.

"Yes, quit it," said Maria. "Next you'll be challenging each other to a duel."

"Funny you should mention that," said Pamela with a grin.

"No!" I said at once. "Heaven forbid that people start fighting duels in the Sirens."

"Have you fought a duel, Pamela?" asked Sandra with interest.

"No!" I said, emphasising my words with a wave of my fork. "No, no, no!"

Thankfully all talk of duels stopped and everyone resumed eating lunch. I eyed Pamela with some misgiving. She was from aristocratic stock and very likely skilled in the art of swordsmanship. A duel would be the last thing we needed.

As we were leaving the dining room, the woman who was fast becoming my nemesis appeared in front of me. Maria stiffened beside me as Linda snapped another lazy salute.

"I see you've left me off the mission list, ma'am," she said with a supercilious smile.

"Yes, I did," I replied. I did not owe her an explanation.

"Well, I could use the break, as it happens," Linda said.

"How fortuitous then," I replied.

She said no more. Instead, she saluted and walked away. I stared after her with irritation. She was doing just enough to annoy me but not enough to cross any lines.

"That's insubordination," said Maria hotly. "Tell me that isn't insubordination!"

"It's not," I replied, shaking my head. "Not in such a way that I can take action."

Maria made a face. "She's mocking you," she said. "I can't stand much more of it."

"Don't take the bait, Maria," I told her. "It's what she wants. If you do, then she's won."

Maria shot me another look of exasperation. "I'm not happy," she said quietly. "Not at all."

"I'm not happy either," I said. "But we've got a mission to fly. That's more important than a dozen Lindas."

"Yes, Boss. If you say so," she replied grudgingly.

CHAPTER NINE

The hour of the mission came around all too soon. I had been standing by the window in James's room, watching the setting sun. He put his arms around me and I leaned my head on his shoulder.

"Are you worried?" he asked. "About the mission?"

"No," I replied. "There's been no time to really think about it. We've just got to do it."

"Yes," he said. "Yes, indeed."

I turned into his embrace as the sun sank below the horizon. It was my cue.

"I've got to go," I breathed.

He sighed. "Must you?"

"You know I must…"

We both wanted just a few more moments together. Moments that might be our last.

I reluctantly kissed him goodbye and made my way to my room. There I changed into my pale brown flying suit, leather boots and sheepskin jacket. I was just checking that I had everything when Maria knocked on the door.

"Ready to go?" she asked.

"As I'll ever be."

I donned my life jacket and picked up my flying helmet, then we quietly made our way downstairs to join the rest of the squadron who were flying with us.

The trucks wended their way down the track towards the airfield. Connie sat alone at the back, smoking a cigarette. It was strange not to see Jennifer sharing it with her.

"What do you think, Boss?" Sandra piped up. "How's it going to go?"

"As well as any other mission, I expect," I said. "Just without the preparation we normally have."

"If only those Resistance guys knew a squadron of women were coming to save their butts," said Sandra with a laugh.

"I don't suppose it would surprise them at all," said Pamela. "There are plenty of women serving in the French Resistance by all accounts. I had thought about it myself before I came to the Sirens."

I couldn't imagine what that would be like, living from day to day with the fear of being caught. I knew that the Marx Brothers had some involvement with the Special Operations Executive, many of whom were women. Pamela seemed an ideal candidate.

"I couldn't do it," said Maria. "They'd clock my Welsh accent a mile off."

We laughed. The trucks came to a halt and we all piled out. I gathered the squadron together for a final word.

"All right," I said. "We don't know exactly what we're getting into here, so let's keep it tight and watch each other's backs. The main thing is to get in and out safely. Let's do the job and make sure we all come home."

There were murmurs of agreement.

"Let's go, Sirens," I said.

We dispersed to our Mosquitoes. Maria and I climbed into our plane, and she pulled the hatch shut and secured it. After the pre-flight checks, I started up the engines. It felt good to be back in our familiar plane, though it was a replacement for the one we had had to ditch.

"Ready?" I said to Maria.

"Ready," she replied with a smile.

"Merlin Leader requesting permission to take off," I said to Control. Merlin was our codename for the mission. It felt appropriate, considering we were being asked to perform some wizardry.

"Merlin Leader, you're clear," said Control.

I waited for the others to check in and when the whole flight was ready, I said, "Merlins, here we go."

I eased the kite out of our standing and started to taxi down to the runway, followed by the rest of the flight. When we reached the end of the runway, I wound up the engines before letting off the brakes. We barrelled down the runway and were soon airborne.

"Merlins, close formation, low level," I said as I took the Mosquito down to the familiar hedge-hopping height while Maria gave out the first bearing.

Then we were off over the patchwork of monochrome fields. Hedges, trees and powerlines loomed up. Maria called them out.

"Lines."

"Got it."

"Trees."

"Seen them."

Having a second pair of eyes was indispensable at the speed we were flying. In no time at all we were past Cambridge and then Chelmsford. It was a route we'd flown several times before, so the landmarks were familiar.

Night flying was inherently dangerous, but if we were going to surprise the Germans and keep our casualties to a minimum, then it was the best time to attack. They wouldn't see us coming, because we were too low for their radar detection. It was a tactic that continued to work and must have been frustrating for the enemy, though they often did the same when attacking our shores.

"There's the big smoke," said Maria, pointing to her left.

Some of the London landmarks could be seen silhouetted in the moonlight.

"Have you ever been there?" I asked her.

"To London? No, I've been a country girl for most of my life," she replied.

"Me too," I confessed. "The big city lights never attracted me."

I had been a homebody for so long and now here I was, flying missions over France. It seemed almost incongruous.

"Here comes the Thames," said Maria as we crossed over the dark water at Gravesend. From there it was a straight run down to Aylesford and Maidstone as we continued on a heading towards Dymchurch.

"Do you think this war will ever be over?" Maria said quietly as we slipped past Ashford.

"I hope so, one day," I replied.

"Part of me doesn't want it to end," she mused.

I flicked a glance at her. "Really? Why?"

"Because flying these missions, being a part of the Sirens, I feel like I'm somebody. A woman with an important job — a matter of life and death. What have I got back home, when I return to my old life?"

"I hadn't thought of it that way," I admitted.

I wondered what I would do. I was supposed to go back and help run the farm, but James wanted me to marry him. What would my life be like then?

"What are you thinking?" asked Maria.

"I've just realised that I'm torn between love and duty," I said.

"Duty to who?" she replied.

"To my family, my father, the farm," I sighed.

"Yes, I see…"

When she said no more, I said, "Well, what do you think?"

"I think that you should look out for that house!"

I took us over the roof of a farmhouse with practised ease, my dilemma temporarily forgotten.

"I think you'll find that love almost always wins," she said softly after a moment.

I didn't answer. I knew which way I was being pulled, and my resistance was crumbling. At least I understood my reluctance to encourage James's marriage proposal.

"We're approaching Dymchurch," said Maria a short while later.

I could see the line of white sand shimmering in the moonlight. Beyond that was the ink-black water of the Channel. I flicked off the navigation lights. The others would be doing the same.

"Merlins, keep them peeled," I said as we left the comparative safety of British shores.

Then we were over the water and skimming the waves, keeping as low as we could and watching out for ships and even the odd U-boat, although we'd never seen one while flying. I recalled the close call we'd had in the life raft. I wondered what we would have done had they decided to investigate and found us hiding inside it. Would I have pulled the pin from the grenade? Perhaps, once the U-boat was close enough. The explosion might have damaged the hull at least.

We were halfway across the Channel when Pamela piped up.

"Radar contact, two possible bandits, heading across our front," she said.

"Sit tight, Merlins," I said. "We keep going. Keep tabs on them, Merlin Six."

"Wilco," said Pamela.

We flew on regardless. At our current height, it was unlikely we'd be spotted. It was possibly a German night fighter patrol. Engaging in a firefight before we reached the target would be bad. We only had one shot at trying to free the Resistance fighters. If we failed or had to abort, then they would all perish.

The French coast was visible as a strip of sand. It came ever closer while I hoped that we wouldn't be detected by the patrol.

"Bandits have passed us," said Pamela.

"Roger," I replied with relief.

The beach flashed by beneath us and then we were over the French countryside. The target wasn't too far away now — around the same distance as the fortress and a little to the west.

We took the same path over fields as we had done on the previous mission. Maria and I were now completely focused. We automatically slipped into our routine.

"Hedge," said Maria.

"Seen it."

"Lines."

"Got it."

Then came yet another distraction.

"Radar contact, two bandits," said Pamela.

"Again?" said Maria in frustration.

"They are behind us, crossing our path," Pamela continued.

"Keep an eye on them, Merlin Six," I said.

"Roger," said Pamela.

I wasn't prepared to deviate now, although there was a possibility the fighters might come to the aid of the Germans when we attacked. Hopefully, the Germans would be taken by surprise and have no time to call in air cover. If they did, we'd just have to deal with it. We had learned to expect the unexpected. In any case, the target was getting nearer and I had no time to worry about anything else.

"Barnyard in ten," said Maria as she adjusted our heading. Barnyard was the codename for the target.

We were close. In just a few minutes, I would split the group into Alpha, Beta, Charlie and Delta. I would lead Alpha group over the top of the farmhouse. Beta and Charlie would take the sides, while Delta would drop the ordnance just before it. This called for some precision, which would all go for a Burton if we couldn't see the target properly. It was crucial for the Resistance to send up the flare.

The minutes passed by and I eased the safety off the guns in preparation. I was glad to have some cannons in our armoury once more. Flying the Highball Mosquito without proper armaments had made me feel vulnerable.

My pulse had begun to race when we got some welcome news.

"Bandits receding," said Pamela.

"Roger," I replied, happy to hear that they would not be an immediate worry.

"Barnyard in five," said Maria.

This was our cue to prepare for the bombing run.

"Merlins, split into attack formation," I said.

Two planes stayed with me, flown by Susan and Patricia. The others moved with their groups into the designated positions. Delta would throttle back and drop back a little.

Now I had to give the coded signal to Control.

"Control," I said. "Luna, Luna, Luna."

This was the codeword for the Resistance to set off the flare. Luna also happened to be the Roman goddess of the moon.

"Roger," said Control. "We're relaying."

We knew the target was rapidly approaching. The only problem was we could not see it. Making out a farmhouse in the dark landscape wasn't going to be easy until we were almost over it, by which time it would probably be too late.

"Where is it?" said Maria. "Where's the bloody flare?"

"Let's try again," I said.

I repeated the codeword over the radio: "Luna, Luna, Luna."

This would tell them the flare hadn't gone up.

"Relaying," said Control.

"Can you see anything?" I asked Maria.

There were shapes and shadows up ahead, but we couldn't be sure. There was no point dropping the bombs in the wrong place.

"No, damn it!" said Maria in frustration.

I was on the cusp of making a decision to abort or at least go around and try again when the sky suddenly lit up. A parachute flare had been sent up at last, casting the landscape into stark relief.

"There it is," said Maria, pointing ahead.

Sure enough, the walled farmhouse could be seen, illuminated by the flare. Surrounding it on all sides were vehicles, trucks, guns and what looked like scores of German troops. This was it. We were going in. I opened the bomb bay doors.

"Merlins, attack, attack, attack," I said.

Tracers streamed out towards us, but we kept going. We had been spotted, but we were over the farmhouse before the Germans could fully react. I caught a glimpse of people waving from behind the wall — the Resistance fighters. Then we were past the farmhouse and above the German troops. I hit the bomb release.

"Bombs away," I said.

Simultaneously Beta, Charlie and Delta released their bombs too. The bombs were on short fuses — just enough to allow us to get clear.

"Merlins, regroup," I said, banking hard left and opening up the throttle. We flew away, and the farmhouse was rocked by several explosions as our ordnance went off. We still had one more thing to do.

"Form up, on me, strafing attack run," I said, banking around to take us back over the ground between the farmhouse and the forest. We had to give the Resistance fighters the best chance of escape.

We fanned out in a line and flew back towards the vehicles, which were now ablaze. The parachute flare went out suddenly, but there was still enough light to see our new target.

"Fire," I said, opening up with the cannons.

Tracers streamed out from twelve Mosquitos, cutting up the dirt. Attempts by the Germans to fire back were cut short. There were more explosions from the vehicles as the fuel tanks ignited. We flew over them and as we banked around to the left of the farmhouse, I opened fire again.

"I can see people running," said Maria. "Hopefully they'll make it."

We had hit the Germans hard. They weren't expecting it. I circled us around the back of the farmhouse, strafing those areas too. We'd done a full circle. It was the best we could do. I caught a final glimpse of figures pelting across the field in the direction of the forest.

I hoped that the Resistance fighters would get away. We couldn't hang around to check on them in any case.

"Get us out of here," I said to Maria. "We've done our bit."

"With pleasure," she replied, giving us a new bearing.

"Merlins, form up. Let's get gone," I said.

I opened up the throttle and we headed away from the farmhouse as fast as we could. The enemy night fighters who had been patrolling might be called out to try and find us. The sooner we were out of range, the better.

"Do you think the Resistance fighters escaped?" Maria asked me.

"I hope so," I said. "It would be all for nothing otherwise."

We returned the way we'd come, flying over the same fields and houses. I wondered if we'd ever go this way again. We rarely hit the same target more than once.

The relief of completing the mission was palpable. I could feel my heartbeat beginning to return to normal as we approached the coastline.

"Wissant, dead ahead," said Maria.

We were passing to the east of the town when suddenly a stream of tracers erupted in our direction.

"Incoming fire," said Patricia.

It was joined by a second. The tracers were coming from the beach area. Perhaps we'd been spotted by a machine-gun nest. Bullets zinged past the canopy but fortunately missed us.

"Merlins, keep going," I said.

There was little point in alerting the Germans any further by returning fire. Twelve Mosquitos could kick up quite a lot of dirt.

"Boss, he's in my sights," said Sandra eagerly. "Can I take him out?"

I glanced at Maria. She nodded in agreement. I decided to risk it.

"Fire, if you're sure of the target," I said.

She opened up with her Brownings. Tracers streaked out from her plane. Moments later we were being fired at from several more places on the beach. It had been a mistake. However, now there was nothing for it.

"Full throttle, Merlins. Fire at will. I repeat, fire at will."

Once again, my heart was pumping as I cranked up the engines, slipped the safety off the guns and fired. The entire squadron cut loose at whoever was on the beach. It was a short-lived engagement as we roared over the sand and were gone.

"At least we made them put their heads down," said Maria with a laugh.

The next moment, Sharon Baker, one of the new pilots, came on the radio with bad news.

"This is Merlin Seven. My navigator's been hit," she said.

"Roger, Merlin Seven. How bad?" I asked.

"She's dead," came the answer.

I hesitated, then asked, "Are you still operational, Merlin Seven?"

"Affirmative, I'll make it. Just keep giving me the bearings…"

"Roger," I told her.

Maria and I looked at each other. We'd had a casualty, after all, hit by a stray bullet. The inky depths of the Channel passed under us as we skimmed the waves once more. I felt numb. This was another loss for the Sirens.

"How did the Jerries get there?" Maria asked. "They weren't on the beach before, when we flew over it."

It was a good point.

"Didn't we fly to the west of Wissant on the way in?" I said, recalling our journey to the target.

"Damn!" Maria swore. "How could I make such a mistake?"

"Hey, it's not a mistake. You weren't to know that troops were garrisoned on the east side. Intelligence said it was just a small town on the coast," I told her.

"It's my fault," she persisted. "And now someone is dead."

I turned to look at her. In the darkness, I could see her eyes glistening with tears.

"Maria," I said firmly, "it's not your fault. We could have gone either side of the town. It's just bad luck. Stop blaming yourself, and that's an order!"

She turned to me and smiled. "You're the Boss."

We both laughed and it broke the tension. What else was there to do? In wartime, things happened so quickly. One moment a person could be alive and the next moment dead. It was a tragedy, but somehow you had to go on.

"Let's focus," I said. "Here's the English coast coming up at last."

We passed back over the beach at Dymchurch and retraced our earlier flight path. To lighten the mood, Maria broke out in a somewhat bawdy sea shanty, and I joined in.

"Goodness," I said when we'd finished. "Where on earth did you learn that?"

"Oh, they used to sing it down at the local pub. I've got a good memory," she said. "Shall we sing another?"

"Why not?"

I learned a few new coarse phrases, to Maria's amusement. It served to pass the time as we flew back over the Thames, up past Chelmsford and Cambridge until at long last the airfield came into view.

"Control, this is Merlin Leader requesting clearance," I said.

"Merlin Leader, you're clear," came the response.

"We've one casualty, Control," I told them as I lowered the landing gear.

"Do you need a medic?"

"Negative."

"Roger."

In a sober mood, I touched down onto the runway. We taxied to the standing and I killed the engine.

I turned to Maria. "I'd better go and see Sharon."

"I'll come with you," she said, unstrapping her harness.

"All right."

CHAPTER TEN

James was pleased to see me back safely. I went back to his room after refreshments — a beef sandwich and a cup of cocoa.

I'd also made sure Sharon was all right. She was stoic about the loss of her navigator; we had all learned to be brave when faced with death, the longer the war dragged on.

"What happened?" James asked as I lay in his arms in the darkness.

"We came under fire at Wissant. There must have been Jerries garrisoned on the east side of the town. A bullet penetrated the cockpit of Sharon's plane. Her navigator was hit in the head. She would have died instantly," I told him.

"That's bad luck," he said.

"We've had a few casualties now," I replied. "Are we going to get some replacements?"

"Yes."

"Another funeral," I mused.

"Let's not talk about funerals, at least until tomorrow," he said.

So, we didn't.

The following day, a briefing was held after breakfast. James, Henry, Gloria and the Marx Brothers were up on the podium as usual.

"First, I just want to say very well done to those who flew the mission last night," said James, catching my eye briefly as he said it. "Second, it is with great sadness that I inform you that one of our own, ASO Wanda Gibson, was killed on the mission." James paused for a moment before continuing. "We will be holding a funeral in due course after her family have been informed."

We all knew the drill by now. Wanda's family would be told that she had died in a tragic flying accident while transporting a plane. Hopefully, nobody was keeping count of how many crew members had died in the Sirens. In wartime, of course, anything could happen. People lived with bad news all the time.

The Marx Brothers, who had been quietly smoking their cigarettes, now stepped forward.

"You will be pleased to know that we've heard from our intelligence sources that the majority of the Resistance fighters managed to escape into the woods from the farmhouse," said Harpo.

"Thanks to your stalwart and prompt action," added Chico.

There was a muted cheer at this news.

"We've also been told that your action accounted for many German casualties among the troops besieging the farmhouse, so it's a double win," Harpo continued, taking a drag on his cigarette.

"Yes, well done, all of you," added Henry, while Gloria beamed at us.

James wound up the proceedings.

"We will be getting some new recruits to the squadron very shortly, to replace those we have unfortunately lost. Selections are in progress." His statement was accompanied by affirmative nods from the Marx Brothers. "In the meantime, there will be another mission along soon, I'm sure. Rather like the buses in London." This elicited a few laughs. "However, please ensure you remain combat-ready."

"Which means practice and more practice," said Henry.

There were some groans on hearing this. However, we all knew that maintaining mission fitness was essential. That meant flying dummy runs, navigation runs and so forth.

"You know what they say about idle hands," said Maria, after the briefing had finished.

We were having a cup of tea in the dining room.

"Yes, we know," said Connie, rolling her eyes.

"I'll put together a practice roster," I said. "To make sure everyone keeps themselves busy."

"Jennifer and Shelly will be back soon," said Patricia, changing the subject.

"Yes," I said.

"Then the gang will all be together again," said Sandra.

A few days later, Jennifer and Shelly returned to Hawberry. They were naturally surrounded by our clan, all eager to see them home. I hung back while they all chattered excitedly in the atrium.

When the hubbub had died down, Jennifer came over to me and gave me a long hug.

"I'm so glad to be back," she said. "I missed this place so much."

"I missed you," I replied.

"Daddy and Mummy send their love," she told me.

"How are things at the farm?" I asked her.

"I'll tell you all the news later…" She trailed off as her attention was taken by the appearance of Connie.

"Go on," I whispered. "She's missed you too."

Jennifer walked slowly up to Connie. Connie smiled.

"Fancy a cigarette?" she said.

"Gasping," said Jennifer.

I watched them slip outside together. Jennifer's hand slid surreptitiously into Connie's. I turned my attention back to the rest of the group.

"What have I missed?" Shelly was saying.

"We went on an exciting mission," Sandra told her.

"Oh goodness! I want to hear all about it. But first let me take my stuff to my room." Shelly picked up her bag.

Since I had nothing more pressing to do, I followed the group upstairs, keen to hear some news of the outside world.

Later that evening, I managed to get some time alone with Jennifer. We walked arm in arm in the formal gardens in the fading light.

"What did you tell them, about what we're doing here?" I asked her, referring to our parents.

"Oh, just a lot of guff about delivering planes, teaching people to fly, you know," said Jennifer airily.

"Did they buy it?"

"Daddy seemed satisfied, though I think Mummy suspects there's more to it. But she didn't say anything."

I chuckled. Our mother had always been perceptive and neither of us was ever able to slip anything past her, no matter how hard we tried.

"Are they worried?"

"About us? Not really, but then they don't know we're flying combat missions into France and getting shot at by Jerries."

We both laughed at this.

"Daddy's very proud of you for getting promoted and becoming Flight Leader," said Jennifer.

"You told him?"

She turned to me in surprise. "Of course, I told him. I'm very proud of my big sister!"

I took a deep breath. "Jenny, have you … forgiven me?" I asked, my voice barely a whisper.

"Oh, Anna," said Jennifer. "There's nothing to forgive. You did your duty. I was sadly lacking in that department."

"Jenny…" I started to cry, unable to help myself. Perhaps it was simply a reaction to leading the flight during the past months.

"Anna, it's all right," said Jennifer, taking me in her arms. "It's really all right."

We stayed like that for a long moment. I had missed Jennifer more than I had realised. The war had made us closer than ever.

A few days later I was called to another meeting in James's office. I arrived to find James and the Marx Brothers seated at the meeting table. My curiosity was immediately aroused as I took the seat indicated by James.

"Our friends from British Intelligence want to run something by you. A possible mission," said James.

"Is this something you've already agreed to?" I asked him. I wanted to know whether I was to give a genuine opinion or simply rubber stamp a decision that had already been made.

"Not as yet, no," James replied with a wry smile. "We want to hear what you think."

"All right then, fire away," I said.

The Marx Brothers, who had been observing this exchange with interest, leaned forward.

"Hitler," said Harpo, "has a bunker in France. Two, in fact."

"But we're just interested in one of them," said Chico.

"All right." This was news to me, though I imagined the Führer had several bunkers.

"The bunker is naturally well defended and probably impregnable to normal ordnance," Harpo continued. "Which is why we need to test a much larger bomb to see how the bunker holds up."

I sighed. I might have guessed it. Another experiment. "Shall we rename this the Guinea Pig Squadron?" I said sardonically.

"Now, Anna, there's no need to…" James began, but I stopped him with a smile.

"I'm joking," I said.

Harpo and Chico chuckled. They had a sense of humour, though they didn't show it very often.

"We can understand why you might think so," said Chico.

"But in reality, tests like these are only given to trusted squadrons, and the Sirens are one of those," said Harpo.

I wasn't fooled. Were we trusted or expendable? I didn't think that Churchill would consider us expendable, given what he had told us. However, in order to give a proper opinion, I needed to know more.

"All right, tell me the whole," I said.

"The bunker consists of several buildings or bunkers. Garrisoned troops and so forth. Hitler has never visited it, according to our intelligence reports," said Harpo, taking a drag on his cigarette.

"So, we're not going after Hitler then, I take it," I put in.

"Not, as such, no," said Chico.

"What the bunker does possess is a very large and well protected telephone exchange. It is used by the Jerries as a relay point for communications within France. It's of major importance in that respect. It is contained within a heavily reinforced concrete building," said Harpo.

"And that is the one we want you to destroy," said Chico.

"You said that it was impregnable to the usual ordnance," I said.

"Yes, that's right. However, we have a high-capacity bomb nicknamed the Cookie," he continued. "It's a four-thousand-pound bomb and only one can be carried by a Mosquito at any given time. As you can imagine, it packs quite a punch."

A bomb that size would carry a lot of explosives by the sound of it.

"And you want to see if this Cookie will penetrate the bunker?" I said.

"Bingo," said Harpo.

"She's got it," said Chico.

"And what's the catch?" I asked. The mission sounded too straightforward for my liking.

The Marx Brothers didn't answer right away. Instead, they finished their cigarettes, stubbed them out and lit up two more. I waited patiently, taking this as an indication that there was indeed more to it.

"The bomb has to be dropped from six thousand feet," said Harpo. "All aircraft need to be that far away in order to be out of the blast zone."

That was quite a blast distance and so potentially a devastating bomb. I could see an immediate drawback.

"That would put us in range of the flak batteries," I said.

"Yes," said Chico.

"And I take it that this bunker is heavily defended?"

"Yes, it is," said Harpo. "But we'd anticipate carrying out a low-level bombing run prior to the big drop to try and neutralise most of these defences."

It was beginning to dawn on me where this was going, and so I pressed a little more.

"Dropping something like this on what is probably not a very large building sounds like a precision job," I said.

"It absolutely is," said Chico.

"And spotting a target like that at night sounds like it might be difficult," I continued, anticipating the answer which Chico immediately gave me.

"It will be. Which is why the raid will have to be carried out in daylight."

I glossed over this point for the moment, although I fully intended to come back to it.

"Is it believed that this Cookie bomb will actually work on the bunker? Will it blow a hole in it?" I asked.

"We're not certain. Experiments have been carried out in Britain, of course," said Harpo, "but we need to know how effective it is in order to provide valuable information for Barnes Wallis, who is developing a new type of bomb to penetrate bunkers."

I took a deep breath, trying to quell my rising irritation. My job was to carry out missions but at the same time protect the squadron. The more I heard about this potential mission, the more misgivings I was beginning to have.

"So let me get this straight: you want us to carry out a dangerous raid that has little chance of actual success," I said.

"Yes," Harpo agreed.

"As an experiment to see if these Cookie bombs will work on bunkers."

"That's right," said Chico.

"Which they might not."

"No."

I sighed again. "In which case the entire raid will have been pointless and Sirens will very likely have been killed," I said.

"Not pointless, no, because then we'll know they don't work. Which is exactly the kind of information Barnes needs to know," said Chico patiently.

I could not help but roll my eyes.

"I perceive you're none too happy," said Harpo.

"You perceive correctly. I want to make a difference in this war, but not at the expense of the entire squadron," I shot back.

"Well, you will make a difference."

"How is this making a difference?" I demanded. I didn't feel that this was a good use of the Sirens' resources.

"Well, you may damage the telephone exchange, so there's that. It would potentially disrupt the enemy's communications. It may even blow a hole in the roof, which will show that it does work," said Chico, completely unruffled by my belligerent tone.

"And it might not."

"No," Chico agreed.

"So, there's *that*," I shot back.

"What can I say? Fortunes of war…"

Harpo shrugged, which served to irritate me even further. I returned to the issue of timing.

"You want us to drop this Cookie bomb in daylight, thereby exposing the squadron to a huge amount of risk," I said. "I have heard reports of the American daylight raids. They sustain a huge amount of damage. We'll be sitting ducks."

"Well, if you put it that way —" began Chico.

"And I assume with no air cover, because you haven't mentioned that," I cut in, fully aware that providing air cover for a Sirens raid would be difficult.

"We didn't, no," admitted Harpo.

"All because someone wants to do an experiment?" I said.

It was Harpo's turn to sigh. "The thing is, we're not sure how we can get you air cover without breaching security," he said, sounding apologetic.

"You can't or won't?" I asked, now thoroughly annoyed.

"Anna," said James lightly, trying to intervene.

It was enough. If we were going to have to do this raid, then I was determined to voice my objections. Protocol could go hang.

"Don't Anna me. This whole squadron was your idea. The brave warriors flying into battle and all that. We've done everything you wanted us to do without question, and yet here you are about to throw it all away. Quite a few of us may never come back from this, including me … then where will the Sirens be? Back at square one … if it doesn't get disbanded…"

"I hardly think —" James began, but I cut him off.

"James, you haven't thought this through. What do I tell the others?"

James looked at me questioningly, but with respect. The normally compliant Anna was gone, and in her place was someone far feistier. I hardly knew myself.

Harpo coughed, interrupting my line of attack. "Look, what you've said makes sense. Now we come to think of it, there might be a way to give you some air cover. We've just got to see if we *can* actually arrange it," he said.

"Really?" I said hopefully.

"Well, yes, there might be a solution to this. Leave it with us. We'll put the whole thing on ice for now, at least temporarily, until we've explored things a little further," he continued.

"If we can arrange air cover, would you be more inclined to consider it?" Chico asked, as if I had a choice.

"It would give us an even chance," I said. "If we were attacked, at least we'd have some air defence while we got out of there."

"All right, then we'll do our very best to sort it out," said Harpo with resolution.

The two of them stubbed out their cigarettes and got up to go.

"Toodle-pip," said Harpo.

"Chin-chin," said Chico.

When they were gone, I got up to leave too. James regarded me.

"Are you going?" he asked.

"Yes," I said bluntly.

"All right. Will I see you later?" He cocked his head to one side and raised an eyebrow in the most irresistible fashion.

"I'll think about it," I told him as I left the room.

As I closed the door behind me, I felt an awful heel. James was only doing his best. His hands were tied in so many ways. I stood in the corridor in a state of indecision. Then I turned around and entered his office once more. He hadn't moved from his seat and looked up in surprise.

"Back so soon?" he said with a smile.

"It's later already," I informed him, smiling too.

CHAPTER ELEVEN

On leaving James's office, I ran into Maria in the corridor.

"Aye, aye," she said with a smile. "I know where you've been."

"Oh hush," I said, though I couldn't quite hide a blush.

I had more than made things up with James. He understood my reluctance regarding the mission and he wasn't happy about it either. He was glad I'd not been quite so acquiescent. I had rather surprised both him and myself.

"Walk with me?" I said to Maria.

"All right."

We headed out to the formal gardens. It was a good place to talk without fear of being overheard. I wanted to canvas her thoughts on the mission. She had become something of a confidante.

"I was in James's office for a reason, and not the reason you think," I began.

"Oh?"

"There's a mission in the offing…"

I explained the situation and what we would be asked to do. Maria exclaimed indignantly when I mentioned the air cover.

"If that don't beat all!" she said. "That's not a stealth mission. It's a suicide mission."

"My thoughts exactly," I replied.

"Do you think the Marx Brothers can get us air cover? I was hoping not to die just yet," she said wryly.

"I don't know. Though I understand the problem," I replied. "We wouldn't be in direct communication with the squadron protecting us, and that might be an issue. We wouldn't be able to relay what we were going to do and when. For example, we couldn't tell them when everyone had to get clear for the Cookie bomb to drop."

"Yes, I see," said Maria. "I wonder how they think it can be resolved?"

"I don't know," I said. "But I hope it can, because without it several of us would die during the attack. Of that, I'm sure."

It was a sobering thought.

"The bunker is bound to be heavily defended," she agreed. "Not to mention Jerry fighter support being called in."

"Exactly. Then we'll be well and truly in the basket," I said.

"Well, they've put it off for now, you said, so I suppose it's best not to worry too much … at least not yet."

She smiled encouragingly and I knew she was right. I looked at my watch. It was nearly lunchtime.

"Shall we?" I asked Maria.

"Most certainly," she replied.

Arm in arm, we made our way to the dining room. The fare was some kind of meat pie, mashed potatoes, gravy and what appeared to be cabbage. I wondered if the estate had a surfeit of it. The taste was a little gamey, so perhaps they were culling some of the deer herd.

We sat down at our usual table, where there was already a lively discussion in progress.

"Pamela's got a boyfriend," Shelly informed me as I was about to take a mouthful of pie.

"Oh?"

"You'll never guess who it is," added Patricia with a grin.

I sighed inwardly, imagining it to be someone entirely unsuitable. "Tell me," I said.

"It's Gary," said Susan.

I almost choked on my food and had to take a large swig of tea. "Gary?" I said, incredulous.

Gary, an erstwhile reporter, had been instrumental in trying to coerce Shelly into telling him about the Sirens. In turn, we had ganged up on him and persuaded him otherwise. As a result, he had ended up becoming a mechanic with the ground crew.

"He's actually rather nice when you get to know him," said Pamela, sounding coy.

"Oh yeah, we know what you mean by *nice*," said Shelly with a wink.

"Stop it, it's not like that," Pamela told her.

"So, you're going out with Gary?" I repeated, just to make sure I had heard correctly.

"Yes," said Pamela, bristling a little. "Any objections?"

"Apart from it being Gary, you mean?" put in Connie.

Pamela looked aggrieved and I decided to call a halt to the baiting.

"Look," I said, "if Pamela wants to go out with Gary, that's her business."

"The Boss has spoken," said Shelly, jumping in with her favourite saying.

"Yes, so lay off," said Pamela, shooting me a grateful look.

I resumed eating my lunch, assuming the subject was closed. However, I was soon disabused of that notion.

"Except it's not that simple, is it?" said Sandra.

"What?" I asked her.

"Gary has been seen with somebody else," said Lucy.

"That's just a rumour!" said Pamela hotly. "I don't believe it, and Gary has denied it."

"Seen with who?" I demanded.

"ASO Betty Watkins," said Jennifer. "I saw them together, and they looked pretty close if you ask me."

"It's not true. I don't believe it," said Pamela. "Gary wouldn't do that."

"Sounds like Gary all over," added Shelly, who probably knew him better than any of us considering her past dalliance with him.

Pamela looked rather upset, which I took to mean that she must be more than just sweet on the unfortunate Gary.

"I'm just trying to warn you, Pamela," said Jennifer.

"All right," I said. "No more talk about Gary. Let Pamela work things out for herself."

Nobody demurred and I hoped that had put the issue to bed. However, I had a nagging suspicion it wouldn't be the last we heard of it.

A few days later Judy came to seek me out. Instead of escorting me to James's office, as I expected, I was shown into the familiar high-ceilinged room where the Marx Brothers usually liked to conduct their interviews. Although this time they weren't alone.

Seated on the sofa at one end of the room was a Section Officer around my age with black hair and brown eyes, alongside an RAF Sergeant of around forty-five, with greying hair and a salt-and-pepper moustache. Harpo stood up from his armchair and came over to greet me.

"Ah, Flight Officer," he said with a smile. "There are some people we'd like you to meet."

I noticed there was a pot of tea and teacups on a low table. This kind of hospitality was unusual for the Marx Brothers. These must be particularly special guests.

"Flight Officer," he said, leading me to where the others were seated, "allow me to introduce Section Officer Angelica Mackennelly and Sergeant Bruce Gordon, from the Mavericks Squadron. Angelica, Bruce, this is Flight Officer Anna Nightingale, Flight Leader of the Sirens."

"Hello," said Angelica, standing up and smiling broadly. She flicked a precise salute and I returned it.

Gordon stood and saluted too. I noticed the embroidered insignia on their uniforms: a blue spitfire silhouette, with the words "Spitfire" in yellow capitals above and "Mavericks" below.

"Hello," I said, dispensing with formality. "Please, call me Anna."

We shook hands and then Harpo indicated one of the easy chairs and I sat down.

"Shall I be mother?" said Angelica.

She set about pouring the tea in a business-like fashion and distributing a cup to each of us. In the meantime, both the Marx Brothers and Gordon had lit cigarettes. The sergeant had a kindly face; he looked like the sort of person you might feel you could confide in.

"As you've no doubt guessed," said Chico, once everyone had tea, "the Mavericks are a squadron we have quite a lot to do with."

I had wondered about the Marx Brothers' other activities. The Mavericks was evidently one of them.

"I think your squadron has come to our aid at least once in the past," I said, recalling a prior incident when we'd been chased by Jerries.

"Very probably, yes," said Angelica.

"Anyway, we shall divulge the reason we've brought them both here very shortly," said Harpo.

"But first," said Chico, addressing himself to Angelica, "you and Bruce will both sign a document which is in addition to the Official Secrets Act, binding you to silence with respect to anything to do with the Sirens in perpetuity. This squadron is perhaps one of the best kept secrets of the war."

"And so it shall remain," confirmed Harpo, taking a drag on his cigarette.

From a briefcase, Chico produced two documents and handed one each to Angelica and Gordon. I wondered why they had not done this earlier but assumed they wanted to reassure me of the secrecy aspect by doing so in front of me.

"You can count on us," said Angelica, taking a copy, perusing it quickly and signing it with the pen she was given for the purpose.

"Most certainly," said Gordon, putting down his cigarette and doing likewise.

The signed documents were returned to Chico, who put them back into the briefcase, snapping it shut with a satisfied nod.

"Section Officer Mackennelly has one of the highest security clearances in the RAF," said Harpo. "It's just a shame she won't join the Intelligence services."

"Not on your nelly," said Angelica firmly.

Chico shrugged. "You see, a hopeless case."

The familiar banter indicated they knew each other well.

"I'm married to my husband and my job, as you know," Angelica told him with a laugh.

"Who is your husband?" I asked her, curious.

"He's Flight Lieutenant Angus Mackennelly, M Flight Leader in the Mavericks," said Angelica with a smile.

"I see."

"Gordon is his batman, and very kindly drove me here," Angelica continued. "I would trust him with my life."

Gordon smiled at this and tapped the ash off the tip of his cigarette.

I sipped my tea and digested this information. Angelica and her husband were married *and* in the same squadron. I resolved to find out more at an opportune moment.

"We've brought Angelica here because we believe she and the Mavericks can assist you with the problem of air support," said Harpo.

"Really?" I said, surprised.

"*And* without breaching our security or protocols," said Chico triumphantly.

"But how?" I said at once.

"Let me explain," said Harpo. "The issue is one of communication, is it not?"

"Yes, that's right," I said.

"The Sirens need to be in touch with their fighter escort in order to relay certain information. For example, dropping a large bomb, which requires all aircraft to get clear, am I right?" he continued.

"So far, yes," I agreed.

He paused to take a pull on his cigarette and Chico took over.

"We don't want the fighter escort to know that the Sirens are an all-female RAF unit. We can't imagine keeping a lid on twelve fighter pilots, as trustworthy as they might be. Someone might let something slip. Some of them may get shot down, interrogated and so on," he said.

"So, we can't have them talking to any of you directly," Harpo finished for him.

"I can see how that might be a problem," I said.

"We couldn't see how this might be overcome," said Chico. "Until we had a brainwave."

"A brainwave," echoed Harpo.

"All right," I said, hoping they would now get to the point.

I noticed a rather fixed smile on Angelica's face and assumed she was also used to their slightly obtuse behaviour.

"Angelica is the key," said Harpo.

"How so?" I asked.

"May I?" said Angelica, cutting in.

"By all means," said Chico.

Anglica turned to me, and now her smile was genuine. "I am the M Flight communicator," she said. "So, I sit on comms listening to the flight chatter, which is useful for intelligence purposes and to know what's going on. Although sometimes one of the pilots, Pilot Officer Jonty Butterworth, likes to sing these dreadful ballads. Pilot Officer Willie Cooper, his best friend, hates them… They do rather quarrel so … but excellent pilots, both of them."

"Right," I said. The Sirens did have a bit of banter in the air, but not on that scale.

"Anyway, the point is that I can be in direct contact with M Flight. So, in the case of your mission, I will act as the relay point. You will talk to me on one channel. I will relay this to the Mavericks on another channel. Easy."

"And you could relay things the other way, to us?" I asked her.

"Yes, of course," she said. "That way, none of you has to talk to the other squadron directly."

"It certainly sounds as if it could work," I mused.

"Of course it can work," said Harpo. "It's a splendid plan."

"Absolutely," said Chico.

Angelica and I smiled at each other. The Marx Brothers would be bound to say so since they had thought of it.

"I think it will work," said Angelica. "You'll keep your secret *and* get the fighter escort that you need."

"Assuming you're happy with this development, Flight Officer," said Chico, "can we count on you as being willing to support the bunker mission?"

There was nothing for it except to agree. I still didn't entirely like the mission, but with an escort we had a fighting chance.

"Yes, all right," I said. "But there's a good deal of planning to be done, and I'll need to talk to Angelica more."

"Yes, yes, of course," said Harpo, dismissively.

"We'll inform the powers that be that the Sirens are ready to take on the challenge," said Chico.

"And I'm at your disposal," Angelica told me.

"Excellent," said Harpo. "We'll leave you to it."

So saying, he and Harpo stood up and left the room.

"They never change," said Angelica with a laugh once they'd gone.

Sergeant Gordon had been sitting quietly, taking everything in.

"Do you need me for anything else, ma'am?" he asked Angelica.

"Not at the moment, no," she replied.

He stubbed out his cigarette in the ashtray on the table. "I can wait in the jeep, read my book." He started to get up.

"I'm certain we can do better than that," I said. "We've a house bar — you could wait there in a lot more comfort."

"Sounds splendid," said the sergeant.

"I'm sure we've got plenty to talk about," I said to Angelica. "But I think we should go and speak to James — I mean, Wing

Commander Donnington. First, I'll show Bruce where the bar is."

"By all means," Angelica replied. "Lead on."

CHAPTER TWELVE

James greeted Angelica with interest when we arrived at his office. I had settled Sergeant Gordon at the house bar, where he had immediately struck up a conversation with the bartender. He assured us he would be perfectly fine.

"Hello," James said to Angelica. "The Intelligence chaps said you were coming."

"So, you knew about this scheme?" I asked him.

He regarded me somewhat apologetically. "They wanted to tell you themselves — they were rather proud of the idea," he said.

"Yes, I certainly got that impression," I said, smiling.

"So, I'm forgiven?" he asked me.

"There's nothing to forgive," I said, trying to sound formal, but it was too late for that.

Angelica looked from one of us to the other. I was sure she wasn't one to miss a trick.

"I just want to be sure that you both think this can work," said James.

"I believe so, yes," I said. "Although we haven't thrashed out the details nor tried it out."

"I've some ideas about that," said Angelica. "We could do a couple of simple rendezvous tests to see if the relay works. You give me coordinates and a time, and I'll relay that to Angus's squadron. Then we'll see if you both turn up at the appointed place and time."

I had been wondering how we might try it out and this suggestion seemed ideal.

"It sounds like a plan," I told her.

"Excellent," said James.

"Angelica is married to Flight Lieutenant Angus Mackennelly, who is the Flight Leader of M Flight in the Mavericks," I informed him.

It was entirely unnecessary for me to tell him that, but somehow I couldn't resist it.

"Is she indeed?" said James with a sudden gleam in his eye. "How does that work out for you?" he asked Angelica.

"Oh, perfectly fine," said Angelica airily. "People are used to seeing us around the base together, as we dated for a rather long time before we were married. We've also got a very good CO in Squadron Leader Bentley."

"I see," he said. "Sounds like it's worked out very well then."

He shot me a look which I assumed would presage a further discussion sometime soon.

"Anyway," I said, changing the subject. "I'll introduce Angelica to some of the squadron, shall I?"

"Yes, yes, of course," he said. "Nice to meet you, Angelica."

We both saluted James and he returned our salutes. Then I took Angelica up to my room, where I had a notion the rest of the gang would be hanging out. I paused at the door and said to her, "This is the unofficial HQ of my closest members of the Sirens."

"All right," she said, not fazed at all.

"Don't be surprised if you're bombarded with all sorts of questions. But obviously we can't say anything about why you are here just yet," I told her.

We entered the room. They were all there. Jennifer and Connie were sitting at the window, sharing a cigarette. Shelly, Maria, Patricia, Pamela, Susan, Sandra, Lucy and Diana were lounging on the beds.

"Everyone," I said, "this is Section Officer Angelica Mackennelly. She's here to help us out with something."

As I had predicted, they all talked at once.

"What is it?"

"Is it a mission?"

"Is she going to be flying a plane?"

I fielded the questions as best I could. I wasn't able to divulge the details of the mission, so I told them she was here to learn more about the Sirens with a view to some possible collaboration with her squadron.

Once the initial interest in having a newcomer waned, Angelica said she needed to get back to the Mavericks, who were situated near Chelmsford at a place called Banley.

I accompanied her down to the bar to pick up Sergeant Gordon and then out to their jeep.

"Come back for longer," I said. "I can arrange a room for you, then we can discuss things in more detail. How exactly it's going to work."

"Yes, I will," she said. "As soon as I can arrange it, I'll let you know."

She climbed into the jeep and I watched as it disappeared from view down the long driveway. There was a touch at my elbow. It was Maria.

"So, why was she really here?" she asked.

"Let's take a walk and I'll tell you."

As luck would have it, all thoughts of the impending bunker mission were set aside when new orders came in. A briefing was called one morning not long after Angelica's visit. We had been enjoying a rather lively breakfast when James stood up and tapped a spoon against his mug for silence.

"If I can have your attention for a moment, Sirens. There will be an urgent briefing directly after breakfast. This will be in around thirty minutes, so there's plenty of time to finish your food."

He shot me a quick glance and then resumed his seat. I wasn't concerned. James would try to discuss missions with me first if he could, but sometimes urgent orders arrived and he didn't have the opportunity to do so.

"Wonder what that's about?" said Shelly.

"We'll find out soon enough," said Maria.

"Just be patient, Shelly," I said and returned my attention to my plate.

"It's not in her lexicon," said Maria wryly.

We had sausages, beans, eggs and toast on this occasion, which was rather special since sausages were in short supply. I was determined to enjoy them.

"What's in these sausages?" remarked Susan. "It's not pork."

"It's venison," said Pamela.

"And how would you know that?" asked Connie, who was sharing a cigarette with Jennifer as usual.

"Because I happen to be acquainted with the gamekeeper, and they are culling the herd," said Pamela.

This was exactly what I had thought. I didn't mind the taste of venison; in fact, I rather liked it. In any case, you couldn't be choosy in wartime.

"Ooh, the gamekeeper now, is it?" said Shelly, latching onto this at once. "I thought you were sweet on Gary."

"I am," protested Pamela. "The gamekeeper is just a friend and useful to know if you want extra rations."

"Enough," I said. "Eat up — we have a briefing soon."

"Have you given up Gary to Betty then?" asked Patricia slyly.

Pamela shot her a look which spoke volumes. She obviously hadn't.

"I sense trouble brewing in that quarter," murmured Maria.

I sighed. Some ruffled feathers were to be expected when you cooped thirty-six people together for long periods of time. To some degree, the war kept us focused.

I finished my breakfast and pushed away my empty plate. The others did likewise. I noticed James getting up to go to the briefing and followed suit.

In short order, we were sitting in the briefing room with James, Henry and Gloria on the podium.

"Sirens," said James, "we've had another polite request to carry out a mission."

There was a ripple of laughter at this. We all knew orders were orders.

"We've been asked to attack an airbase that's causing a bit of trouble," he continued. "It's also home to some of the night fighters that you might encounter on your missions, so disabling it for a while will serve a useful purpose."

Henry stepped forward and the lights were dimmed. An aerial photograph appeared on the projection screen.

"This is the *Fliegerhorst Volkel*," he said. "Also known as the Volkel Airbase, in the Netherlands. It's home to Junkers Ju 88 night fighters, and the Messerschmitt Bf 109s. The Luftwaffe recently expanded it into a fully operational base. So, it has strategic importance."

I exchanged a glance with Maria. We'd not attacked the Netherlands before. This was something new.

"Your job will be to bomb the runway and put it out of commission, albeit temporarily, and also strafe as many planes as you can. One plane less is one enemy less to fight."

A few more photographs followed and then a map appeared on the screen.

"Here is the airbase," said Henry. "It's a fair way into Holland, around a two-hundred-mile round trip all told. For a Mosquito that's a fairly quick jaunt."

This elicited further amusement. The lights came on again and James took over.

"This is part of Operation Stinger, which comes under Operation Scorpion. Yes, I know, it's all very convoluted. However, the main point is that you've flown this kind of mission before, so while it won't be a walk in the park by any means, you won't be unfamiliar with how it goes. Am I right, Flight Officer Nightingale?"

He paused and looked over at me. It was typical of him to put me on the spot.

"Yes, sir," I said, forcing a smile. "We should all be perfectly au fait with this type of bomb-and-strafe mission."

"You'll have two days to prepare," said Henry. "The mission will be flown at night, as per usual. It will be a twelve-plane assault. The good news is that Holland is pretty flat for the most part, so that will make low flying a lot easier, although you will have to look out for the odd windmill."

We all laughed at this. Holland was well known for its windmills.

"We will post up the mission roster later today," said James.

This meant that he would consult with me first before assigning the crew.

"We'll hold a full briefing on mission day, in two days' time," said Henry.

"Until then, dismissed," said James.

Not long after, I felt a touch at my elbow. It was Judy, right on cue.

"Wing Commander wants to see me?" I asked her with a smile.

"Of course," she said, smiling too.

I accompanied Judy to James's office. She let me in as usual and then shut the door behind me.

"Ah, Anna," said James affably. "Come and have a seat."

He was with Henry and Gloria. I sat down and waited, although I had a pretty shrewd idea of what it would be.

"We'd like to settle the roster for the mission," he said. "What are your thoughts?"

"I'll take Jennifer, Patricia, Sandra, Susan…" I began reeling off the names.

I made sure to include Linda, because I couldn't be seen to be discriminatory. The irony was that she was a good pilot, particularly in combat. If only she hadn't taken such a dislike to me, we might even have become friends. Something that I knew could never happen now.

James raised an eyebrow at Linda's name, but he didn't demur. There were some new names on the roll, as the Marx Brothers had been busy bringing in replacements for those we'd lost. The newcomers were absorbed into squadron life, undergoing training, but it wasn't the marathon effort that had been needed at the start. All of them would be tested in combat as soon as they were ready.

"Sounds all right to me," said James when I'd finished. "How about you two?"

He always made sure to include Henry and Gloria in operational decisions. I admired him for it. As Flight Leader, I tended to make the decisions myself, but leading a mission required something of an autocratic approach. Combat, as many of us had discovered, was a very different beast.

"Sounds good," said Henry.

"Agreed," said Gloria. "I think they'll do a good job."

Gloria knew the squadron well. She ran the place like a tight ship, and I was fairly sure she knew everything that went on at Hawberry.

"It's settled then," said James. "I'll get Judy to type it up and post it today."

"Have you any thoughts about the attack?" Henry asked me.

I had anticipated this question and had been mulling it over in my head.

"We could fly in three groups of four, spread across the base including the runway. Then the leading group can drop at the end of the runway. The others will drop simultaneously. If it's all on timed fuses, we'll be able to get clear, turn around and come back for a strafing attack. One line of twelve should probably do it," I said. "Perhaps a broadside on the airbase?"

"Do you think you'll need a practice run?" asked James.

I considered this for a moment and decided that a couple of dummy runs would be useful for the newcomers.

"We'll try it a couple of times without ordnance," I said. "On the range. That should be enough for the new recruits to become au fait with the routine."

"All right," said James. "Unless there's anything else, perhaps you could stay for a quick word, Anna?"

"Certainly, sir," I said.

Henry and Gloria took that as their cue to leave.

"What did you want to discuss?" I asked James when we were alone.

He came around to my side of the table. "I don't want to discuss anything," he said.

"Well then…"

His lips curved into the familiar smile that I knew so well.

The first practice session went without a hitch. The newer members of the squadron kept up without problems. We flew low level out to the range, split into three groups of four, and simulated the bombing run and then the strafing run.

After dinner, some of us went to the house bar for a drink. I sat nursing a glass of Coca-Cola with ice, though the others seemed to prefer beer. Sandra drank her beer cold, which apparently was an American habit. The barman would keep a bottle or two on ice just for her.

"Today went well," Patricia said. "Here's a toast to that."

"Cheers!" said Shelly. "Let's hope the actual mission goes well too."

"What say you, Boss?" asked Sandra, taking a sip of her drink.

"I say here's to a successful mission," I said with a smile.

Jennifer and Connie slipped into their seats. They had been outside for a walk. Connie lit up a cigarette, took a drag on it, and passed it to Jennifer.

"I'm off to powder my nose," said Pamela, getting up from her seat.

I watched her go and as she left the bar, Connie and Jennifer started talking in low voices. To my mind that could only mean trouble of one kind or another. I wasn't wrong.

"What are you two whispering about over there?" asked Sandra. "You all are acting mighty suspicious."

Connie quickly looked around and then lowered her voice. "You'll never guess who we saw in the formal gardens," she said, obviously brimming with news.

I decided that it must be something concerning Pamela, since Connie had waited until she had left the room.

"Go on, try us," said Susan.

Connie had left it too long. Out of the corner of my eye, I saw Pamela making her way back to the table. I surreptitiously tried to divert Connie's attention, but it was to no avail.

"Gary and Betty … walking arm in arm as bold as you please," said Connie. "Anyway, don't tell Pa…" She trailed off.

Everyone had stopped talking and she now perceived the reason. Pamela, who was standing directly behind Connie, let out an oath.

"Oh, Pamela, I didn't see you there," said Connie, looking around. "I didn't mean —"

Pamela cut her off angrily. "When was this?" she demanded.

"Just a few minutes ago," said Connie, desperately trying to backpedal. "I'm sure it was nothing…" She stopped. She'd already said too much.

She and Jennifer exchanged guilty looks.

"I'll give them nothing!" said Pamela, looking grim.

"But I thought you and the gamekeeper were a thing now. The other day at breakfast when we were talking, I thought…" began Connie, trying to mitigate her mistake.

"Well, you thought wrong!" Pamela informed her. Then she turned and stalked resolutely out of the bar.

"What did you have to go and bring that up for?" said Maria.

"I didn't know she was there," said Connie.

"I'd better go after her," I said.

I hurried out of the bar in the direction Pamela had gone. I was aware that the others were following me. The last thing I needed was an audience, but I hadn't time to worry about it. I was more concerned about preventing a fight which might have disastrous consequences for both Pamela and Betty.

I arrived at the formal gardens, which were bathed in the half-light that accompanied twilight. I peered into the gloom; I could certainly hear the argument that was currently underway.

"How dare you!" Pamela was saying.

"I dare! What have you to say to it?" Betty countered.

"Gary is mine!"

"No, he's not. He's mine."

In the midst of it all, Gary was attempting to calm things down.

"Now, ladies, please, can't we talk about this in a civilised manner?"

"I'll show her civilised!" said Pamela.

"Go on then, I dare you," said Betty.

It seemed that I had arrived just in time.

"Stand to attention!" I said in my best parade ground voice.

To my relief, they did exactly that.

"What is the meaning of this?" I asked.

"I was out here having a nice walk with my boyfriend when *she* came along and started threatening me, ma'am," said Betty with righteous indignation.

"He's not your boyfriend, he's mine!" said Pamela.

I could see this line of questioning was only going to result in more of an altercation. I decided to try another tack and addressed myself to the object of the argument.

"Gary," I said, "kindly enlighten me as to which one of these ladies you are going out with."

He looked a little shamefaced.

"Well?" I said, when he didn't answer.

"I … well, ma'am … er … both of them."

"Both of them?" I was aghast at hearing him be quite so barefaced about it.

"Typical! Men, they never change."

It was Shelly. I looked around to discover that the rest of the gang gathered behind me at a discreet distance.

"You lot can keep out of this," I told them. "And that's an order."

"Sorry, Boss," said Shelly. "Couldn't help it. Can't see what either of them see in him anyway."

I ignored this interjection and turned my attention back to the three miscreants before me.

"Whatever this is that you've got going on," I said, "it's not conducive to discipline or good conduct for the squadron. So, it needs to be resolved."

"That's easy," said Pamela. "She just has to give him up."

"Damned if I will," said Betty.

I could see that neither woman was about to step back from her position, so I appealed to Gary instead.

"All right then, Gary, let's settle this once and for all. You choose."

He was silent for a long while and then he shrugged. "Sorry," he said. "I can't."

"Typical," said Shelly.

"Hush," said Jennifer.

I had become exasperated and said so. "You are being ridiculous, all of you," I informed them. "How about I just order you all not to see each other?"

"Wait, Boss," said Pamela. "What if we can settle this another way?"

"How?" I asked with a sense of foreboding. "If you're suggesting fisticuffs or something, then no."

"Not fisticuffs precisely. A more old-fashioned remedy. A duel. Winner takes all."

I stared at her, unable to believe my ears. "A duel? Have you taken leave of your senses?"

Pamela was unabashed, and then Betty piped up.

"I'm game for it if she is, ma'am," she said.

"Good grief!" I exclaimed. "You as well? Quite apart from the impropriety of such a suggestion, one of you might be killed. How am I supposed to explain that to the Wing Commander?"

"I'm not talking pistols or anything," said Pamela. "Just, you know, swords, first blood and all that. No hits on the body, so no fatal wounds — just superficial."

"Are you serious?" I said furiously. "Let me inform you that I most certainly do not condone this tomfoolery! We are not living in the eighteenth century." I took a deep breath and tried to calm down. "Apart from anything else, we've got a mission to fly," I went on in a more even tone. "That is of paramount importance for now. I'm ordering you to cease and desist from any further interaction until after the mission. Leave Gary alone, both of you. After the mission, we will talk again to see if this can be resolved in a sensible manner. Can you do that?"

"Yes, ma'am," said Betty and Gary together.

"Yes, Boss," said Pamela, realising that I actually meant it.

"Then you're dismissed, all of you. I don't want to hear about this again until after the mission, is that clear?"

They saluted. I watched Betty and Gary walk away, thankfully in different directions.

"Boss…" Pamela began.

I raised an admonishing finger. "Not another word!"

I turned on my heel and started back for the Hall. Behind me, I could hear the gang breaking into muted chatter.

"Well, I thought a duel was a splendid idea."

"It would be so much fun."

I realised there was someone beside me, hurrying to keep up. It was Maria.

"Wait up," she said with a laugh.

I slowed down but kept on walking.

"You did the right thing," she said.

"A duel indeed! Whatever next?" I replied as we made our way back into the Hall.

CHAPTER THIRTEEN

Pamela and Betty's rivalry was forgotten in the preparation for the mission. I knew I would have to find a way to resolve it one way or another, but it would have to wait. Thankfully, my orders were heeded, and it seemed as if both of them stayed away from Gary as I had requested.

The second day of practice went as well as the first, and by the third day, the day of the mission, we were ready. A final briefing was held where the route, call signs, timings and bearings for the navigators were gone over in detail. We would be flying over unfamiliar territory. I couldn't help but feel a little anxious.

"You'll be fine," said James, as we said a fond farewell in his rooms.

"I love you," I told him as we stole one last kiss.

"I love you too. Come back safe," he said.

"I will."

Those same words spoken every time. A last kiss, like a talisman. My good luck charm. I left his rooms and returned to mine, where Jennifer was putting on her flying suit. I proceeded to do the same.

"I'm glad to be flying another mission," she said.

"Glad isn't quite the word I'd use," I replied with a laugh.

She laughed too. "Perhaps I just need more excitement than you do, Anna."

"Perhaps you do, Jenny. You always were the one who took all the risks."

"Now, that's not fair. Remember that time you…"

I finished dressing to a friendly sisterly squabble and put on my life jacket. Then I gave Jennifer a hug.

"Just be safe and try not to die," I said.

"I won't if you won't," she quipped.

She was flippant in the face of danger, but I knew that underneath, as with all of us, there was also fear. The fear of dying far from home and never seeing your loved ones again. Yet each of us found the courage to keep going, again and again.

Maria knocked on the door. She was accompanied by Shelly.

"Ready?" she asked.

"As we'll ever be," I replied.

We began the familiar walk down silent corridors in the dead of night, gradually joined by those who were also flying the mission.

We emerged from the front door into the warm autumn air and climbed into the waiting trucks. As they trundled down the track to the airfield I wondered, as always, how many of us would be coming back.

"Come on, people, cheer up," said Shelly, picking up on the mood. "Let's have a jolly sing-song."

A burst of laughter eased the tension. Then Maria broke into a bawdy ditty ridiculing Hitler and various other Nazi figures. Those who knew it joined in. Jennifer and Connie looked on from the back of the truck while sharing a cigarette.

"There you go," said Shelly as the truck came to a stop. "Worked a treat, didn't it?"

"It certainly did," I replied.

The Sirens congregated around me for the final words.

"We don't know what we're getting into here," I said. "But let's just get this done and come home. All right?"

"All right!" came the enthusiastic response.

"Then let's get to it," I said.

Victoria was waiting by the aircraft in her usual mechanics' overalls. "All set for you, ma'am," she informed me, snapping a smart salute. "Fully fuelled and loaded."

"Thanks, Victoria," I replied, returning the salute.

"Give them hell, ma'am," she said with a smile.

"We'll certainly try."

Maria and I climbed into our Mosquito, strapped in and after going through the preflight checks, I fired up the engines. The two Merlin engines purred to life, a familiar and reassuring sound.

"Control, this is Fox Leader requesting clearance," I said once we were ready.

Fox was our codename for the mission. Foxes were stealthy. I felt it suited our mission that night.

"Fox Leader, you're clear. Good luck."

"Roger, thanks," I replied. "Foxes, let's go," I said over the radio to the rest of the flight.

I let off the brake and eased the Mosquito towards the end of the runway. Once there, I applied the brakes and wound up the engines.

"Shall we do this?" I said to Maria with a grin.

"Let's do this," she replied, grinning back.

I let off the brakes and the Mosquito barrelled down the runway, picking up speed. Then we were airborne. We circled around, waiting for the rest of the flight. Once everyone was in the air, Maria gave us a bearing.

"Foxes, on me, low-level flying," I said.

I dropped the Mosquito down low and opened up the throttle. The other planes settled into formation. All at once the landscape started flashing by and all my attention was on the terrain in front.

We were to make our way cross-country towards Ipswich and then to Harwich before crossing the Channel. East Anglia was fairly flat, which made flying at night a lot easier. The familiar routine with Maria kicked in.

"Lines, lines, lines."

"Seen them."

"House."

"Seen it."

"Hedge."

"Got it."

The chequerboard fields passed beneath us. White, black and grey depending upon the crop, or lack of it. Some fields of grain still remained glowing white. I assumed there was a late harvest. Being a farm girl, I had memories to match.

"I used to help bring in the harvests," I remarked to Maria.

"It must have been fun," she said.

"Hard work," I laughed. "But those were golden days."

"And now look at us," said Maria wryly.

We fell silent as we passed Ipswich and then Harwich. The port was used by Navy ships and we could see several dark hulks anchored in the harbour. Our passage would be noted, but flak batteries would have been told of our passing by Anti-Aircraft Command.

"Here's the Channel," said Maria as we passed over the port.

"Foxes, kill the lights and keep them peeled," I said, flicking off the navigation lights as we effectively crossed into enemy territory.

Then we were just black shapes skimming the inky water just above the waves. The still air meant the Channel was thankfully reasonably calm.

We were heading for a point just south of Rotterdam. This was an estuary and marshland. An easy way for us to pass into

Holland unseen, since for the most part it would be uninhabited.

"All these places I've never been," Maria said wistfully. "Yet we're dropping bombs on them."

"It seems strange," I agreed.

"I wonder what will happen after the war," she mused.

"It depends if we win…" I trailed off.

We both knew enough about the Nazi yoke that had spread across Europe to realise that this war was truly about survival. Our way of life would be forever changed if the unthinkable happened and we lost. It was what kept us going and flying missions.

The strips of white sand which made up the beaches at the start of the estuary came into view.

"Here we go," said Maria. The coastline flashed by beneath us and then we were over the marsh flats.

For ease of navigation, we followed the course of the river that flowed west from the flats towards a town called 's-Hertogenbosch, where it petered out. The airbase was not too far from there.

I kept us on the landward side of the river, but we could see the water glinting in the moonlight. It was possible there might be German patrol boats on the river, and we didn't want to be spotted. This might result in Jerry scrambling some night fighters, which might impede our attack.

Halfway there, my fears were realised when tracers suddenly streaked out towards the flight.

"Incoming fire," said Patricia.

"Steady, keep it steady," I said.

The shots seemed to have come from the other side of the river and not the river itself. They stopped as abruptly as they had started.

"What do you think it was?" said Maria.

"It may just have been a German hearing the sounds of aircraft and having a go with a machine gun," I replied.

Twelve Mosquitos were quite loud, although we'd have been hard to spot and moving too fast.

"Radars, keep a lookout," I said, just in case.

"Here's hoping they don't send up some fighters to look for us," said Maria, picking up on my thoughts.

"They won't know where we're going," I replied, although it might be an easy guess that the airfield was our target.

Nothing further happened and I began to relax, though not completely. There were still the usual hazards, plus those exclusive to Holland.

"Windmill!" said Maria suddenly.

"Oh yeah!"

We flew up and over the tall, white wooden structure with sails. I was surprised not to have seen more of them on the way.

We reached 's-Hertogenbosch then flew on a little further west before turning onto a south-westerly bearing and down towards the airbase. The route took us across the least populated areas, avoiding towns and villages and keeping low all the way to avoid radar detection by the Germans.

"Not far now," said Maria.

I immediately felt my heartrate increase as the tension begin to mount. No matter how many missions I flew, I could never become insouciant about any of them.

Endless fields flashed by and then we eased between two towns, Uden on one side and Mariaheide on the other.

Maria and I had laughed when we'd seen the name of this town on the map.

"It's a good omen," said Maria.

"Let's hope so," I replied.

Now it was simply another dark town, and we had other things to concentrate on. In a few moments, we would turn due west again and begin our attack run.

The minutes crawled by, but soon enough it was time.

"We're here. Over to you," said Maria, giving out a new bearing.

"Foxes, attack formation," I said.

The squadron split into the prearranged groups. Sandra, Dorothy and Patricia moved into position behind me as the leading group. Behind us, Jennifer led the middle group and Susan the final group. After the last mission, I knew that Sandra and Dorothy made good wingwomen; I could rely on them. I had chosen Jennifer and Susan as group leaders for the same reason.

"Opening bomb bay doors," I said to Maria.

These were nerve-wracking moments, not knowing what was waiting for us at the target. Would the flak batteries open up? Would they spot us? I hoped not.

We flew right over a small town, probably making their windows shake as twenty-four Merlin engines roared above their roofs.

"Big Bertha in sight," said Maria. This was the codename for the target.

There was the airbase, laid out in front of us. The runway, buildings and planes were neatly lined up in rows. No lights, no incoming fire, nothing. We had caught them well and truly napping.

"Here we go," I said as we approached the airbase at speed. "Foxes, drop on my command."

We had rehearsed this several times; all of the ordnance had to go at once. Then we had to make a fast exit.

My heart was pounding and all I could hear was the thrum of the engines. I eased off the safety on the guns. My fingers hovered over the bomb release.

Then we were over the runway and there was no more time to think. I gave the command.

"Bombs away."

I let the bombs go and then banked sharp right. I opened up the throttle and the Mosquito surged forward.

"Foxes, on me, get out, out, out," I said. We had only seconds before all hell broke loose.

As the airbase receded behind us, a series of explosions lit up the sky.

"Yeah!" cried Maria. "We did it."

"Almost," I replied. We still had to go back for a strafing run. I banked around, ready for the second attack.

"Foxes, strafe formation," I said.

Twelve Mosquitos fanned out in a line, trigger fingers poised to unleash a hail of cannon fire. The airbase was awash with burning planes, and hopefully the bombs would have damaged the runway too.

This time we met with some ack-ack and machine-gun fire.

"Incoming," said Sandra.

"Keep it steady. Fire on my command," I said.

Bullets zinged past us, but we had to get closer. Flak exploded around us. Searchlights lit up the sky. Figures were seen running on the base. I ignored it all, intent on one thing only.

We finally closed the distance.

"Fire," I said, opening up with the cannons.

Tracers streamed from twelve Mosquitos, cutting up the dirt and silencing the guns. It was almost a textbook attack. Then came an unwelcome distraction.

"Fighter," said Dorothy, on my wing. "Taking off."

Over on the airbase, one lone Junkers night fighter was attempting to take flight.

"Fox One One and One Two," I said. "Stop it before it leaves."

We had to prevent it from getting airborne. If it made it, we'd be in trouble. We didn't need a dogfight in the air.

Dorothy and Sandra broke off and banked sharply in the direction of the plane, which was picking up speed.

As we zoomed over the base, I watched their progress with bated breath.

"I've got it," said Sandra.

"On it," said Dorothy.

"He's getting away," said Patricia as the Junkers started to take flight.

"The hell he is," said Sandra, cutting loose with her guns.

She and Dorothy hit the Junkers amidships and it exploded, to my immense relief. We had crossed the airfield now; there was nothing more to be done.

"Foxes, form up on me," I said. "Let's get out of here."

Maria gave us a bearing and we were away. We took the same route back because it was the safest option. It was funny how the return journey always seemed shorter. We could breathe just a little easier, having done our part.

Once more we flew over the town and then turned northeast over fields until we hit the river once more. I took us to the north side, not wanting to risk Jerry having another pop at us. We'd lost a navigator to a stray bullet. I didn't want to lose another.

"There's the windmill," said Maria.

"Got it."

It loomed up as we hopped up and over and continued over the flat countryside, with the river glinting on our left.

Shortly afterwards we were over the estuary south of Rotterdam once again. I breathed a sigh of relief as we left the coast of Holland and streaked over the waves of the Channel.

The wind was up but not so much as to cause a problem. Harwich came into view. We passed over the ships and onto the flat landscape beyond.

"We did it," said Maria.

"Yes," I said. "We did."

"If only every mission was as easy as that," she said.

"Yes," I agreed, knowing full well that the next one might be quite a different story.

CHAPTER FOURTEEN

"You're back," James murmured as I slipped under the covers beside him.

"Yes," I said.

"And safe?"

"As you see."

He wrapped his arms around me and we didn't talk any further. I had been to my room and given Jennifer a brief hug before making my way to James's room. It had become a familiar pattern. In earlier times, I was sure what I was doing would have been considered most improper. In wartime, things were different. You never knew if you'd return safely from a mission, or at all. Normal society mores seemed to have been at least temporarily suspended.

The following day a briefing was held after lunch with James, Henry and Gloria. The Marx Brothers didn't always attend briefings. I now knew they also spent time with the Mavericks squadron.

"Well done, Sirens," said James. "The mission last night appears to have been quite a success."

"Many planes were destroyed," said Henry. "In addition, the runway was damaged, putting it out of operation for at least a while." He signalled for the lights to be dimmed. "Hot off the press are these reconnaissance photographs taken in the early hours," he went on. Images appeared on the projection screen, showing a cratered runway and damaged planes.

I wondered how they had got the photographs to us so soon, but assumed they must expedite these things.

I exchanged a glance with Maria. We smiled. There was a feeling of satisfaction all round at a job well done.

"This was an important strategic target," said James as the lights came on again. "Bomber Command no doubt intends to attack it again, but your mission was a softening-up exercise, as it were. Every fighter put out of action is one less to threaten our bomber squadrons." He paused momentarily. "In any case, you can chalk up another win for the Sirens. Another feather in your cap."

This brought a few smiles, but no cheers. The extraordinary now seemed almost ordinary. Perhaps we had simply come of age. To some degree, we were combat-hardened. We'd stared death in the face one too many times. At the start of my journey with the Sirens, I had wondered if I would ever get used to it. Now I knew that I had. We all had.

"There will be a new mission very shortly," James continued. "But for now, you're dismissed."

As I left the briefing room, I found myself collared by Pamela and Betty.

"Boss," said Pamela, "have you had any thoughts about my suggestion?"

I stared at her blankly. "What suggestion?"

"Our idea for settling our dispute," put in Betty.

"Can't you settle it yourselves in a civilised manner?" I said, a little exasperated.

"Not really, no…" Pamela trailed off. She'd been rather circumspect with me since the incident in the gardens.

I sighed. I could see that I was going to have to find a way of sorting it out.

"Leave it with me," I said. "And stay away from Gary."

"Yes, Boss," said Pamela meekly.

"Ma'am," said Betty.

I turned to find Maria at my elbow.

"Honestly," I said in a low voice. "You'd think they *wanted* to fight a duel."

"Maybe they do," said Maria.

"There has to be another way," I told her.

"Maybe there isn't," Maria replied.

I looked at her. She seemed serious.

"Don't tell me you're now condoning this idea?"

She shrugged. "I'm just being practical."

I laughed. "Oh, you're impossible."

"So I've been told," she said, laughing too.

The exigencies of war waited for no one. I'd discovered that fairly early on. Now the airbase mission was over, there was a push to move forward with the Cookie bomb mission. It was an infinitely more complex arrangement. Even with the Mavericks' involvement, it was far more dangerous than any other mission we'd been on to date.

We held a proper debrief in James's office with Henry, Gloria and the Marx Brothers. I took Maria with me, as she was in effect my number two in terms of mission planning. As the lead navigator, she played a key role.

The debrief didn't take long, and there were more congratulations all round for the success of our attack on the airbase. I was particularly happy since nobody had been injured or killed. When we'd finished, matters turned to Hitler's bunker.

The Marx Brothers took the lead.

"We're getting a little agitation," said Harpo, tapping the ash from his cigarette into the ashtray on the table, "with regards to the Cookie bomb."

"Yes," said Chico. "The powers that be are anxious for the results so that Barnes can finalise work on a much bigger bomb that he's developing."

"If he's making a bigger bomb anyway, then why do we need to drop this Cookie bomb?" I knew it was probably a pointless question, but I asked it anyway.

Neither of the two spies was fazed by this. They were almost always phlegmatic, I had learned that they were deceptively thorough. What appeared at first glance to be a somewhat hare-brained idea had usually been considered in great detail behind the scenes. They were certainly not a pair to underestimate.

"Because," said Harpo patiently, "Barnes needs more information on how much bigger a bomb he needs to make."

"What is more," added Chico, "he needs to know how the bomb behaves when it's dropped."

"Why does that make a difference?" asked Maria, who had been listening intently.

"The Cookie, as we previously explained to the Flight Officer here," said Harpo, "is four thousand pounds of high explosive contained in what is effectively a metal cylinder, with a shallow cone on one end that contains the detonator."

"Obviously tests have been carried out with the Cookie, but they want to know what it does on a live target," said Chico.

"And in particular on an enemy bunker," added Harpo.

I thought of another point. "We're not going to be able to hang around to watch it drop," I said. "We have to get clear."

Harpo smiled and took a drag on his cigarette. "That is true, but the Mosquito you will be flying will be rigged up with a camera in the bomb bay. When you release the bomb it will begin filming, and continue to do so until the film runs out."

"That way, we'll get at least some of the bomb's behaviour in flight," said Chico.

Maria cut in before I could say anything. "I assume from what you're saying that we'll be getting a Mosquito specifically fitted out to drop this bomb?" she said.

"Yes," said Harpo. "In fact, you'll be getting two."

"Two?" I exclaimed in surprise.

"Fail-safe," said Chico. "No sense in going to all that trouble if something happens to one of the bombs before it gets dropped…" He trailed off, but I had already caught his drift.

"You mean in case one gets shot down?"

"Exactly so," he replied.

Maria and I shared a look. Getting shot down was a distinct possibility.

"Are we to drop both, otherwise?" Maria asked them.

"No sense in taking it all that way and not delivering it to Jerry," Harpo said with a light laugh.

"Won't that muck up the experiment, if two are dropped on the same target?" I wondered.

"I sincerely doubt they'll both land in exactly the same place," said Chico. "And reconnaissance photos will give Barnes a chance to evaluate the damage, which is what he needs."

"Nevertheless," I said, thinking aloud, "the second Mosquito will have to wait for the blast before making its run. Both will be exposed to risk."

"There is that," said Harpo.

"But you will be performing an extremely valuable service to the war effort," said Chico.

I didn't answer. That was the reason given almost every time we went on a mission. Who was I to naysay it? The missions were all planned at a high level. Strategies were formulated from Churchill downwards. In many ways, we were just a cog in a very big war machine.

"I know what you're thinking," said Harpo as if I had articulated my thoughts out loud. "But the truth is that this *is* strategically important. It's a high-profile mission and it's been given to the Sirens because you're recognised as one of the best."

"By Churchill himself," said Chico. "Word is that he insisted on it."

"Well, if Churchill insisted," I said with a laugh, "then who am I to demur?"

"Precisely," said Harpo.

"She's got it," said Chico.

James decided he'd taken a back seat for long enough and pitched in to ask a pertinent question. "Who exactly will drop the Cookies?"

Although I had not factored two bombs into the equation, the choice was still easy. I wasn't sure that James was going to like it.

"I will fly the first Mosquito," I said. "And Patricia will fly the second."

There was a flash of concern on James's face on hearing this, then it was gone.

"I guessed you would make those choices," he said quietly.

"It makes sense to me," said Henry, cutting in. "After all, Anna and Patricia both flew the Highball mission, plus they now have two reasonably experienced bombardiers in Maria and Connie."

"We'll still need to practice," I put in. "We've got to get the timing right for a start. Maria and Connie will need to become au fait with whatever bombsights will be used. We will need to drop dummy bombs from the correct height too."

"It can all be arranged, I'm sure," said Henry.

"Yes, indeed," said Harpo.

"Absolutely," said Chico.

I had suddenly become all businesslike. James seemed to find it amusing.

"You can tell she's the boss," Maria quipped.

"And a very capable one at that," said James.

I felt a little embarrassed at the compliment. Although I enjoyed it when James paid me one, I still wasn't used to it.

"I've got a great navigator too," I said, not wanting to be singled out.

"You will need to liaise with Angelica," said Gloria. "Get all that properly underway."

"I'll get in touch with her pronto," I said. "Perhaps she can come here for a couple of days so we can finalise various details."

"I'll make sure she has a room," said Gloria.

"Thank you."

"If there's nothing else, for the moment?" said Harpo.

Both he and Chico stood up. They would have plenty of other things on their minds, I was sure of that.

"No, I think we're done for now. If I could just have a quick word with Anna?" said James.

This was the cue for everyone else to depart, which they did with alacrity. It made me wonder just how much of our relationship was known to them. It wouldn't surprise me if the Marx Brothers knew, as they seemed to know just about everything else that went on in the Sirens.

"So," said James, coming around to my side of the table once we were alone. "Putting yourself in danger once again."

"But I do every time we fly," I shot back.

"I know," he said with a sigh. "I still can't entirely get used to it."

"Would you rather it was the other way around?" I quizzed him.

"No, not that."

"Well, get used to this instead," I said, applying my lips firmly to his.

After a little while, we took a seat together on the sofa. James made some tea and poured it out for both of us. I took the cup from him gratefully. A notion occurred to me, and I wanted to ask him about it. I wasn't sure how he'd take it, though.

"James?" I said, sipping my tea.

"Yes, darling?"

"Is there anything in the RAF rules about duelling?"

He had been in the act of taking a drink of tea and almost choked at the question. "What did you say?"

"Duelling, you know, with swords. Is there anything that forbids it, specifically?" I asked innocently.

"Anna Nightingale, what on earth are you planning?"

"Nothing in particular. Just asking a question, that's all," I told him.

"About duelling? That's not just a random question. Are you planning to fight a duel with someone? Tell me at once!" he demanded, setting down his cup and fixing me with a beady eye.

"No, I wasn't… Well, not me…" I trailed off, realising that perhaps it wasn't such a good idea to ask him after all.

However, he immediately relaxed. "Thank goodness for that," he said, picking up his cup and taking a few sips.

I realised his initial reaction had been about me. Perhaps he had visions of me being skewered by a sword. Now that wasn't the case, he seemed a bit more approachable on the topic.

"Is it … forbidden?" I persisted.

He sighed. "I suppose you're not going to tell me what this is about?"

"No," I replied.

"It's probably not something I want to know either," he said with a wry smile.

"Trust me, you don't."

He drank the rest of his tea and set the cup down.

"Technically, I've never read anything in the rules forbidding such a practice," he said. "But that's probably because nobody expects anyone to engage in something quite so outrageous in these modern times."

I didn't reply, since I had elicited the answer I wanted.

"I'm not going to ask you any more. I trust you have your reasons. But you know, Anna, that you're completely impossible," he said, moving closer.

"So, you've said."

"And incorrigible."

"You've said that too."

"Just don't go letting anyone get seriously hurt or killed, while you're resolving whatever dispute this involves," he said softly, removing my cup from my grasp.

"I'll try my best," I said.

"That's what's worrying me…"

I wound my arms around his neck and soon all talk of duelling was forgotten.

I contacted Angelica and arranged for her to come for a short stay. She was more than happy to oblige, and not long afterwards I met her at the front of the Hall. She arrived in a jeep driven by Sergeant Gordon. She jumped down with a small bag and walked quickly up the steps to greet me.

"Hello, Anna," she said with a smile.

"Hello, Angelica. Glad you could make it," I replied, smiling too.

Having dropped her off safely, Sergeant Gordon left with a wave, promising to pick Angelica up again at the appointed hour.

"He could have stayed," I said as we watched the jeep disappear down the driveway.

"He's got his duty," said Angelica. "He'll be driving Angus around as usual. Anyway, the two of them will probably go to their favourite tearoom."

"Tearoom?" I said, surprised, thinking they'd be more likely to go to the pub.

"Yes." She laughed. "Annie's Kitchen. They go there to discuss things. Gordon's more of a friend to Angus than a batman. I've been to Annie's too. It's not exclusively a male preserve. The crumpets are to die for."

I refrained from asking what things they might be discussing and instead accompanied Angelica up to the room Gloria had arranged for her. It was nicely appointed and reasonably large for one person, with its own bathroom.

"I say," she said. "This is grand. A bit like where Angus and I are billeted."

"Oh?"

"We're staying at Amberley Hall near Banley. We've a small suite of rooms. Some of the other pilots are there too," she said, noting my surprise.

Of course, I had no idea what billets the Air Force put their pilots up in. There had been suggestions from some people from other squadrons that the Sirens were lucky.

"What did you tell Angus about your trip?" I asked her.

"I just said it was some top-secret thing and that I couldn't tell him anything about it. He didn't enquire further, particularly when I mentioned the Marx Brothers' involvement. They're not exactly his favourite people."

I laughed on hearing this.

"He doesn't like me to be away too long," she said. "I don't like it either."

"When you've freshened up," I said, "we should make a start on planning the mission."

"Of course," she said. "I'll just a be a few moments. You can wait for me, if you prefer."

I did so and a little while later, I sat with Angelica and Maria in the same meeting room the Marx Brothers used. It seemed quite a convenient place to go over the logistics of the mission. First, we talked about squadron-to-squadron communications, which was the nub of the issue after all.

"So, you will be on one radio frequency," said Angelica. "The Mavericks will be on another."

"Won't that be difficult to manage?" I asked her.

"Not really," she replied. "I will have two separate radio sets. I'll have them running independently. That way I can keep an eye — or rather an ear — on both."

"It sounds like a lot," said Maria. "You'll have your hands full."

"Yes," said Angelica. "But I think I can do it all right."

"Who else knows about this at your base?" I asked.

It was a perfectly reasonable question, since the existence of the Sirens was theoretically compromised the more people knew about it.

"Well," she said, "I've had to tell Squadron Leader Bentley, since it would be virtually impossible to use the Mavericks for the job without doing so. His adjutant Section Officer Audrey

Wilmington also knows, but then she's privy to virtually every secret that he is."

"Why don't you have Audrey on one of the radio sets then, if she already knows? That way, you'll be able to relay between you and won't miss anything," said Maria.

Angelica looked much struck by this. "That's certainly an idea. I hadn't thought of it, but it might be a better option. Thank you."

Maria laughed. "Three heads are better than one," she said.

"I think that speed of response from our escort is the main consideration," I told Angelica. "If and when we get into a situation on the mission, I need to know they'll be there."

"Oh," said Angelica. "You need not worry about that. They are used to escorting the American Bombers from the base next door. You'll find that M Flight is exceptionally reactive and we've some of the best pilots around."

I was relieved to hear that and said so.

"It's not a problem," Angelica replied. "I want this mission to succeed just as much as you do."

"What does Angus think about the arrangements? Doesn't he think it's odd?" I asked her bluntly.

"I've told him that this is a secret squadron. That's all he needs to know. I've said that you fly very important stealth missions. Not, of course, that you're all women…"

She laughed at this. Maria and I joined in.

Maria placed a large A3 folder on the desk and opened it. Inside were reconnaissance photographs, maps and various other things pertaining to the mission. There had been a fair bit of planning already completed by the Mission Department on our end.

"We need to go over the flight plans, the route and so on. It's quite a distance — about a four-hundred-mile round trip," said Maria. "We haven't asked about the Spitfire range and just assumed it will be okay."

"They'll have extra tanks under the fuselage. We've done it before on a different mission, so it won't be a problem," said Angelica.

"You've thought of everything, by all accounts," said Maria.

"I've tried to," Angelica agreed. "I'm not usually quite so involved in mission planning as this, but needs must."

By contrast, I had become increasingly involved in planning missions as time went on. However, that was because I also had to fly them. In any case, Maria and I had been over the details with Henry before meeting with Angelica.

"The bunker is located west of Paris," said Maria, pointing it out on the map. "We suggest we rendezvous with your squadron over Chelmsford. We will then take a direct route down to Hastings, where we will cross the Channel. We'll be flying at hedge-hopping height and then wave height to avoid radar detection."

"Oh, the boys will love that," said Angelica with a light laugh. "Particularly Jonty."

I wondered what this Jonty was like. In fact, I wondered what they were all like. We'd never get to meet any of them in all probability.

"He's a bit wayward," said Angelica, seeing my expression. "He's been in trouble more times than I can count. Remind me to tell you about the time he took his parrot up in his Spitfire for a spin."

"Really?" said Maria.

"Oh yes. He's had a few carpetings from Bentley for getting into various scrapes."

I resolved to find out more about the parrot incident later. Maria gently guided our attention back to the map.

"So once over the Channel, we'll cross into France here."

She pointed to the mouth of a river at a place called Le Crotoy.

"I'm glad it's not Wissant," I said. "Bearing in mind we got shot at last time."

"Yes, we think this is a better option and there's less time over land to the target," said Maria. "We will get up-to-date reconnaissance before we go just to double-check."

"All right," I said. "You know what you're doing."

Maria laughed. "That's debatable."

"You and the boys would get on well," Angelica said. "If only things were different."

We all reflected on that for a moment. However, I knew the only reason we were flying in combat at all was because we were living in such extraordinary times. Otherwise, fate would probably never have brought us together.

"Once we've made landfall, it's low level all the way to the target," said Maria, tracing the route with her finger. "Once we reach the target, we will split. The two Cookie planes will circle over the countryside out of the way. The rest of the flight will carry out a bombing run over the target in order to try and neutralise the ack-ack. The aim is to drop as much ordnance as possible. The bombing runs go in at low level on timed fuses and then get out fast."

"So, they'll need an escort," said Angelica.

"Yes, they will, but the Spitfires accompanying them will need to get clear once the bombs are released, as will all the Mosquitos," Maria continued.

"Yes," said Angelica. "They will probably be circling just out of the target zone in any case to provide cover in case of enemy planes."

Maria nodded. "The two Cookie planes will also need an escort at all times. Once the main squadron has dropped their bombs, we will start our approach, go to six thousand feet and drop the bomb once over the target. Then we'll all get the hell out."

"You two are flying one of the Cookie planes?" asked Angelica.

"Yes," I replied.

"How many planes are you taking on the mission in total?"

"We're taking the full eighteen for maximum effect."

Angelica was thoughtful for a few moments. "I think that your Cookie planes will need at least two Spitfires each," she said. "So that only leaves us eight to protect sixteen planes. So, we might need to borrow about six more from the other flight to make up the numbers... I'll talk to Bentley."

"Thank you," I said. "As I see it, our biggest problem is going to be *after* the attack and not before it. We should manage to reach the target without too much trouble, unless we are spotted by a patrol. We can't help that, though. Once the shooting starts, then we will probably see a response from Jerry. So it's the journey back that is likely to be the most perilous."

Angelica looked concerned. "Then perhaps we need both Maverick flights," she said. "It might be safer."

"We're grateful for whatever you can spare," I replied. "I want to get us home in one piece, if possible ... *all* of us."

We regarded each other in silence. What would the German response be? Until we were actually on the mission, we would have no idea.

"What if you do get spotted on the way in? What then?" Angelica asked.

"I'll have to make a call. If necessary, we may have to abort the mission, but that would be a last resort."

"Once the Germans know you're there, they'll keep coming after you," said Angelica. "The American Bombers have been taking huge casualties."

What she said brought home to me even more the precarious nature of our mission. We hadn't the luxury of the huge bomber wings that attacked German targets. If we kept going, we'd all potentially get shot down. If the Cookie planes were lost, then the whole point of the mission was over. If we were detected, it would simply depend on how near or far we were to the target. The closer we were, the more pressure we'd be under to keep going regardless.

"It's a decision only I can make when it happens," I said. "I am the Flight Leader and also the Mission Leader. I will lead the formation and so the Mavericks will need to follow our lead accordingly."

"All right, it's your show, of course," said Angelica.

"We're going to be relying on the Mavericks completely," I replied. "Without them, it's more or less a suicide mission for us."

"Then I'm glad we can help," said Angelica.

"Let's take a look at these reconnaissance photographs of the target and the route," said Maria. "We'll be sticking to the countryside as far as possible, and that will help us avoid detection."

It wasn't a night mission, but if we left at dawn then we'd have a better chance of stealing in undetected. I articulated my idea to the other two.

"I think that we should leave at dawn," I said. "Or just before."

"The Spitfires can't fly at night," said Angelica. "Well, not many of them. They have to have a special glare shield fitted and our day fighters don't have those."

"Then it needs to be dawn," I said. "It will give us the edge we need."

"You're right," said Maria.

"I agree," said Angelica.

"I will inform Henry and James that's what needs to happen," I said decisively.

There were more things we had to discuss. For example, the Mosquitos could outrun the enemy if we were pursued on the way home, but then we might leave the Spitfires behind. This would have to be a tactical decision depending on how close to the French coastline we were and other such factors.

"We can't plan for everything," I concluded at the end of the session. "Some decisions will have to be made on the fly."

"I think we've covered all the important stuff," said Angelica, and Maria agreed.

"We'll have to go over it all again with James and the others," I told them.

"How about lunch first?" suggested Maria.

"I second that," said Angelica.

CHAPTER FIFTEEN

The rest of the day passed quickly. James, Henry, Gloria and the Marx Brothers concurred with the decisions we'd made. Now it was all agreed, the next thing would be to practise the communication link. Once that was established, we'd brief the squadron. There would be plenty more to practice before the mission proper.

That evening after dinner, I managed to get Angelica alone by suggesting a stroll in the formal gardens. There was something I wanted to ask her.

"What's on your mind?" she asked as we walked between the well-maintained low hedges and beds. Even in wartime these were looked after, although most of the beds were given over to growing vegetables to feed the Sirens and all of the ancillary staff.

I hesitated for a moment, and then said, "I was wondering about your relationship with your husband, as you seem to work quite closely together on the same airbase."

Angelica laughed. "I'm sort of unofficially Angus's adjutant, but I would never tell him that. We spend a lot of time working together. You might say I've engineered it that way."

"But how does that work, you being married to the boss?"

"Angus is definitely not the boss. Let's rather say it's a détente. I let him think he's in charge when it suits me. But to answer your question, it works just fine. Nobody bats an eye."

She had evidently found her métier with regards to her marriage. It made me more than a little envious.

"So nobody cares that you two are in the same squadron?"

"The Mavericks are not an ordinary squadron. We're misfits and outsiders — at least the pilots are. Thrown out of other squadrons for all kinds of reasons. So unusual arrangements are countenanced, and we have a good CO."

This wasn't quite what I'd expected to hear, but it seemed like there might be some similarities to my situation.

"Oh… Then I suppose the Mavericks are a bit like the Sirens. We're out of the ordinary too."

She smiled and turned to face me. "*And* your boyfriend is the CO…"

I blinked. Was our relationship that obvious, if Angelica had guessed? I sighed and took the plunge.

"You're right. I am in a relationship with James," I said. "He wants to get married."

"And do you?" Angelica probed gently.

I let out another sigh. "I don't know."

"If you want my advice, Anna, don't wait like I did. The only thing that held me back was my own scruples."

"And now?"

"I couldn't be happier. I wish I'd done it sooner," she said.

"I see."

She hadn't told me exactly what I wanted to hear, but it was reassuring to know that her marriage had been well received.

"I'll consider it," I said.

We both laughed. There didn't seem to be much more to say.

"Tell me about flying into combat — what's it like?" Angelica asked as we resumed walking.

She listened with interest to my anecdotes about our missions. Then a thought occurred to me.

"Have you ever wanted to fly in combat?" I asked her.

"Goodness, no. I'm quite happy as I am, but it's hard when Angus flies out on a mission."

"James says the same."

"A complete role reversal," she laughed. "How funny."

"It's getting dark — we should go inside. I have to deal with a problem between two of my pilots," I told her.

"Oh?" she said. "What kind of a problem?"

Since we seemed to be on good terms now, I elaborated. "They want to fight a duel," I said.

She laughed out loud at this. "A duel? Whatever for?"

I explained Pamela and Betty's dispute over Gary.

"Fighting over a man? Oh dear!" she said.

"And I'm still not sure what to do," I replied.

"What does James say about it?"

"I asked him if there was anything in the rules against duelling, and he said not specifically. He was fine once he realised that *I* wasn't intending to fight someone."

"Goodness," exclaimed Angelica. "And I thought we were a bit wayward in the Mavericks."

"Yes, well, this isn't how it usually goes," I said hastily. "But they seem adamant, and I'm starting to come around to allowing it before it escalates into something I can't control."

"Are you going to talk to them about it this evening?" she said.

"Well, yes…"

"Might I listen in? It sounds so intriguing."

I smiled at this. "As it happens, there might be a way for you to do just that."

"Well, then let's get to it," she replied, a little too eagerly for my liking.

After dinner I convened a meeting in the room the Marx Brothers usually used. Maria and I sat on one side of the ornately decorated table, facing Betty and Pamela on the other.

The room housed a secret hidey-hole accessed via a panel in the wainscoting. Before everyone else arrived, I had conducted Angelica into the secret room through the panel and up a small stairway.

"Oh, this is exciting," she said, looking out through the filigree screen higher up in the wall. From there one could view the entire room and everything that went on in it.

"Yes," I said. "Not many people know it's here."

"Thank you for letting me sit in," she said.

"You're welcome."

From where I was sitting, I glanced surreptitiously up at the screen. It was impossible to tell that it wasn't just a part of the panelling.

I had asked Maria to attend, because I needed a witness. I also respected her advice. I supposed she had become my right-hand woman.

"All right," I said to Betty and Pamela. "The two of you seem set on the idea of a duel."

"Does that mean you're going to allow it?" asked Pamela, her eyes wide.

"That is not what I said," I replied firmly. "I am simply considering it."

"Oh." She looked a little crestfallen.

"This is not a game," I said. "This is the RAF. I would be breaking all kinds of protocols. But the two of you have put me in an impossible situation."

"I understand," said Betty.

"Clearly you do not, because if you did, you'd find another way to settle your blasted disagreement," I said, becoming annoyed.

"What the Boss is saying," Maria told them, "is that you're a pair of idiots who want your heads banging together. But since she's a kinder soul than I, she's minded to let you to carry out this hare-brained scheme of yours."

I suppressed a laugh. "Thank you, Maria. It's not quite how I'd put it, but I imagine the two of you get the gist."

"Yes, Boss," said Pamela, looking a little abashed.

I sighed. There seemed to be nothing for it. "If — and I do mean *if* — I allow you to fight this duel, explain to me how it will work," I said.

"Oh, well, we would fight outdoors, because that's best, at dawn … traditional and all that … and we'd need seconds, because that's traditional too," Pamela explained excitedly. "Then we'd choose our swords and fight … until one of us drew first blood." She saw my expression and hurried to reassure me. "No hits on the torso or the face, so it would have to be the arms or the legs, which are also harder to hit. No deadly thrusts and so forth."

"I see," I said, not particularly liking what I was hearing. "And if one of you does draw first blood, as you call it, then it is over? One of you will withdraw and I will never hear any more about it again?"

"You have my word," said Pamela, nodding enthusiastically.

"And mine," said Betty.

I looked from one to the other. "Have you both engaged in sword fighting before? You seem incredibly keen about it."

"I used to do fencing, Boss, so yes," said Betty.

"I was brought up in a household where it was part of my education," said Pamela.

I knew she was from aristocratic stock, so I didn't enquire too deeply.

"Right," I said. "What about the swords?"

"Oh, I've already got those," said Pamela.

"Of course you have," I replied with a sigh.

I felt as if I had been outmanoeuvred somehow, and I didn't feel easy about it.

"You can't just toss a coin or something?" I ventured in a last-ditch effort to avoid actual bloodshed.

"No," said Pamela.

"No," said Betty. "It needs to be the best woman who wins."

"I hope that Gary is worth all of this," I said coolly.

They didn't answer and I sat in silence for several minutes, thinking. The others waited patiently for my verdict. I felt that I had no option. At least this would get it out of the way as discreetly as possible.

"All right," I said at length. "I will allow this farrago to go ahead on the following conditions. We keep it between ourselves. It can *never* go any further. Understood?"

"Yes, Boss," said Pamela.

"Of course, Boss," said Betty.

"If one of you manages to wound the other person more than just superficially, then there will be hell to pay," I continued. "If I have to explain to the doctor how you got cut up, I'm not going to be happy at all. Have I made myself clear?"

"Perfectly," said Pamela.

"Absolutely. We'll be careful, I promise," said Betty.

I doubted that this would be the case once the heat of battle commenced.

"And when is this damned duel going to take place?" I asked.

"Tomorrow at dawn," said Pamela.

I eyed her somewhat askance. It was almost as if they'd anticipated that I would agree.

"All right, but I will be there to witness things. You can go and gather the others in my room, but say nothing to them until I get there, understood?"

"Yes, Boss, thank you, Boss," said Betty.

"You won't regret this, I promise," said Pamela.

"That remains to be seen," I replied with a healthy amount of scepticism in my voice.

Pamela and Betty hurried out of the room and when they had gone, I beckoned to Angelica to come down and join us.

"I say, well done you," she said. "Isn't it splendid that it's happening tomorrow morning?"

"Why is that?" I asked with some suspicion.

"Because I can come and watch!"

I returned to my room, along with Maria and Angelica. Then I laid down the law regarding the duel. Shelly, Patricia, Connie, Susan, Sandra, Lucy, Diana, Dorothy and Jennifer were all present, along with Pamela and Betty. It would have been impossible to exclude any of them.

"I am allowing the duel…" I began and was immediately interrupted by excited exclamations.

"Hush, for goodness' sake," said Maria. "The Boss is talking."

"Thank you, Maria," I said. "Not one word of this is to leave this room. Is that understood?"

There were eager nods.

"You can all come to witness the duel. Afterwards, none of you are to ever mention it again!"

"We won't," said Shelly.

"We promise," said Sandra.

I relaxed a little after this. There were still the arrangements to be made.

"Apparently there need to be seconds," I said. "For the two protagonists."

"I'll be Pamela's second," said Susan, which made sense since Pamela was her navigator.

"I'll be the other," said Connie.

"Diana and I will be Betty's seconds," said Dorothy.

"All right, that's settled," I said.

"We also need a Mistress of Ceremonies, to tell us when to start and stop," said Pamela.

"Surely that should be you, Boss?" said Shelly.

"No!" I said emphatically. "I've had far too much to do with this already."

"I'll do it," said Jennifer.

The others agreed and the time and place were finalised.

"Gosh," said Sandra. "This is like one of those gunfights in the Old West."

"Heaven forbid," I said firmly. "I'm going to leave you lot to discuss the finer details. We'll meet at dawn tomorrow… God help us all."

With that, I departed from the room with Angelica in tow. We headed for the house bar, where we spent a pleasant hour chatting amicably. The others came down and apart from an air of suppressed anticipation, there was thankfully no mention of the duel.

I didn't go to see James that night because I felt that I wouldn't be able to stop myself from telling him. It was better that he didn't know, at least before the event. He might insist on coming too, and that would not be seemly for him as the CO. He might try to stop it, and that also could cause even more problems than letting it go ahead.

Nevertheless I slept fitfully, thinking of the worst that could happen. Jennifer stirred beside me.

"What's the matter?" she murmured.

"It's the damn duel. I'm worried about it," I whispered.

"Don't be," she said. "It's just their way of letting off steam…"

"Letting off steam!" I exclaimed, firing up.

"Hush," said Jennifer, holding me tight. "It will be all right. I'll make sure of it. Stop worrying and get some sleep."

She began to sing softly. It was the lullaby our mother used to sing to us when we were young. Finally, I slipped into a deep sleep.

CHAPTER SIXTEEN

The alarm woke me with a start and a feeling of dread. Jennifer and I got up and dressed quickly. There was a quiet knock at the door. I opened it to Maria and Shelly.

"Are you ready?" Maria asked me.

"I feel sick to my stomach, but yes," I said quietly.

"It will be all right, you'll see."

"The others will be waiting downstairs," said Shelly. "We'd better get going."

Silently we made our way down the corridors, treading as quietly as we could. It was very much like going on a mission, except this one felt incredibly foolish. I wondered for the umpteenth time if I should have allowed it.

On the way we collected Angelica, who seemed far more excited than I.

"I'm rather looking forward to this," she whispered. "Aren't you?"

"That's not entirely my sentiment, no," I replied.

"Oh, well, I'm sure it's going to be fun."

Fun wasn't how I would describe it either, but I refrained from commenting further as we continued on our way.

I realised that we were at the point of no return. We arrived at the foyer, where the others were waiting. Pamela was carrying an ominous-looking slim wooden case. Softly we slipped out through the main entrance and made our way to a little-known part of the gardens.

The air was a crisp and there was a slight mist rising off the grass. The grey light of predawn began to appear on the horizon. We walked down stone paths and through avenues of trees before emerging into what seemed to be a secret garden.

It had a long, flat and well-kept lawn surrounded by high hedges. There were statues at either end with beds of shrubs around the sides.

"Nobody will disturb us here," said Pamela.

"How on earth did you find this place?" asked Shelly.

"Oh, I went scouting for a suitable spot," Pamela replied airily.

All of this served to increase my suspicion that I had been somehow coerced into allowing the duel.

"I suppose we'd better get on with it," said Jennifer, taking charge.

"I've brought a first aid kit," said Diana, producing a bag which presumably contained bandages and the like.

"Where did you get that?" I demanded.

"Borrowed it from the Sirens' hospital, for first aid practice," she told me.

I shook my head in despair.

"It's going to be fine, I'm sure of it," Angelica whispered.

"Duellists," said Jennifer in an assertive tone, "prepare yourselves."

She seemed to be taking her role very seriously. No doubt she had consulted Pamela further regarding the protocol.

The two protagonists, Pamela and Betty, removed their hats and jackets. Then they rolled up their shirtsleeves to the elbow. I noticed they were wearing trousers rather than skirts, presumably to assist their movement. They then proceeded to take off their shoes and socks so that they could fight barefoot. I assumed this would be something to do with getting a better purchase on the ground while fighting.

When they were ready, Jennifer called for the duelling weapons. Susan and Dorothy brought up the long wooden box and opened it.

There was a collective gasp. Lying on the red velvet lining were two wicked-looking swords.

"These are my family's sixteenth-century Elizabethan rapier duelling swords," Pamela informed us. "They are also razor-sharp."

I could have done without hearing that part but held my peace.

"Choose your weapons," said Jennifer, maintaining her formal tone.

I assumed the swords were the same so neither duellist had an advantage, although the handles were wrought slightly differently. The guards were fashioned from gilded steel styled in an ornate wraparound open weave. Pamela gestured for Betty to go first.

Betty selected a sword and drew it out. Then Pamela selected the other.

"Seconds, have you been able to persuade the protagonists to settle their dispute amicably by other means?" said Jennifer.

"No," said Dorothy.

"We haven't," said Susan.

It was supposedly the duty of the seconds to try and persuade the duellists to call it off. I doubted very much whether any such persuasion had been attempted. Jennifer was simply repeating what I assumed was the form of the duel.

"In which case, the duel will now go ahead," said Jennifer. "Seconds and others must withdraw."

We all moved away to a safe distance from where we could view the action.

"Duellists," said Jennifer, "this must be a clean fight. You will instantly break if I order it. The fight will be to first blood. You must desist at once should that occur. Is that understood?"

"Yes," said Betty.

"Yes," said Pamela.

"No hits to the body or head," Jennifer continued. "If you do, then you will be automatically disqualified. Do you both agree that the winner of this fight will withdraw all claim to Gary and leave the field clear for the other?"

Again, Betty and Pamela confirmed that they would.

"Very well," said Jennifer. "Take your positions."

Betty and Pamela moved more than the length of two swords apart.

"That's called being out of distance," murmured Connie. "So, they have to lunge in order to get each other."

"How do you know that?" Lucy asked her.

"I know a bit about fencing," said Connie cryptically.

"Hush," said Shelly. "They're about to start."

We fell silent. There was a definite air of anticipation.

"*En garde*," said Jennifer.

Betty and Pamela raised their swords and took up a fighting stance. Their free arms went behind their backs, presumably for balance and to keep them out of the way. All of their attention was on each other.

"Engage," said Jennifer.

They moved forward so that the tips of their swords were now touching.

Jennifer stepped back out of the way. "Fight!" she said.

The duellists began to move slowly back and forth, never taking their eyes off each other. Each was waiting for the other to attack. The swords gleamed as the sun began to rise behind us.

Suddenly, Pamela circled Betty's blade and lunged forward. Betty parried it and thrust back, causing Pamela to leap away.

Betty was now on the attack. She feinted a cut from the right, circled under and cut left. Pamela swiftly parried and countered with a raking cut. Betty leaped backwards in turn.

The clash of steel echoed around the garden. I looked around to reassure myself that nobody else had appeared.

The two of them circled warily, changing position. There were a couple of feints from each of them, easily parried.

"Give it up, Betty," said Pamela. "Gary is mine!"

"Damned if I will," Betty shot back.

She cut left, then right. Pamela parried each time. Then Betty's sword thrust forward, sliding over Pamela's guard. But Pamela was quick — she pushed the blade away before it could do any damage.

Without hesitating, Pamela crouched down and whipped her sword towards Betty's legs. Betty jumped and Pamela's sword cut thin air. As Betty landed, she attempted a cut to Pamela's arm. Pamela rolled away in the grass and scrambled to her feet, taking up a defensive posture once more.

Pamela pressed forward a series of fast attacks, cuts left and right, thrusts, one, two, three. Betty was pushed back, barely parrying any of them. It seemed perhaps that Pamela was the better swordswoman.

But Betty wasn't to be beaten so easily. She countered with her own furious set of attacks, cuts and thrusts, pushing Pamela back in turn. But Pamela countered all. Then the two of them stood *en garde* a short distance apart, panting from exertion.

I had to admit it was a thrilling spectacle. Just when we thought they would give it up, they engaged their blades again.

Pamela tried several feints, but Betty parried them. Then Betty attacked, feinting left, cutting right, then the opposite way — all to no avail.

"What if neither of them win?" whispered Lucy.

"Then I guess it's a draw," said Connie.

I reflected that we would be no further forward, should this prove to be the case.

More cuts, thrusts and parries ensued. Back and forth, they went, now grunting a little with the exertion of it all. I had never wielded a sword, but I imagined it would feel heavier as the fight went on. The sound of steel on steel rang out, with neither duellist gaining an advantage.

"They're good," said Connie. "Very good."

"Who is going to win?" said Shelly.

"The way they are going, it's hard to say," Connie informed us. "But one of them might just make a mistake."

Meanwhile, Pamela was pressing her attack on Betty, one cut to the right, one to the left, a circle attack and thrust. Betty was defending well, but even I could tell that she was tiring.

Betty's sword was wavering a little, but Pamela held hers rock-steady. Pamela certainly had the advantage.

"Give up?" Pamela asked her.

"No, damn you. If you want to win, then you have to *win*," Betty shot back.

"As you wish," Pamela replied.

She attacked again, left and then right. Betty barely parried the blade each time.

The two of them stood panting with blades engaged. Suddenly, Betty circled Pamela's blade and leaped forward with a flying attack like an arrow as her feet left the ground. Had

Pamela stayed in place, the blade would have neatly grazed her arm. It was a last-ditch effort by Betty. All or nothing.

However, Pamela was far too quick. She stepped aside with ease, keeping her blade on her inside. She caught Betty's upper arm as she flew by and sliced it neatly.

"Oh hell, I'm cut! I've been cut!" shouted Betty, dropping her sword and clutching her arm. I could see a red stain spreading out over her uniform shirt.

"Seconds!" shouted Jennifer, running to help.

Diana was there quickly, tearing open the first aid kit.

Then everyone else crowded around.

"Is she okay?" said Shelly. "Has she been badly cut?"

"Give them some space," I ordered, taking the situation in hand.

We all moved back and waited while Diana saw to the cut. Betty looked a little pale, and by the state of her shirt the wound appeared to have bled quite a lot.

Finally, Diana looked up. "I've bandaged the cut," she said. "But I'm pretty sure it's going to need some stitches."

"That's all we need," said Patricia.

"Now we're in the basket," said Shelly.

However, I wasn't having that. Not after all the care we'd taken.

"We're not in the basket if I can help it," I told them. "Get those swords squared away, then Maria, Jennifer, Diana and Angelica can help me get Betty to the infirmary. We'll go up the back stairway. Get her jacket on, and her shoes. The rest of you get back to your rooms and hide those blasted swords. Not a word of this to anyone."

There was a chorus of "Yes, Boss," and then they bustled around, carrying out my orders.

Shortly afterwards, the main group dispersed. The rest of us took Betty back to Hawberry Hall and up a little-used stairway to the Sirens' hospital.

Flight Officer Sophie Carpenter was the doctor in charge of the unit. I was glad to see she was at her desk. She got up to greet us as we arrived.

"What have we here?" she asked.

"A casualty, ASO Betty Watkins," I said. "She has a cut on her arm."

"All right, come through to the treatment room."

Dr Carpenter was businesslike and obviously an expert at her profession. We all stood back while she helped Betty remove her jacket and then the bandage on her cut.

"Well, it's a clean cut, but a little deep," she said. "How did this happen, Betty?"

Betty shot me a helpless glance.

"A knife," I said, prevaricating. "A very sharp knife."

"A knife," said Dr Carpenter in disbelieving tones. "And how exactly did she manage to cut her upper arm with a knife?"

"Carelessness?" I ventured.

"Really?" Dr Carpenter's tone was cynical, but she said nothing more and instead addressed herself to Betty's wound.

"Fortunately, I've got some local anaesthetic," she said, bustling around.

I watched her disinfect the cut with iodine, which brought tears to Betty's eyes. Diana went to sit beside her on the bed and put her arm around her.

"Who bandaged this up?" Dr Carpenter asked us.

"I did," said Diana.

"As it happens, you did a very good job. Well done," said Dr Carpenter.

Then she deftly sewed up the cut with neat stiches. Afterwards she put a bandage over it.

"There you are," she said to Betty. "All right and tight, but I'll need to check on it tomorrow. If you start feeling feverish, come straight away and we'll give you some antibiotics."

"Thanks, Doctor," said Betty.

"You're welcome," said Dr Carpenter. "Now, run along while I talk to your Flight Leader."

Betty put on her jacket and left with the others. I told them to meet me in my room. When they had gone, Dr Carpenter turned to speak to me.

"How did it really happen?" she asked quietly.

"Well —" I began.

"Let me just tell you that the last time I saw a cut like that, it was from a sword fight," Dr Carpenter said, cutting me short.

"Really?" I said, trying to feign innocence.

Dr Carpenter wasn't fooled. "You know, if people *are* fighting duels, then they should always have a doctor on hand."

"How did you know it was a duel?" I said, flabbergasted.

"I don't, not for sure," she replied. "But I'm pretty certain that was a sword wound."

"Have you been to many duels then?" I asked. There wasn't any point in trying to prevaricate further.

"You'd be surprised what we doctors get up to, particularly at medical school," she replied.

"All right," I said. "But please —"

"It goes no further than me," said Dr Carpenter before I could finish. "I'll record the incident as an accident with a knife, just as you said."

"Thanks, I appreciate it."

"Sometimes people do the most extraordinary things," she said. "I've just learned to take them in my stride. You should too."

I thanked her profusely and made my way back to my room. On the way, I ran into Linda. I made to go past her, but she stepped in front of me. My heart sank.

"Condoning duels now, ma'am?" she said. "Tut-tut."

"What do you know about that?" I demanded, annoyed at once.

"Oh, I saw it all. Just another black mark on your record, don't you think? Oh, don't worry, your secret is safe with me. As long as I get the second-in-command position."

"I haven't decided about that," I told her. "And I don't like being blackmailed."

It was her turn to look annoyed. I knew, however, that if push came to shove, James would send her packing.

"You'll come around to my way of thinking eventually," she told me. "I can wait."

I was infuriated by her manner and her tone. She knew exactly how to get under my skin.

"Dismissed," I said in icy tones.

Linda saluted and walked off down the corridor. I suppressed an exclamation of exasperation and continued on to my room.

As I expected, all the gang was there, chatting nineteen to the dozen about the duel. When they saw me, they all went quiet.

"How are you, Betty?" I asked. She was lying on one of the beds.

"I'll live," she said.

"Remember," I said to all of them. "Not a word to anyone about this."

"Yes, Boss," came the chorus.

I directed my attention to Pamela. "So, Pamela, I suppose you get your man. Lucky old Gary. I hope he makes you happy," I said.

Pamela took a deep breath. "Betty and I have talked, Boss, and we've decided that Gary isn't worth it after all."

"What?"

"I've decided I don't want him. Betty doesn't want him either," she said.

"Unbelievable!" I said furiously. "Then we've been through all this for no reason at all."

"It was fun, though, wasn't it, Boss?" said Sandra.

I could contain my anger no longer. "Get out, all of you! I've had enough of your shenanigans," I told them. "I don't want to see you again until breakfast."

They all looked at me, a little startled. Nobody moved.

"Go on," I said. "Get out, all of you … except Jennifer, Maria and Angelica. The rest of you, vamoose, *now*!"

I watched them leave with alacrity, then sat down on the bed.

"What's up, Anna?" said Jennifer.

I let out a big sigh. "Well, for one thing, that blasted duel appears to have been entirely unnecessary, and for another thing, Linda knows about it…"

"Oh dear," said Maria. "Tell us what happened."

CHAPTER SEVENTEEN

By the time breakfast came around, I had calmed down. When I told Maria, Jennifer and Angelica about Linda, they were equally furious.

"Good Lord," said Angelica. "She sounds perfectly horrid."

"Oh, she's more than just horrid," said Maria, going into more detail.

"Don't worry about Linda," said Jennifer eventually. "I mean, there's always the B-17."

Angelica looked puzzled. "The B-17?"

I sighed. "Maria will tell you." After this recent escapade, I had no desire to threaten to drop Linda out of a B-17 to get her to withdraw her blackmail attempt. "I need to freshen up before breakfast."

"Yes, do tell me. I want to know," I heard Angelica saying as I closed the bathroom door behind me. I could hear her chuckling as the others related the story regarding Gary and the B-17.

I sat down at our usual table in the dining room with a full plate. I discovered that the adventures of the previous night had made me hungry. I started to address my plate of eggs, beans, spam and sausage with gusto. After I had eaten a few mouthfuls, I noticed that everyone else at the table was very quiet.

"What's going on?" I asked them, sipping my tea.

"Are you still angry with us, Boss?" Sandra asked tentatively.

I sighed and looked around at their concerned faces. "I'm not angry anymore, no," I said. "I'm still rather displeased, if I'm honest, because I feel like I've been hoodwinked."

"It wasn't like that, Boss, I swear," said Pamela earnestly.

"We're the best of friends now," said Betty, who had also joined us at the table. "We've seen the error of our ways."

"There were easier ways of finding that out," I said, resisting the temptation to roll my eyes. "But let's move on now. We will have another mission to fly soon, and we need to focus our attention on that."

Now that I had broken the ice, the conversation resumed.

"How's the arm?" I said to Betty as I finished my food.

"It's fine, Boss," she replied. "It only hurts a bit."

"Make sure you go and get it checked, like the doctor asked you to," I instructed her.

"Yes, Boss, I will."

I smiled and pushed my plate away, satisfied that we could put the incident to bed. I glanced over at the table where James usually sat. I caught his eye. Not long after he left the dining room, I wasn't surprised when Judy appeared at my elbow.

"Wing Commander?" I asked her.

"Yes, ma'am," she replied.

"Very well."

I pushed back my chair and accompanied her up to James's office. Judy opened the door and ushered me in.

James was sitting on the sofa. He got up to greet me. I went over to him and wound my arms around his neck.

"You're a sight for sore eyes," I said, kissing him.

"Am I?" he said, leading me to the sofa.

I sat down while he poured some tea.

"You didn't come to see me last night," he said mildly. "Did something detain you?"

"I was just tired," I told him, feeling like a heel for dissembling.

He passed me a cup of tea and I sipped it with pleasure.

"I thought perhaps something occurred regarding that duel you asked me about the other day?" he said.

My hand trembled slightly, rattling the cup in the saucer. "Duel?" I asked innocently.

He pretended not to notice but continued to press me, nevertheless. "Yes, duel."

I looked at him, wondering how much he knew. "It didn't come to anything," I said, lying through my teeth.

"Really? Because I heard tell of some unusual activity at dawn this morning. Perhaps you could tell me more about it?"

So he *did* know something. I decided to ameliorate the situation, if I could.

"Oh well, we all just decided to go out for a stroll, you know…" I began.

"Anna," James said with a smile, "you really are not the best liar."

I sighed. "I wish you wouldn't quiz me on the subject any further, because it's not something you need to know about, James. I've dealt with it and —"

"It's all right," he interrupted. "I trust you. But perhaps you'll tell me one day?"

"Yes," I said. "One day, I will, I promise. Just don't ask me today."

He laughed. "All right. Let's talk about something else."

I gulped my tea down with some relief and handed him the cup for more.

After I'd left James, I went to see Angelica. She was in her room, packing her bag.

"I should go back to Banley. I think we're done here," she said. "I asked reception to call up Gordon to collect me."

"I understand," I replied, accompanying her downstairs. I knew she wanted to get back to Angus as much as anything else. There wasn't any reason for her to stay any longer. We had gone over the mission planning the previous day. She had the folder with all the plans, photographs and other information she needed. Now it was down to us to practise for the real thing.

Pretty soon, Sergeant Gordon's jeep wound its way up the drive and came to a stop.

"Get in touch to arrange the first practice," she said.

"I will."

"It's been fun." Angelica grinned and then gave me a spontaneous hug. "See you soon, I hope."

"I hope so too."

I watched her climb into the jeep. Sergeant Gordon gave me a wave, let out the clutch and away they went. I watched them disappear down the drive and then went back inside in a pensive mood. There was much to do to get ready for the mission. I went to find Maria.

For the first practice, I took Jennifer and Patricia with me. Three planes, I felt, was enough for a trial run.

I had arranged a rendezvous point with Angelica. However, the Mavericks were not to set off until we were airborne and had contacted Angelica. She would be on our frequency, as discussed. Apparently, she had taken our advice and put Section Officer Audrey Wilmington on the Mavericks' frequency. The two of them were working in tandem.

"Are you going to tell us what this mission is about?" asked Jennifer as we made our way to the airfield in the truck.

As always, she sat at the back with Connie, sharing a cigarette.

"All in due course," I said. "When James is ready for it to be revealed."

Jennifer made a face but said nothing further. Perhaps it irked her that I could not always share the burden of my command with her. Maria was different. As lead navigator, she needed to be involved.

The truck came to a stop and we all jumped down from the tailgate.

"All right," I said, "this is a simple test. We fly to the rendezvous and meet the Mavericks. Assuming it goes according to plan, we'll do some low-level flying with them and then return home."

"Let's go then," said Patricia.

Maria and I were soon strapped into the Mosquito. I started the engines and went through the usual protocols. Maria gave me a thumbs-up, signifying we were ready.

"Control, this is Bluebird Leader requesting clearance."

"Bluebird Leader, you're clear," came the response.

"Here we go Bluebirds," I said, letting off the brakes and wending our way to the runway.

Shortly afterwards we were airborne.

"Bluebirds, form up on me," I said as Maria gave us the bearing.

Now I had to establish comms with Angelica. I gave out the agreed call sign.

"Red Fox, this is Bluebird Leader, do you read me?" I said over the radio.

I was pleased to receive an instant response.

"Loud and clear, Bluebird Leader," said Angelica.

I looked over at Maria and she smiled.

"So far, so good," she said.

"Red Fox, Bluebirds on route to Waypoint One," I said.

"Roger, Bluebird Leader," said Angelica and then, "Blackbirds are airborne."

Blackbirds was the Mavericks' codename during practice runs.

"Roger," I replied.

"Now let's see if we can both arrive at the same time," I said to Maria.

We'd arranged a rendezvous at a landmark near Colchester. I took our flight down to low level and the ground rushed by beneath us.

"Trees," said Maria in her role as lookout.

"Got it."

"Lines."

"Seen them."

Suddenly the radio crackled to life.

"Radar contact, twelve planes," said Shelly.

I wasn't fazed. It was obviously the Mavericks.

"Roger, that will be them," I replied, then, "Red Fox, we have Blackbirds on radar."

"Roger," said Angelica.

As we neared the rendezvous point, I started to keep a lookout for the Spitfires.

Right on cue, Patricia said, "Blackbirds at nine o'clock."

Sure enough, I could see twelve Spitfires in formation heading our way.

"Red Fox, we have a visual on Blackbirds. Ask them to form up on us."

"Roger," said Angelica.

Moments later the Spitfires settled just above our wings, almost like a protective umbrella.

"Red Fox, Blackbirds in formation," I said. "Now we're going to practise manoeuvres — tell them to follow my lead."

"Wilco," said Angelica.

Maria gave out a new bearing and we commenced some point-to-point flying. We continued at low level and the Mavericks matched our flight pattern with ease, never wavering from the formation.

Angelica could hear Maria as she gave out each bearing and relayed it to the Mavericks, so they were not flying blind. All seemed to be going well.

After half a dozen short waypoints, I felt we'd proved our point. The system was workable. We flew back towards Hawberry. When we were close enough, I signed the Mavericks off.

"Red Fox, that's all for today, thanks. Blackbirds can return to base," I said.

"Roger, Bluebird Leader. Blackbirds Leader says it was a good show."

"Tell him thank you," I replied.

"Roger, Bluebird Leader. Blackbirds signing off."

The Mavericks squadron wheeled away from us and headed home while we continued to Hawberry. We landed shortly afterwards and were soon heading back in the truck.

"That went well," said Jennifer, puffing on a cigarette before handing it to Connie.

"Yes, it seemed to work a treat," I replied, satisfied with the result.

"Now are you going to tell us what it's all about?" she asked.

"I have to discuss the test run with James first, and then no doubt there will be a briefing, since we're going to have to start practising properly for the mission."

"Oh fine," Jennifer replied, rolling her eyes.

"Leave her be," said Connie. "If she can't tell you, she can't tell you."

"But she's my sister," Jennifer complained.

"She's also your Flight Leader," Maria reminded her.

"Don't you think it's hard to be both?" I put in.

Jennifer sighed. "You're right. I'm sorry, Anna."

When we arrived at Hawberry, Jennifer gave me a hug.

"You're doing a great job. Just ignore me. Sometimes it's hard to forget we're sisters," she whispered.

"It's hard for me too, but one day I'm sure we will be just sisters again."

She regarded me seriously. "Will we?" she said. "The war has changed us all, Anna."

Her words struck a nerve. Perhaps our relationship would never be quite the same. Only time would tell.

After informing James that the communications test had been a success, things got serious. The following day a briefing was called after breakfast.

"So, we're finally going to hear what this is all about," said Jennifer at breakfast.

"Yes, you are," I told her.

"Not sure how much you're going to like it," said Maria.

"Well? What is it?" demanded Shelly.

"In approximately thirty minutes you'll find out," I said, cutting into my eggs on toast.

"Can't you give us a hint?" Shelly persisted.

"It's another mission," Maria shot back. "Now eat your breakfast."

"You're not my mother!" Shelly replied, poking out her tongue.

"Oh boy," said Sandra. "Here we go…"

While the two of them traded insults in their usual fashion, I thought about James. After my talk with Angelica, I was starting to come around to the idea of marriage. How to broach it with him so that it didn't seem like I was prompting him, however, was a question I was mulling over.

Susan's voice jerked me back to the present. "Boss, can't you tell them to stop?"

I lifted my fork and pointed it in Shelly and Maria's direction. "Stop it, you two, and that's an order!" I said in a half-hearted manner.

This elicited some laughter from the others, but it at least had the effect of making them stop. I finished my food, pushed away my empty plate and sipped my tea.

"It's time," said Lucy, glancing at her watch.

"Let's get to it then," I said.

I joined James, Henry, Gloria and the Marx Brothers on the podium while everyone took their seats.

"Welcome," said James. "We have a rather unusual mission for you."

Henry stepped forward, the lights dimmed and an aerial photograph of what looked like a series of concrete buildings appeared on the projection screen.

"Wolfsschlucht II," he said. "Otherwise known as Hitler's bunker…" There were a few gasps at this. "Not Hitler's main bunker, but just one of several he's had built. He's never been there, but had he successfully invaded England he may well have visited it."

The screen changed to show a map of France. Henry took a long pointer and indicated a spot on the map.

"The bunker is located in Margival, about ten kilometres northeast of the main town of Soissons. It is also northwest of Paris, for orientation purposes. It's an approximately two-hundred-mile straight trip from here."

The screen changed again to show the aerial photograph once more.

"The bunker consists of several heavily reinforced buildings, including barracks and ack-ack batteries. Also, this." He pointed to a long rectangular building. "This is the telephone exchange. It facilitates Nazi military communications over many parts of France. It's housed in a bunker, and it's this bunker that we want to try and damage."

There was silence as everyone absorbed this. The squadron would be aware that our normal bombs would have no hope of penetrating it.

"The mission itself is fairly straightforward," Henry continued. "The main part of the squadron will drop their ordnance over the entire installation in order to neutralise the anti-aircraft defences as much as possible. Following which, two Mosquitos will drop two four-thousand-pound bombs known as Cookies on top of the bunker. We hope that these will effect a great deal of damage, but we don't know for sure."

There were signs of unease in the room — a few anxious glances, people shifting in their seats. They hadn't yet heard the worst of it.

"There's a catch," Henry said quietly. "Well, two. Firstly, the bombs have to be dropped from six thousand feet and, secondly, the raid has to be carried out in daylight."

There was a collective gasp at this.

"I will let Flight Officer Nightingale explain the finer details of the mission. It's not quite as bad as you may think. But before that, our Military Intelligence colleagues will brief you on the strategic importance of the mission."

The lights came on again and Henry stepped back. The Marx Brothers, who had been quietly observing the proceedings, stubbed out their cigarettes and stepped forward.

"Sirens," said Harpo, "make no mistake, this is a dangerous mission. However, it is also a hugely important one."

"I am sure you all remember Barnes Wallis," Chico said, taking up the refrain.

There were murmurs of acknowledgement.

"Barnes is developing a bomb to take on bunkers like the one you attacked recently with his Highball. However, it's crucial for him to know how much damage a bomb like the Cookie can do to a bunker," he continued.

"So, your mission will provide the essential information he needs to build something that can put places like the Mimoyecques Fortress out of action for good," said Harpo.

"This mission," said Chico dramatically, "has been sanctioned at the highest levels, and the Sirens were requested by Churchill himself."

There was a more positive response to this. We all remembered Churchill's visit, and the fact he had requested the Sirens to fly the mission carried a lot of weight.

"As you will shortly discover," said Harpo, "we've taken every step we can to protect the Sirens on this mission."

The two spies nodded to James, who stepped forward again.

"Let's not sugarcoat this," he said. "This mission is highly dangerous and certainly has more risk attached than any of the missions you've flown in the past. I know that you will carry it out with the ruthless efficiency that has come to be a hallmark of this squadron. Now, your Flight Leader will enlighten you further on the details."

This was my cue.

"Sirens," I said, "the codename for this mission is Operation Firecracker, which I suppose is appropriate. We will be taking eighteen planes for maximum effect. Take-off will be a little before dawn so that we're approaching in daylight but will hopefully catch Jerry napping."

I paused and looked at the expectant faces. I could see the penny had dropped for some of the squadron at least.

"Recently we hosted Section Officer Angelica Mackennelly from the Mavericks squadron. She is now one of the few people who know what we do here. She is also the communicator for the Mavericks, which consists of two flights of Spitfires. The arrangement is that the Mavericks will be riding shotgun for us on this mission — they will be our escort.

"In order to preserve security, we will relay our communications to the Mavericks through Angelica and vice versa. She will be the conduit. We won't be communicating directly with the Mavericks, for obvious reasons. However, what this means is that we will have as much protection as possible on this mission. In case you're wondering, we've already tested the comms procedure, and it all works fine."

I noticed that most of the Sirens had relaxed now they had heard we had an escort.

"This mission will require a fair bit of practice," I said. "Timing and coordination are essential. Two Mosquitos will carry the Cookie bombs specifically modified for the task. I will be flying one of these and SO Patricia Batley will fly the other. I will lead the flight to the target and then break off to wait for the first attack. SO Jennifer Nightingale will lead the rest of the squadron on the attack to drop their ordnance over the target zone."

I could see Linda's barely suppressed fury out of the corner of my eye. I ignored it. I was determined not to give in to her demands.

"Once that's done, the squadron will get clear. The Cookie planes will fly in with an escort, climb to six thousand feet and then drop their bombs. Everyone has to be at least six thousand feet from the blast zone. Once that's done, we will catch up with the squadron and head home."

I paused. Linda was looking daggers at me.

"The return journey will be the most perilous and when we are most likely to need the escort. I anticipate Jerry fighters will be scrambled against us, and we won't have the cover of darkness like we normally do. Over the next few days we'll carry out dummy practice runs with the Mavericks, so that the mission itself will hopefully run smoothly."

I smiled at James. He stepped forward once again and looked around.

"Are there any questions?" he asked.

We fielded a few, including what to do if we were attacked on the way in. Then the meeting broke up. As we were leaving the briefing room, Linda walked past me and paused momentarily.

"You've made a big mistake, ma'am. I hope you know that," she said, before disappearing into the throng.

I wondered what on earth Linda really thought she could do that wouldn't damage her own standing in the Sirens. Then I put it from my mind.

The next few days were taken up with flying exercises. First, I had to get the squadron into shape for the bombing mission. Even though we hadn't got the right Mosquitos yet, we simulated flying to the target, splitting up and doing a dummy bombing run.

My concern about the Cookie bomb run remained. The more time we spent waiting while one bomb was dropped, followed by the other, the longer we were exposed to enemy fire or fighters.

Eventually, I asked to see James and the Marx Brothers about it.

We sat in James's office drinking tea while I explained my point.

"I don't think we should try to drop the Cookies separately," I told them.

"Your reasoning?" said Harpo.

"It's the time factor. We're already exposed in daylight, and even with an escort the longer we hang around, the more we are at risk," I said.

"Fair point," said Chico.

I thought of another thing. "When that first bomb drops, it's going to create a big explosion. That might make it harder to zero in on the target for the second one. So, we might miss. Why not either only drop one bomb, or drop them both in tandem?"

James, who had remained silent while I made my point, spoke up. "I think Anna is right," he said. "There is no sense in increasing the risk."

"We do indeed take your point, both of you," said Chico.

This only served to increase my frustration. James flicked a glance at me and could tell I was also quite irritated by the spies' phlegmatic attitude to something that was rather important.

"Look," he said, "how specific are the mission orders?"

Harpo took a long drag on his cigarette. "Well, as I recall, the orders are to drop two Cookie bombs on the bunker if possible —"

This was all I needed to hear.

"Ha!" I cut in. "So they don't say they can't be dropped at the same time?"

"Technically, no," said Chico. "Although Barnes has expressed a preference."

This time it was James's turn to express his frustration. "Barnes's preference can go hang," he said, standing up and pacing the room. "We've already gone the extra mile for him with his Highballs. And that was under cover of darkness. We have an entirely different scenario here. Operational priorities need to take precedence. As the CO, I say that the operational priority is for the Sirens to return from this mission intact. Dropping two bombs on the target at the same time, exactly like *all* other bombing raids, is the sensible thing to do and mitigates the risk."

I looked at James with admiration. I'd not witnessed him being quite so assertive before and I found the trait rather attractive in him.

As far as the Marx Brothers were concerned, his outburst seemed to do the trick. They leaned forward as one and stubbed out their cigarettes.

"Well, if that's how you feel, old man, there's no more to be said," Harpo told him.

"Nothing," agreed Chico.

"What?" said James, flabbergasted at their capitulation.

"You're the CO," said Harpo, getting up.

"So, it's your call," Chico added, joining him.

"So that's settled then?" I said, wanting to make sure. "We'll drop the bombs at the same time?"

"Absolutely," said Harpo.

"Must be going," said Chico. "Chin-chin."

"Toodle-pip," said Harpo.

The two of them left the office in some haste.

"Well, I'm blowed," said James. "I expected them to put up more of a fight."

"I'm not sure I'll ever understand them," I said, laughing.

"Me neither," he said.

"Anyway, if you've got some time before your next practice?"

"I think I just might," I said softly, edging closer.

CHAPTER EIGHTEEN

The two Cookie bomb Mosquitos arrived shortly after that conversation. The ordnance was loaded on the planes and promptly removed by the ground crew. A pair of dummy Cookies filled with concrete had been sent by road. We would use these for target practice. Both Maria and Connie would have to get used to the bombsight. We'd never dropped ordnance from anything other than fairly low level. This was a whole new thing.

Practice for the others was suspended while we spent a couple of days working on our bombing runs. An area the approximate shape and size of the telephone exchange was taped out on the range.

It was fortunate that the telephone exchange was at the bottom right of the bunker complex. The other buildings were all separate. This made it easier for the squadron to drop their ordnance without affecting our view of the primary target.

I flew out to the range with Patricia. Then we circled around for an approach, rapidly gaining height to six thousand feet. We had to fly in at that height in order for the bombardiers to zero in on the target. Patricia flew directly behind me, almost on my tail. That way she could line up with us.

"Here we go," I said as we made our first practice approach. Maria had slid forward into the familiar position to aim the bomb correctly.

"Steady," she said. "Steady … left a little … straighten up… That's it, we're on target. And … bombs away."

Connie would have been listening and lining up her bombsight too. Neither of them dropped the dummy bomb on the first few goes.

"Are you ready to try releasing a bomb?" I asked Maria after we'd been around several times.

"Let's do it," she said.

"Bluebird Two, we're going to try releasing the dummy," I said.

"Roger," said Patricia.

We circled around, dropped down low and then gained height.

"Bombing formation," I said to Patricia as I lined up on the building.

"Steady … left… now right … perfect, you've got it," said Maria. "Bombs away."

"Bombs away," said Connie.

This time they released the dummy bombs. The two bombs dropped rapidly to earth. I banked around to check where they had landed.

One of them was within the target and the other slightly off to the left.

"Bother," said Maria.

"The one on target must be mine," quipped Connie.

"Yeah, sure," said Maria sarcastically.

"Never mind," I said. "We'll return to base and then we'll try again."

It took a while for the ground crew to retrieve the bombs, bring them back and install them in the Mosquitos. I wondered why they'd not sent two sets of dummies.

"Would have been useful," said Maria.

"And quicker," said Connie.

We waited at the airfield. Once the bombs were loaded we tried again, with a similar result. After a couple more attempts, the sun was beginning to set and I called a halt to the practice.

"Maybe we just can't get them on target," said Connie. "They're falling from a great height and the roof of the target is very narrow."

"You're probably right," said Maria.

"Well, wherever they drop," said Patricia, "there's going to be one hell of an explosion."

"Tomorrow," I said, "we'll practise getting out fast once the bombs have been released."

I wanted to be as far as possible from the target when they exploded. We'd have a few seconds while they were falling, and that meant a full-throttle exit.

"Sounds good," said Connie. "Anyway, I'm starving."

The conversation turned to food and speculation as to what was for dinner.

The following day, we tried again. This time we accelerated out of the target zone as fast as we could. The bomb landing was still not completely accurate, but it couldn't be helped. It was as close as we could get it. We'd probably be under fire on the mission, which would make it even harder. Nevertheless, I felt Barnes would get the information he needed.

After this, I decided to include the full squadron in our practice drills and then we'd be ready to add the Mavericks. After a couple of days, I felt that it was time for a proper full rehearsal. The idea was to rendezvous with the Mavericks, then fly a route leading back to the target, thus simulating the mission, at least in part. Navigators were handed sheets containing waypoints and coordinates to follow.

The main flight would carry out a dummy bombing run and then we'd go in for our Cookie run. After that we'd simulate the return trip from the mission before signing off.

On the day in question I took off as normal with the main flight in tow.

"Bluebirds on me, close formation, low level," I told them once we were all in the air.

Maria gave out a bearing for Chelmsford.

"Red Fox, we're heading for Waypoint One," I said to Angelica.

"Roger, Bluebird Leader. Blackbirds are airborne," she replied.

As expected, the radar planes spotted the Mavericks squadron — consisting of two flights this time — and we all came together at the rendezvous as planned.

"Red Fox, we're heading for Waypoint Two," I said, then Maria gave out the bearing.

"Blackbirds moving to escort position," said Angelica.

The Mavericks took positions on either side of and just a little above us. We all had to remain under the radar, so they couldn't fly too much higher. It was comforting to know they were there, and I felt well protected. However, I had to remind myself this was just a practice run, not the real thing, and we weren't over enemy territory.

We flew from waypoint to waypoint and headed back towards the range. As it came into view, I gave the order to split.

"Bluebird Four, take the flight," I said to Jennifer. "Bluebird Two, on me to hold."

"Bluebirds on me," said Jennifer, splitting off. We banked in the opposite direction once they were clear.

The bulk of the Mavericks stuck with them. Four planes remained with us on our wings. I flew to the holding position and waited, circling around.

"Bluebirds, attack formation," said Jennifer as they spread out for the bombing run. We waited for what seemed like a long time but was in reality only minutes. Finally, Jennifer said, "Bombs away. Get clear, clear, clear."

This was our signal to go.

"Red Fox, we're going for the target," I said.

"Roger."

"Bluebird Two, Cookie formation," I told Patricia.

"Roger," she said.

We banked sharply and climbed to six thousand feet, just as we had practised. Then we started our run. Maria slipped down to the bombardier position.

"Steady," she said. "Steady … left … right a little, that's good… Keep going… Bombs away."

"Bombs away," said Connie.

"Clear, clear, clear," I said, knowing that Angelica would also hear me.

I banked the plane sharply and throttled up. In moments we had left the target behind us. Jennifer would already be taking the flight on the return leg but a little slower, so we could catch them. Maria gave out the bearing and I maintained a fast speed. I looked around to ensure that the Spitfires were keeping up. We could go slightly faster than them and run at high speed for longer. I didn't really want to lose our escort, though, so full throttle wasn't an option unless we were attacked.

The main flight came into sight. I took over the lead from Jennifer. We continued on the prearranged course, which took us near the south coast, flying at low level. It was all going perfectly when Shelly piped up.

"Radar contact, five or maybe six planes coming in fast," she said.

"Confirmed," said Pamela.

"Bandits?" I asked.

"Possibly — they're coming in from the Channel," replied Shelly.

We were flying parallel to the coastline at this point. Sandra, who had pretty sharp eyes, suddenly shouted, "Bandits on our three o'clock!"

I glanced over and could just make out six Focke-Wulfs in the distance.

"Red Fox, bandits sighted," I said.

"Already on it," said Angelica. "Blackbirds breaking now."

Half our escort peeled off and headed in the direction of the bandits.

"Maria, give us a bearing away from the coast," I said.

She gave out a bearing and I turned the flight away. Behind us, the Mavericks closed with the Focke-Wulfs.

"Blackbirds have engaged the bandits," said Angelica.

"Look at those tracers," said Maria, craning her head around to see.

There wasn't any more to be said. We left the dogfight behind us. A short while later, Angelica came on the radio.

"Bandits have retreated. Blackbirds returning."

"Roger," I said.

"Well, I wasn't expecting that," said Maria.

"Me neither."

It was a reminder of what was likely to happen on the real mission.

We made the sign-off waypoint without further incident, by which time the other half of the Mavericks had got back on station.

"Red Fox, Blackbirds can sign off," I said. "Tell them thank you for the timely intervention."

"Bluebird Leader, they say it's all in a day's work," said Angelica.

"Any casualties?" I asked her.

"I think they got one bandit. Nothing on our side."

"Thank goodness for that."

"Catch you next time," said Angelica.

"Roger."

The Mavericks left us on our own and we headed back to Hawberry. In the truck on the way back to the Hall, all the talk was about the Spitfires.

"I wonder what it's like to fly one," mused Dorothy.

"Ask Sandra," I said wryly. "She's done it."

"It was glorious," said Sandra.

"I'd love to try it if I could," said Jennifer.

"Nobody is going up in a Spitfire," I said firmly. "We had enough trouble last time."

"The Boss has spoken," said Shelly.

We all burst out laughing.

It was only a matter of time before the mission came around for real. There were several more dress rehearsals and thankfully no more bandit incursions. Finally, I went to see James to tell him that we were ready.

He was having a meeting with Henry, Gloria and the Marx Brothers when I entered his office.

"Anna," he said. "What can we do for you?"

"I've come to tell you that we're ready as we'll ever be for the mission," I said.

"That's good news," he said. "In fact, we were just discussing the timing of the mission. Why don't you join us?"

I took a seat at the table while the Marx Brothers leant back in their chairs, blowing smoke up into the air.

"We would like you to go in three days' time," said James.

"All right," I replied. "I will warn the rest of the flight."

"That's settled then," said Harpo.

"Absolutely," said Chico, looking pleased.

I would need to contact Angelica too and get the Mavericks on standby for the mission. After we finished our discussion, I stayed behind to talk to James.

"Can I ask you something?" I said as we sat together on the sofa.

"Anything," he replied with a smile.

"Could you … could we … go away together … just for a night… to a hotel somewhere … not far … just where nobody knows us?"

"What's brought this on?" James asked in surprise.

"I was talking to Angelica and she mentioned…" I hesitated. "She mentioned that she and Angus like to go to a hotel … before an important mission … just to be away together and…" I trailed off and looked at him anxiously. "James, I'm not used to this…"

"Not used to what?" he said.

"Romance, courtship, all of that…"

He moved closer and took my hand.

"Well, I could certainly get used to it … and I think it's a splendid idea. I'll sort something out for tomorrow night. How's that?"

"It would be marvellous," I said.

James was as good as his word and the very next afternoon I packed an overnight bag. In order to maintain discretion, Jennifer drove me a mile down the road where I waited at a bus stop for James to pick me up.

He had laughed when I informed him of these arrangements, but he didn't demur.

Earlier in the day I had also borrowed a staff car and taken Jennifer, Maria and Sandra to the nearest large town.

As we approached the lingerie shop, which was the object of my visit, the other three thought it most amusing.

"Have you never purchased lingerie before?" asked Maria in surprise.

"I've never had any reason to," I said.

"Well then, you're in for a treat," said Sandra, who was more worldly-wise than I.

With the precious purchase safely stowed in my bag, I waited for James. He picked me up in short order and we drove through the countryside to a small country hotel. James said it was unlikely anyone would know us there.

The hotel turned out to be rather cosy and quaint. We registered as Mr and Mrs Donnington, but nobody questioned it. Our room was nicely furnished and warmed by central heating.

We ate dinner together in the dining room and it felt incredibly pleasant to pretend we were a married couple.

"Have you ever done this before?" asked James as we tucked into a welcome plate of roast beef, roast potatoes and vegetables.

"Never," I said.

A faint smile curved his lips. "Do you like it, so far?"

"I like it excessively," I told him.

After dinner, we repaired to our room. I bade him sit on the bed while I went into the bathroom with my overnight bag. I pulled out the black silk negligee I had bought and put it on. I stared at myself in the mirror for some time, hardly able to recognise myself. Then, suddenly feeling shy, I returned to the room.

"Good Lord," exclaimed James in surprise. He had dimmed the light suitably, but I could see that he was smiling.

"Don't you like it?" I asked.

He reached out and ran his hand down the sheer fabric. "I like it … excessively," he said, echoing my words from earlier. "Whatever gave you the idea?"

"Angelica," I replied.

"It seems I have rather a lot to thank her for," James said.

Later, lying in his arms, I decided to broach the subject which had been on my mind.

"James," I said softly.

"Yes?"

"You know that thing we've talked about…"

"Which particular thing was that?" he said.

I took a deep breath and took the plunge. "Getting married," I said.

He turned to look at me. "What about it?"

"Well … the thing is … if…" I stumbled over my words and tried again. "I just want you to know that if you were to ask me, well, it's highly possible and in fact very probable that I might say yes…"

I finished the speech with some trepidation. It had taken a lot for me to even bring myself to the point of mentioning it. James said nothing for a long time. I wondered if I had somehow overstepped.

"Do you really mean that?" he said at length.

"Yes, yes, I do," I whispered.

"Then I will bear it in mind."

I saw the grin appear on his face and couldn't help laughing.

"Oh, you beast," I said. "Do you know what it took me to tell you that? Are you intending to ask me or not?"

"Wait and see," James said, pulling me close.

"Don't make me wait too long," I replied before my lips met his.

The hotel interlude was over all too soon. We left after an early breakfast and drove back to Hawberry.

"Are you wanting me to drop you at the gate?" James asked with interest.

I laughed. "Certainly not, I don't want to walk all the way up the drive. Just park and I'll wait for you to go. Then I'll follow in a little while."

"All right."

Things were different all of a sudden. I felt more at ease and less uncomfortable with the situation.

When I felt the coast was clear, I left the car with my bag and went inside. It was still fairly early, but Martha was at her desk. She looked up and smiled. I made my way down the corridors. They were quiet and it was probable a lot of the Sirens were still at breakfast themselves. As I neared my room a shadow detached itself from the wall. My heart sank. It was Linda.

She saluted and I returned it, anticipating what was coming.

"Been somewhere?" she asked in the mocking tone I'd come to hate.

"Is it any of your business?" I retorted.

"Perhaps it is, perhaps it isn't," she said.

"Kindly step aside," I told her, feeling exasperated already.

"I know about you and the Wing Commander," she said suddenly. "That's where you've been, isn't it? I've seen you sneaking to his room at night. I know your sordid little secret."

My heart jumped into my mouth on hearing this. At the same time, I felt a surge of contempt for a woman who would stoop so low.

"What do you want?" I said, keeping my voice even.

"You know what I want," she replied. "And if you want this to remain a secret, then you'll give it to me."

I thought quickly. She obviously thought she had me at *point non plus* and that I had run out of options. After all, she wasn't to know that James and I might soon be engaged, which would put paid to her little scheme. I decided to play along for the moment. It would buy me some time.

"And if I arrange what you want, you'll leave me alone?" I said.

"Absolutely." She smiled unpleasantly.

"Well, it will have to wait until after the mission," I said. "It's too late to do anything before that."

She took my words as capitulation. It was nothing of the sort, of course, but I knew it would keep her off my back a little longer.

"I can wait, as long as I get what I want," Linda said. "I'm glad to see you're coming around to my point of view. I'm sure we're going to deal very well together."

With that she saluted in a perfunctory way and walked off as casually as she pleased. I was slightly worried when I entered my room. I sat down on the bed to think. Even if I wanted to, there was no way I could let Linda be second-in-command. The rest of the gang would all hate her. James would never allow it. I certainly had no intention of doing it.

Just then, Sandra slipped silently into the room. "What did she want?" she asked.

I knew she could only mean Linda. "You heard us?"

"I was coming up the corridor when I heard you both talking." She sat down beside me.

"She wants what she's always wanted, but this time she thinks she's got a winning hand," I told her.

Sandra was silent for a while. Then she said quietly, "Boss, do you want me and the others to arrange a little … accident?"

"What? No! Of course not. I was just playing for time because I know something she doesn't."

"All right." Sandra looked at me seriously. "But if you need my help, *our* help, just say the word."

"I will, and thanks."

I squeezed her hand, and she gave me a spontaneous hug.

"Anyone coming after you has to get through us first," she told me.

CHAPTER NINETEEN

The day before the mission, a final briefing was called. We'd be leaving just before dawn the next morning to make our rendezvous with the Mavericks. I joined James, Henry, Gloria and the Marx Brothers on the podium.

"Sirens," said James, "there's an old saying which I take the liberty to change: cometh the hour, cometh the woman. Over and over again you have proven your worth, your courage, your commitment without wavering. You've done everything that's been asked of you and more. Yet while this war continues, you will be asked to step up again and again. For that you have our greatest respect. I just want to thank you, for your service. I know you will do your duty and do it well. This is probably your most daring and dangerous mission yet. I'm sure you'll carry it out with the same resolution that makes you, every one of you, not just a Siren but a true heroine in my book."

Shelly began the chant, which was shortly taken up by everyone in the room.

"Sirens, Sirens, Sirens…"

It resonated around the walls. I felt my heart swell with pride to be a part of this squadron.

As the chant finally died down, James spoke again. "Good luck, Sirens, and Godspeed. Above all, come back safe."

Henry stepped forward. "Not sure how I can follow that," he said, to a ripple of laughter. "Make sure you study your charts, photographs and routes, and as the Wing Commander said, come home safely."

"Sirens," said Gloria, taking her turn, "you know that my heart always goes out with you all. You've a tough mission ahead, but I'm certain that you will all acquit yourselves with honour and courage."

Then the Marx Brothers stepped forward to say their last few words too.

"We're honoured as always to be part of this endeavour," said Harpo.

"Our hats go off to you," Chico.

"Godspeed," they said together.

James indicated to me that I should speak, so I did.

"Sirens," I said, "we're not sure exactly what we're getting into, but we're still going because that's who we are."

"Damn right!" yelled Sandra.

I smiled at her exuberance. "This is going to be a tough mission for us in daylight. Even with an escort, there are plenty of things which can go awry. Let's keep it tight and do our job. Whatever happens, try to make it back to Blighty at all costs. That's all."

"Dismissed," said James.

The next hour or so was spent going over everything again. It was always useful to try and memorise the route, imprint the photographs in one's mind. This time it would be easier because we'd be able to see where we were going more clearly. But it also made us easier to spot.

Eventually it was time for bed. I went up to James's room to say goodbye. He was waiting for me and took me in his arms at once.

"Will you stay a while?" he asked.

"I need to get some sleep," I said quietly.

"Of course."

We embraced for a long time, saying nothing. I felt this goodbye more keenly than any other so far.

"If I don't come back…" I began, but James put a finger to my lips.

"You'll come back," he told me.

"All right," I said with a tremulous smile. "If you say so."

"I do say so. Now kiss me and get off to bed."

He was smiling as my lips met his. Eventually we drew apart.

"I love you, James," I said.

"I love you too, Anna."

I left him reluctantly and slipped back to my own room. I checked the alarm was set and snuggled in beside Jennifer. I closed my eyes and found myself drifting off to sleep.

All too soon the alarm sounded. I sat up at once, conditioned to do so from previous missions. Jennifer was stirring.

"Is it time?" she asked, opening her eyes.

"Yes," I said. "Let's get ready."

We completed our ablutions and put on our flying suits, sheepskin jackets, boots and lifejackets. Right on cue there was a knock at the door. It was Maria and Shelly.

"Are we set?" Maria asked.

"Yes," I said. "Let's go."

I heard soft footfalls in the corridors as the entire squadron turned out for the mission. It was still dark outside. We had got up well before dawn to ensure our rendezvous with the Mavericks was just around the time dawn was breaking. After many missions we had the timing down to a tee.

In the back of one of the trucks, Jennifer and Connie shared a cigarette as usual. The rest of us looked a little bleary-eyed.

"Come on, wake up, you lot," said Maria. "We've got a mission to fly."

"Oh, goodness! You're so loud," said Shelly.

I couldn't help smiling at the irony of Shelly complaining that someone else was loud. Maria ignored her.

"Let's have a few verses of 'The Quartermaster's Store'," said Maria, breaking into song. We followed her lead and soon the whole truck was singing. It was infectious, and then the Sirens in the other trucks followed suit.

By the time we reached the airfield we were all in high spirits.

"See," said Maria. "A song works wonders."

"You're right," I said as we jumped down from the tailgate.

The squadron gathered around for the last words as always.

"Sirens," I said, "we've practised for this, now let's get it done. Watch each other's backs out there, and let's all come back safe."

There were a few whoops and shouts of agreement as we made our way to the planes. Victoria was waiting for me and saluted.

"Everything's ready, ma'am," she said. "The Cookies are loaded."

"Thank you, Victoria," I replied.

"We wrote 'Happy Birthday, Hitler' on the Cookies," she said with a chuckle.

"You know he won't be there," I told her.

"More's the pity," she said. "And it's probably not his birthday either … but anyway, give them hell, ma'am."

I laughed. "We'll do our best."

Maria and I climbed into our Mosquito and strapped in. I went through the checks and then started the engines.

"Isn't that a glorious sound?" said Maria, who was evidently in a poetic frame of mind.

"It is," I agreed, then, over the radio, I said, "Ospreys, check in." Ospreys was our codename for the mission. I thought it rather suited our stealthy daylight attack.

"Osprey Two ready."

"Osprey Three ready."

One by one the calls came back. Once I had heard from Osprey One Eight, I radioed Control.

"Control, this is Osprey Leader requesting clearance," I said.

"Osprey Leader, you're clear, good luck," said Control.

"Roger and thanks," I replied. "Ospreys, here we go."

I let off the brakes and taxied down to the end of the runway, followed by the rest of the squadron. I applied the brakes once more and glanced at Maria.

"Are we going to do this?" I said to her.

She smiled. "Let's do this."

I wound up the engines and eased off the brakes. The Mosquito leapt forward and within a few moments we were airborne. We circled around waiting for the rest of the flight. Once everyone was in the air, Maria gave out the first bearing.

"Ospreys on me, low-level flying," I said, dropping the kite down to hedge height.

I opened up the throttle and we were away. The sky was just beginning to grow lighter. Our timing was spot on; we should reach Chelmsford as dawn began to break.

"Red Fox," I said to Angelica over the radio, "this is Osprey Leader. Ospreys are airborne on route to Waypoint One."

I had to rely on her being on station. She didn't reply instantly. I glanced at Maria. Was it going to go wrong before we'd even left?

"Red Fox," I tried again. "Red Fox."

"Osprey Leader, this is Red Fox, reading you loud and clear," said Angelica, to my relief.

"Everything okay, Red Fox? Are we green to go?" I asked her.

"We're green, Osprey Leader," she said. "Sorry about the delay — small glitch here. Don't worry — we're here for the duration."

She didn't elaborate so I let it go. There was no sense in fretting about it. We'd practised many times over.

"Ravens are airborne, heading for Waypoint One," said Angelica, referring to the Mavericks. Ravens was their codename for the mission.

I put my attention on the terrain. Maria was looking out as usual.

"Lines, lines, lines," she said.

"Got them."

"House!"

"Seen it."

In this fashion we made our way over the countryside as the minutes ticked by. The sky was turning grey, and dawn was upon us. Eventually the sun would rise, but we had some time before that happened.

"Radar contact, two squadrons," said Pamela.

"Confirmed," said Shelly.

"It's the Mavericks," Maria said to me. "And bang on time — there's Chelmsford up ahead." We could see the town in the distance.

"Ravens at nine o'clock," said Patricia.

Sure enough, two flights of Spitfires were rapidly approaching.

"Here they come," said Maria.

The Mavericks settled into their positions on each side of our flight.

"Ravens are on station," I said to Angelica.

"Roger," she replied.

Maria gave out a new bearing, which would also be relayed to the Mavericks. The flight turned as one towards Gravesend. Soon afterwards we crossed the Thames, a familiar sight, but this time the Navy ships were visible in the grey light of dawn as we roared over them. I could see some of the sailors waving as we passed. A couple of the Spitfires dipped their wings.

The next bearing took us on a direct line towards Hastings. We'd be passing just east of the town. I turned my attention back to the terrain and watched the ground flash by beneath us. In daylight it almost seemed faster, perhaps because we could see more clearly.

We passed Rochester and Maidstone. Nothing stirred below as it was so early in the morning. I could see mist curling off the grass in the fields and lying low in swathes of white. We flashed past Bodiam Castle standing in its moat, a remnant of ancient times.

"Coast coming up," said Maria.

I could see the blue water of the Channel ahead. There were a few white tops to the waves, indicating a slight swell.

"This is it," said Maria.

We crossed over the small cliffs at Fairlight Cove.

"Ospreys, keep them peeled," I said as we flew out over the water.

I kept us as low as I dared. In the dark it would be less of a concern, as the enemy wouldn't see us coming. In daylight, if their coastal defences were alert, they might well spot a large flight of planes. I felt myself growing tense and we hadn't even made the French coast.

"It will be all right, Boss," said Maria, sensing my unease. "Just stay focused."

She reached across and touched my arm lightly. I shot her a grateful smile. We were streaking over the water at high speed. It made no sense to hang around.

After what seemed an interminable time, but in reality had not been so many minutes, the river mouth at Le Crotoy loomed up ahead of us.

"Here we are," said Maria. "Just where I wanted us to be."

"You're the best navigator," I said, laughing. "We all know it."

"Damn right," she said, laughing too.

It broke the tension. I took her advice and put my attention wholly on the terrain. We had the radar planes. We had an escort. Aside from pray, what more could we do?

We followed the course of the river, keeping as low as I dared. The sun was starting to show itself and the rays of red and orange cast deep shadows across the landscape.

The trip so far had been uneventful, aside from a few spooked cows. I fervently hoped it would stay that way. The fact we were exposed put me on edge.

Reaching Amiens at last meant we were three quarters of the way there. It wouldn't be long before we made the bunker.

Maria kept up her hazard-spotting while simultaneously reading the map and navigating.

"Treeline," she said.

"Got it."

"Hedge."

"Seen it."

Below us, the fields were now bathed in light as the sun rose higher in the sky. Minute after minute passed. Field after field. All the time the possibility of detection preyed on my mind.

Just then Shelly came on the radio with the news I dreaded.

"Radar contact."

"Confirmed," said Pamela.

I flicked a glance at Maria. She pursed her lips.

"How far? How many?" I asked them.

"A couple of bandits maybe, out of visual," said Shelly.

"Red Fox, we've detected two bandits. They might be too far away," I told Angelica.

"Roger, I'll pass it on," she said.

"Ospreys, stay on course," I said.

We were close now. We couldn't deviate. It was possible it was just a German patrol. The best we could hope for was that they wouldn't spot us and would remain at a distance. If they did, then we'd just have to deal with it accordingly.

The seconds ticked by as I scanned the skies. I knew that the Mavericks would be doing the same. They were far more experienced in combat. I willed myself to stay calm and take comfort from their escort. Finally, there was some better news.

"Bandits moving away," said Pamela.

"Confirmed," said Shelly.

I breathed a sigh of relief. We hadn't been detected. I continued peering into the distance, in case I could see a speck on the horizon. Fortunately, there was none. We were very low in any case, so against the terrain we would hopefully be harder to spot. The scouts would be flying at a much higher altitude. My attention was brought back to the mission.

"Big Tent in ten," said Maria, referring to the target, which was codenamed Big Tent.

"Roger," I said.

In five minutes, we would split off and go to our holding position. The rest of the flight would continue to the secondary target. The primary target was ours — the telephone exchange. My heart began to race. No matter how many times we rehearsed for a mission, it never removed the trepidation of the real thing.

"In eight," Maria said.

The adrenaline was beginning to flow, putting me on high alert. Now all my focus was on reaching the target intact. We *had* to make it.

"In five," said Maria.

I acted at once, all the training kicking in.

"Ospreys, split; Alpha group to Big Tent, Charlie group to hold," I said over the radio.

"Alpha, on me," said Jennifer, taking control of the main flight just as we'd rehearsed.

"Charlie, on me," I said, peeling out of formation and heading for our holding area. Four of the Spitfires followed suit, staying on our wings. Maria gave us a bearing and I made for the designated spot. We'd circle at low level over empty fields just northwest of the bunker. Hopefully far enough from any Jerry outposts or ack-ack. None had shown on the reconnaissance photographs.

"Alpha, attack formation," said Jennifer.

They would be lining up, splitting into their designated groups. They'd drop the bombs simultaneously and make a fast exit. They were close. Jennifer was perfectly capable of leading the flight. I knew she would carry it out well. Still, I felt my heart beating faster as we waited for our signal to go.

"Incoming fire."

It was Sandra. It was inevitable. The flight would be in range of the ack-ack guns and close to the target. I hoped their attack would take down most of the enemy's air defences.

"Bomb bay doors open," said Jennifer. "One minute to Big Tent."

Moments later came the words we were waiting to hear.

"Bombs away, get clear, clear, clear," said Jennifer.

They would be turning, streaking away from the target as fast as they could go. There was no more time to think; it was time to act.

"Charlie group, let's go," I said as Maria gave us the bearing for the target.

"Red Fox, this is Osprey Leader. We are taking the Little Tent," I told Angelica. This was the codename for the telephone exchange.

As I gained height I could see the fire and smoke from the bombing run of sixteen aircraft. It would have created quite a stir. The downside was that now the Jerries would know we were here, and fighters would be scrambled. We reached six thousand feet. Maria set us on course for the primary, unstrapped, and slipped into the forward position. Once there, she was in control. My job was to keep the plane on track, no matter what.

"Stay on target," she said. "Steady … that's it… I have a visual on Little Tent… Keep going … steady … steady…"

The next moment, flak burst all around us. I swore under my breath. Alpha group hadn't managed to hit all the batteries and now we were in range.

There was no choice but to keep going as grey puffs of smoke blew up around us. The enemy was trying to gauge our distance. We wouldn't be around long enough for them to zero in — at least that was the hope.

I kept the Mosquito steady as we approached the primary target. Patricia would be following behind. Over the radio I could hear Connie giving her course corrections. The flak was heavy, bursting left and right, but our escort didn't waver.

"That's it … nearly there…" said Maria.

Just then, two of the escort Spitfires peeled off from us.

"Osprey Leader, bandits incoming, Ravens going to intercept," said Angelica.

That wasn't good news, but I kept the kite on course. The Mavericks had a job to do.

"Roger, Red Fox." I glanced over to where the Spitfires were racing towards some specks on the horizon, which were getting larger by the second. Focke-Wulfs.

I tore my eyes away from the ensuing dogfight and kept my focus on the job in hand. The flak had stopped. This was probably a sign that more fighters had been scrambled.

"How are we doing?" I asked Maria.

"Almost there … hold on… We are almost…" She trailed off before finally saying the words I needed to hear. "And bombs … away."

"Bombs away," echoed Connie.

"Charlie group, get clear, clear, clear," I said, banking away sharply and opening up the throttle. We only had seconds before the Cookies hit the ground.

Maria scrambled back into her seat and strapped in. Over to the right, I glimpsed the two Mavericks wheeling and diving. Tracers were flying. I hoped the Mavericks would prevail.

"Do you think you got it?" I asked Maria.

The next moment there was a tremendous explosion below us. Smoke billowed up high into the air and then we were buffeted by the wind created from the blast, despite our altitude. I fought the controls momentarily before the Mosquito was steady once more.

"Wow," said Maria. "That was one hell of a firework."

"Speaking of which," I said, "let's get the hell out of here."

Maria gave us a bearing to the rendezvous. I started to drop lower now the bombs had exploded. We cleared the blast zone and headed for the main squadron. They would be on a return route, but just slow enough for us to catch them up.

One of the Mavericks that had engaged the Germans returned to our wing. I wondered where the other one was, but Angelica soon gave me the story.

"Osprey Leader, we lost one, but both bandits are down," she said.

"Sorry to hear that, Red Fox," I replied.

I glanced at Maria. We both knew the risk of casualties was high. You couldn't hit one of Hitler's bunkers without consequences. The Sirens had been lucky so far. I hoped our luck would not run out.

Although not out of danger, at least we were back to low level and flying at speed. I hoped we'd make the main squadron soon. We had no guns onboard and were relying on three Spitfires to keep us safe. Without the escort, we were highly vulnerable.

Angelica came on the radio. "Ravens have spotted bandits on your six o'clock. They are going to engage," she said.

I glanced to the side. All three Mavericks were peeling off. Now we were completely alone.

"Roger, Red Fox. We're going to full speed," I told her, opening up the throttle.

There was nothing for it but to run. Maria craned her head around to see what was going on behind us.

"The Mavericks are outnumbered."

I hadn't time to think about it. I just hoped they could hold out. The Spitfires only had so much ammo, so they had to use it sparingly. Hopefully they could prevent any enemy planes slipping through and coming after us.

"Osprey Four," I said, radioing Jennifer. "We're on route. We've lost our escort."

"Roger, Osprey Leader. We're going as slow as we can. Get here soonest," said Jennifer.

"Roger," I replied.

We had to fly for our lives. I kept my focus on the terrain as we hopped over trees, hedges and the odd farmhouse. Animals scattered beneath us in the fields. My heart was hammering and all I could think of was catching the main pack.

"Radar contact," said Pamela, who was with the Alpha group. "Two incoming."

"Confirmed, on our six o'clock," said Shelly.

It was a relief. We were almost there.

"Osprey Leader, we've got you on radar," said Jennifer.

"We'll make it," said Maria. "I'm sure we'll make it."

We had passed Amiens and found the river. Nothing had been heard of our escort. I wondered if they were still alive. Then Maria gave a shout.

"There they are!"

Sure enough, up ahead was the rest of our squadron.

"We have you on visual, Osprey Four," I told Jennifer.

"Roger, Osprey Leader. We've seen you too," she replied.

They must have slowed down a little more, because within a few minutes we passed over the top of them.

"Osprey Leader, take over," said Jennifer.

"Roger, Osprey Four. Ospreys on me," I said as I settled in to lead the formation. Then I opened up the throttle.

"All right, Ospreys, let's go," I said as Maria gave us a bearing for the river mouth. With a palpable sense of relief, I took over command of the flight once more.

"Red Fox, Osprey Leader back on station," I told Angelica.

"Roger, Osprey Leader, well done..." There was a pause. "We lost two more Ravens... One lone Raven is heading for home."

Two more of our escort had been shot down.

"Sorry to hear it, Red Fox," I told her.

"They took down three bandits," she continued.

It was small consolation. I glanced at Maria. I felt suddenly sad; three Mavericks had died saving our lives.

"They did their duty. It's what they had to do," she said softly. "Anyway, perhaps they managed to bail."

That at least was an option for the Mavericks. For us, being shot down in enemy territory meant certain death. Then Maria said the words I needed to hear.

"Get us home, Anna. That's what *you* need to do."

I put my attention back on the terrain and kept going. There was nothing for it but to run for home. We'd done what we came to do and dropped the Cookie bombs. Whether they had hit their mark or not was no longer our concern. We had done our best to deliver the payload. As we neared the Channel, it seemed like we might make it.

As we approached the river mouth, Shelly piped up. "Radar contact, at least one squadron coming in on our three o'clock."

"Confirmed," said Pamela.

"Red Fox, we've got incoming bandits," I told Angelica.

"Sit tight and keep going. Ravens will take care of it," she said.

"Roger."

I could see the river widening out into the blue water of the Channel beyond. It almost seemed to be beckoning us. As we crossed over the water at wave height, several of the escort peeled off.

"Ravens on route to engage bandits," said Angelica.

"Roger, Red Fox. Ospreys stay on course."

Maria gave us a bearing to take us towards Hastings. I glanced over to see one squadron of Mavericks fast disappearing to meet the incoming Jerries. We continued with our now depleted escort. They were down to eight planes. We couldn't see the dogfight that was probably now ensuing. Would the Germans give up? I had a feeling they would not.

Hitler's bunker was their prize. No matter that he wasn't in it; we had struck at their heartland, albeit on French soil. They would want revenge.

We were halfway across the Channel when Shelly gave us more unwelcome news.

"Radar contact on our five o'clock, closing fast," she said.

"Confirmed," said Pamela. "Looks like six planes."

"Red Fox, we have more incoming bandits — six, we think," I told Angelica.

"Roger, Ravens have spotted them. Engaging," she said.

We lost another six from our escort. We were now down to two Mavericks still on our wings.

"I think we stirred up a beehive," quipped Maria.

"We certainly have," I replied.

There was nothing to be done but to keep going.

"We're nearly there," said Maria, studying her map.

I was on tenterhooks as we ate up mile after mile of blue water below us. The English coastline finally came into view. I was about to breathe a sigh of relief when Maria suddenly shouted.

"Bandit on our nine o'clock, coming in low and fast."

I flicked a glance over to the left. A lone Focke-Wulf was streaking towards us at wave height. He'd not been spotted by the radar.

"Red Fox, we're under attack. One bandit, nine o'clock," I said frantically.

"We've got you," said Angelica as the two escort planes left us.

I really hoped they had. One lone Wulf could cause a lot of damage.

"Ospreys, keep going," I said, opening up the throttle.

The coastline was invitingly close when Maria said, "He's evaded them. He's broken through. He's coming for us."

"Full throttle," I said. "Let's go."

I opened up the Mosquito to maximum and it leapt forward.

"Ravens are in pursuit," said Angelica.

"Not quick enough," said Maria, who was looking over her shoulder.

"Tracers!" shouted Sharon Baker. She was flying with a new navigator, ASO Letitia Church. "We're hit. We're going down."

"Get down safely, Osprey One Seven," I said.

They were close enough to England to ditch in the Channel.

"I'm trying," said Sharon, sounding a little desperate.

The Wulf, however, wasn't finished, and the Mavericks hadn't managed to catch him.

"He's coming in again!" shouted Maria.

My heart sank.

"Incoming fire!" It was Linda. "We're hit! We're hit!"

"Ospreys, keep going," I said. We couldn't afford to falter now.

Suddenly, Sandra cut into the chatter. "He keeps evading the Ravens," she said. "Come on, Osprey Leader, I've had enough of this."

"Osprey One Three, what are you doing?" I asked her, although I had already guessed.

Sandra was gutsy and an expert flier. She had already proved her worth in combat.

"There are two of us and one of him — he's not picking us off one by one," she replied.

I flicked a glance at Maria. Extraordinary times called for extraordinary measures.

"All right, take him, Osprey One Three," I told her.

She peeled out of formation.

"Tracers!" shouted Susan. "He missed! Thank goodness."

Surely the Wulf must be out of ammo? And where were the Mavericks? We were almost over the English coastline now. All the action was going on behind us. I wondered what Sandra was doing. Just then, her voice came over the radio.

"All right, Mister Wulf, here comes Grandma," she said.

"They're closing in on him from two sides, and the Mavericks too," said Maria.

"All right," I replied as we made landfall at Fairlight Cove.

"Now I've got you," said Sandra, and then, "Bullseye! Mr Wulf is down. Yeeha!"

Maria and I both laughed. Sandra had done it again.

"Ravens confirm kill by Osprey One Three," said Angelica.

"Roger, Red Fox, great news. Osprey One Three and One Two, return to formation. Well done," I said.

"Wilco," replied Sandra.

I remembered Sharon and called to check on her.

"Osprey One Eight, do you read me?"

There was silence.

"Osprey One Eight?"

Angelica came on the radio and told me what I needed to know. "Ravens confirm Osprey One Eight ditched and are in a life raft."

"Roger, thanks," I said.

I turned my mind to Linda. She had also been hit. Regardless of my feelings, it was my duty to check on her.

"Osprey Seven, what's your status?" I asked her.

"I'm … okay… Thanks for asking…" she replied, but her voice sounded strained.

"Are you hit?" I continued.

"I'll … live…"

"Roger. Get back to base as best you can," I told her.

"Wilco."

I put Linda from my mind. We still had to get home. We continued towards Gravesend. Maria adjusted the bearing. I throttled back just a little; there was less need for speed now we were back over Blighty. The two remaining Mavericks reappeared on our wings.

I decided to enquire as to how the rest of our escort had fared.

"Red Fox," I said, "how about the Ravens?"

"A bit of a bunfight," said Angelica. "But they're on their way home, no casualties."

"Good to hear," I told her.

My heartrate had finally returned to normal as we eased over the Thames once more. As we passed Chelmsford, the two remaining Mavericks slipped away towards home.

"That's our final two Ravens signing off," said Angelica.

"Thank you, Red Fox, and thank you for the escort. Please thank the Ravens for their help — we wouldn't have made it back without them," I said.

"Ain't that the truth," muttered Maria beside me.

She was right. The Mavericks had been indispensable to our mission. I was glad to have insisted on an escort.

"Don't mention it, Osprey Leader. See you soon. Over and out," said Angelica.

The rest of the return journey was thankfully uneventful. The familiar post-mission fatigue started to kick in. I felt quite drained by the time Hawberry came into view.

"We made it," said Maria, smiling.

"Control, this is Osprey Leader requesting clearance," I said.

"Osprey Leader, you're clear to land. Welcome home," said Control.

"Roger," I replied. "We've one potential casualty, Osprey Seven. One to be picked up, Osprey One Eight crew."

"Roger, Osprey Leader. We've been informed of Osprey One Eight's position and rescue has been requested. We will have a medic standing by for your casualty."

"Roger," I replied. Angelica must have phoned in Sharon's position.

I lined up our approach and touched down onto the runway once more.

"It's good to be home," said Maria.

"I'll second that," I replied.

I taxied the Mosquito to its standing and killed the engines. We unstrapped and jumped down from the plane. My first thought was for Linda. It was my duty to check on my team. Over by her plane, the medical team looked as if they were putting her onto a stretcher. I walked over with Maria.

Linda was lying on the stretcher, looking pale. A dark red stain was spreading through the front of her flying suit. She looked up and saw me.

"Oh," she said, her breath coming in a rasp. "It's you."

"How the hell did you make it back?" I said, taking in her serious condition.

"Sheer willpower," she replied.

"Janice?" I asked, referring to her navigator, ASO Janice Kipling.

"Dead," she said. "Bullet to the head."

"Sorry…"

I glanced at Dr Carpenter, who was standing over Linda. I caught her eye. She shook her head. It was obviously too late. Linda was dying.

"I was determined … to make it home," Linda gasped. "I wanted to look you in the eye one more time … and tell you … how much I bloody well hate your guts…"

I stared at her aghast, but Linda wasn't finished.

"You took … everything from me … everything that should have been mine… Damn you … damn you to hell!"

I became aware that most of the squadron had gathered around and was listening to what Linda was saying.

Her breath was coming in hard rasps now and she was struggling to talk. "I should have been leader … of this squadron … not you… I deserved it … I … deserved…" Her voice trailed off and I heard a final rattle in her throat. Her eyes became glassy as the life went out of them.

Dr Carpenter put two fingers on Linda's wrist to feel for a pulse. "She's dead," she said, closing Linda's eyes.

"All right," I replied, not knowing what else to say.

I was shocked that someone could hate me so deeply that even at the point of death they couldn't let it go. I stood stock-still, aware of the silence around me. What must they all be thinking?

"Boss," said Sandra suddenly, "none of that is true — she was just too bitter. You always deserved to be Flight Leader. We all think so."

There were murmurs of agreement from the others. Ever practical, Maria stepped into the breach.

"Let it go," she said. "It's done."

I turned away and the crowd parted to let me through. Then one by one they all turned to follow me, leaving Linda's body alone on the stretcher.

"I'll say one thing," said Shelly as we neared the truck. "That was one hell of a mission."

This broke the ice. People started to laugh and talk at once. Death in war was a transient thing, often soon forgotten, unless the person meant something to you. Linda didn't mean anything to me, so I ruthlessly put her out of my mind as we climbed into the back of the trucks.

When we arrived at the Hall, James was waiting for our arrival. He congratulated everyone as they passed him on their way into the Hall, until finally there was just him and me.

"Anna?" he said.

"Yes?"

"Can you come with me? There's something I want to talk to you about," he said.

"All right."

I wondered what it was, since he sounded so formal. Perhaps it was something to do with Linda. Word had surely not reached his ears that quickly.

We soon found ourselves in a secluded part of the formal gardens, surrounded by high hedges and roses. James stopped and turned to face me. I tried to divine his intention from the look on his face, hardly daring to hope.

"Anna," he said, "I'm not sure if this is the right time or place, or if there will ever be a right time or place ... but I don't want to wait another minute."

James paused and reached into his pocket. Suddenly my heart started to beat rather fast. It was really happening. He extracted a small box from his pocket and dropped down onto one knee. I randomly wondered when on earth he had found the time to get a ring and at the same time tried to focus on the words he was saying.

"Anna Nightingale," he said, "would you like to marry me?"

I hesitated, but only for a second, and then I was all smiles. A sense of relief washed over me but more than that, I finally understood that love really can conquer all. The sun was shining and it seemed as if the birds were singing only for us.

"I would like it excessively," I told him.

HISTORICAL NOTE

The three main targets described in this book were in fact real places. The Mimoyecques Fortress presented a real danger to the Allies, and London in particular, were it ever to have come to fruition. Eventually, the fortress was abandoned by the Nazis when larger bombs were manufactured, which were able to penetrate the bunker's defences.

The Highball bouncing bomb was designed by Barnes Wallis. It was originally designed to bounce or skip across the surface of the water to destroy enemy shipping. However, it was also tested against railway tunnels. Ministry of Defence footage shows the bombs being dropped on land and water by Mosquitos. It's not too much of a stretch to imagine that a live test could have been carried out against the fortress railway tunnel entrance. In reality, the Highball bombs were never used, although there was talk of them being deployed in the Italian campaign.

The Fliegerhorst Volkel, or Volkel Airbase in the Netherlands, was an operational Nazi base. It was extensively bombed by the Allies on various occasions until the runways were finally put out of action. It is still in use today by the Dutch Air Force.

Wolfsschlucht II was one of two bunkers built for Hitler in France. He never visited this particular bunker. Remnants of it still stand today and are a tourist attraction. The bunker had a telephone exchange which was heavily fortified.

The Cookie bomb was a sizeable bomb used by the Allies and was the largest bomb the Mosquito could carry. Barnes Wallis was working on bigger bombs and produced others which were actual bunker-busting bombs. Hitler's French bunker is not noted as having been attacked by the Allies.

There are several recorded cases of duels being fought by women in times gone by. Technically, duelling was illegal in England, but was a common practice between the seventeenth and nineteenth centuries, after which it declined. In the sixteenth century in France, it was fashionable for women to learn the art of swordsmanship.

In 1792, Lady Almeria Braddock and Mrs Elphinstone fought a duel in London over remarks the latter made about the former's true age. The duel was fought with pistols and then swords. Mrs Elphinstone received a wound to her sword arm and honour was satisfied.

In 1886, two doctors of different nationalities fought a duel over which country had the better female medical practitioners. The French doctor won and the other was forced to concede that France had the better doctors.

In 1892, two Austrian noblewomen, Princess Pauline Metternich and the Countess Anastasia von Kielmansegg, engaged in a duel following a disagreement about a flower arrangement at the Viennese International Exhibition. Bizarrely, the duel was fought with the two protagonists wearing only petticoats. Those men present were required to move far away and avert their gaze. Both women ended up drawing blood, thus leaving the result rather undecided.

As in this book, a duel between two women over a prospective beau took place in Mexico in 1900, when two society ladies fought over a man with too much of a roving eye. The duel ended with one lady being severely injured and being forced to give up the beau.

As always, bringing history to life is a pleasure for this writer. I hope you find the same as a reader.

A NOTE TO THE READER

Dear Reader,

I hope that you have enjoyed this third instalment in the Secret Sirens series. In this book I wanted to show the Sirens as a now combat-experienced squadron. The life of any squadron was not simply flying missions. In my books I like to weave in the other aspects of their lives, the inevitable ups and downs. Characters develop just as they do in real life, friendships and relationships too.

In this book the Sirens fly several important missions. I wanted in particular to show Anna coming into her own as the Flight Leader. She started off shy and retiring in the first book, but has grown into the role over time. I understand something of leadership, having managed teams in my erstwhile career. The dynamics can be challenging, as Anna discovers.

The duel between Pamela and Betty is completely fictional, of course, but then again such things could easily have taken place. The age of chivalry was not entirely past. I was once a fencer and a professional fight director, so I know a thing or two about sword fighting. I thought a duel would inject some excitement of a different sort into the storyline, particularly between two women. We know there are just as many accomplished female fencers as male, and in earlier times some notorious women also fought duels. For more on this, please see the Historical Note.

With the missions, I tried to stick to real places and targets, which made for some interesting research. Whither next for the Sirens? Only time will tell.

I hope you enjoyed reading this novel as much as I enjoyed writing it. If you did, then I would be very grateful if you could spare the time to write a review on **Amazon** and **Goodreads**. As an author, these reviews are hugely important, and always appreciated. You can connect with me in other ways too, via my **website**, **Facebook**, **Twitter**, **Instagram**, and a special **Secret Sirens Page**.

I very much hope you were entertained enough to read the next book in the Sirens series.

Warmest regards,

D. R. Bailey

Sapere Books is an exciting new publisher of brilliant fiction and popular history.

To find out more about our latest releases and our monthly bargain books visit our website: **saperebooks.com**